Aberdeenshire
COUNCIL

Aberdeenshire Libraries
www.aberdeenshire.gov.uk/libraries
Renewals Hotline 01224 661511

1 7 AUG 2018

2 0 JUL 2022

2 3 FEB 2023

0 2 MAY 2023

THE MILLIONAIRE MYSTERY

'THE DETECTIVE STORY CLUB is a clearing house for the best detective and mystery stories chosen for you by a select committee of experts. Only the most ingenious crime stories will be published under the THE DETECTIVE STORY CLUB imprint. A special distinguishing stamp appears on the wrapper and title page of every THE DETECTIVE STORY CLUB book—the Man with the Gun. Always look for the Man with the Gun when buying a Crime book.'

Wm. Collins Sons & Co. Ltd., 1929

Now the Man with the Gun is back in this series of COLLINS CRIME CLUB reprints, and with him the chance to experience the classic books that influenced the Golden Age of crime fiction.

THE DETECTIVE STORY CLUB

FURTHER TITLES IN PREPARATION

THE MILLIONAIRE MYSTERY

A STORY OF CRIME BY

FERGUS HUME

PLUS TWO SHORT STORIES

WITH AN INTRODUCTION BY
PETER HAINING

COLLINS
CRIME
CLUB

COLLINS CRIME CLUB

An imprint of HarperCollins*Publishers*
1 London Bridge Street
London SE1 9GF
www.harpercollins.co.uk

This edition 2018

First published in Great Britain by Chatto & Windus 1901
Published by The Detective Story Club Ltd
for Wm Collins Sons & Co. Ltd 1930
'The Greenstone God and the Stockbroker' and 'The Rainbow Camellia'
first published in *The Dwarf's Chamber* by Ward, Lock & Co. 1896
Introduction excerpted from *The Golden Age of Crime Fiction* published
by Prion Books, copyright © Peter Haining 2002

A catalogue record for this book is
available from the British Library

ISBN 978-0-00-813762-5

Typeset in Bulmer MT Std by
Palimpsest Book Production Ltd, Falkirk, Stirlingshire
Printed and bound in Great Britain
by CPI Group (UK) Ltd, Croydon CR0 4YY

INTRODUCTION

THE growth of the railways in Britain, from the 1850s on, gave rise to the success of Victorian books of sensation. Coinciding with a shift from handmade books to machine-made paper and mass-produced bookbindings which dramatically reduced the costs, books became attractive with their two-, three- or four-colour illustrations—principally yellow but sometimes replaced by green, blue or grey—and their handy, pocket-sized format made them ideal for travellers, just like their descendants: today's paperbacks. Railway bookstalls were springing up at all the big stations, and those of W. H. Smith & Son in the south and John Menzies in the north were soon piled high with books and posters declaring, 'YELLOW-BACKS—High Quality Reading Only Two Shillings'. The books varied in length from 256 to 420 pages and offered customers a full-length novel or numerous short stories to while away their hours of travel. Although naturally enough the early titles from the publishers were cheap editions of the classic authors such as Jane Austen, Daniel Defoe, Henry Fielding, Captain Marryat, Samuel Richardson and Sir Walter Scott, the 'yellow-backs' were not slow to include crime, mystery and detection stories. Among the early successes were the Chatto & Windus reprints of Wilkie Collins' *The Woman in White* (1860) and *A Rogues' Life* (1870), and *The Masked Venus* (1866) by the American soldier-turned-storyteller Richard Henry Savage. The rights for Savage's book were purchased from America by Routledge, whose 'Railway Library', claiming to be 'The Cheapest Books Ever Published', began in 1848 and published some 1,200 titles over more than 50 years, making the company's fortune. The cover illustration for this and many other Routledge titles was by Walter Crane, who later provided the artwork for another popular title, Edgar Allan Poe's *Tales of Mystery & Imagination*, in 1919.

A typical example of the publishing phenomenon of cheap fiction that took the British reading public by storm in the 1860s were the books featuring Mary Paschal, 'one of the much-dreaded, but little-known people called Female Detectives'. A dark-haired beauty with arching eyebrows and ever-alert eyes, she made her debut as the first lady crime fighter in Britain in the pages of *Experiences of a Lady Detective* published in 1861. The book, with its predominantly yellow illustration on strawboard covered by glazed paper, epitomized the 'yellow-back era', named after the unmistakable characteristic of the books (also dubbed 'mustard-plaster novels'), and tales of crime and mystery now became major elements of this incredible success story.

The author of *Experiences of a Lady Detective* was given as 'Anonyma' and the publisher, George Vickers of London, implied in the book and advertising that the 'experiences' had been written by the heroine herself. Just as the yellow covers were used to identify these inexpensive works, so the idea that the texts were written by real detectives was used to enhance their appeal. Whether Mary Paschal had any basis in fact or not, she is undoubtedly a worthy pioneer of crime fiction, and sold so well that in 1864 Vickers issued a second volume, *Revelations of a Lady Detective*, in which the intrepid heroine described tackling a further cross-section of rogues and villains, not to mention bringing about the downfall of a prominent Member of Parliament who had been using his position to pervert the course of justice and amass a fortune.

The picture of the criminal fraternity that Anonyma's titles offered readers was very different from the subject of the two books credited with starting the 'yellow-back era'. These were a culinary guide, *Letters Left at the Pastry Cooks* by Horace Mayhew, and *Money: How To Get, How To Keep, and How To Use It*, both issued in April 1853 by a London firm,

Ingram, Cooke & Co. The two books with their eye-catching, illustrated covers were in stark contrast to the plain cloth or leather-bound volumes of the time. They were aimed unashamedly at providing inexpensive reading for the masses, and it was the pioneer 'self-help' title, *Money*, with its vivid yellow covers, that gave the entire series its name and established the format that other publishers were soon following. The major players in this area of publishing would soon prove to be Vickers, George Routledge & Sons, Chatto & Windus and Ward Lock; the latter would become even more famous for publishing the first Sherlock Holmes case, 'A Study in Scarlet', in 1887.

Far and away the single most popular crime 'yellow-back' was *The Mystery of a Hansom Cab*, a novel originally published in Melbourne, Australia, by the author, Fergus Hume (1859–1932), at his own expense. There is, in fact, probably no more unlikely success story in the history of crime fiction publishing than this tale of a brutal crime in which the identity of the killer is actually given away in the preface! Hume had been born in England to Glaswegian parents, but emigrated with his family to Dunedin in New Zealand, and Fergus was educated at the High School there. He afterwards passed through the university of Otago with distinction and qualified as a barrister in 1885. Rather than go into legal practice, he sailed to Victoria, finding work for three years as a law clerk in Melbourne while attempting to further his ambitions as a playwright. In an attempt to augment his income, he asked a local bookseller what kind of book sold best. Hume wrote later, 'He replied that the detective sales of Émile Gaboriau had a large sale; and as, at this time, I had never heard of this author, I bought all his works and determined to write a book of the same class containing a mystery, murder and a description of the low life of Melbourne.'

Unable to find a publisher for *The Mystery of a Hansom*

Cab, Hume decided to publish the book himself and just about covered his costs on the first printing. One purchaser of the book, however, was an Englishman who evidently had an eye for a commercial prospect. He promptly bought the rights from the author for just £50, set up 'The Hansom Cab Publishing Company' in London, and launched the book on to the nation's railway bookstalls. With its simple yellow cover and illustration of a hansom cab, it rapidly sold 350,000 copies, a figure which was doubled when the story was reprinted in America. By the end of the century, *The Mystery of a Hansom Cab* had also been translated into twelve foreign languages.

Hume, who was still in Australia while all this was happening, scraped together enough money for a fare to England and arrived in London to find his book everywhere and his name on everyone's lips. It should have made him wealthy, but having sold the copyright he was not entitled to another penny. Disappointed but not downhearted, Hume settled in Essex and in the years that followed tried desperately to repeat his success, writing over 100 more novels—including *Madame Midas* (1888), *For the Defense* (aka *The Devil-Stick*, 1898) and the optimistically entitled *The Mystery of a Motor Cab* (1908)—but none achieved anything like the popularity of the first book. Today, in most histories of crime fiction, Hume is dismissed as a hack whose books are unreadable and whose most famous story was 'tedious from start to finish'. Yet *The Mystery of a Hansom Cab* outsold the works of Poe, Collins and even Conan Doyle for years, and more copies were bought in its 'yellow-back' format than any other title. Furthermore, the original 1886 Melbourne edition printed by Kemp & Boyce has the distinction today of being one of the rarest books in the world—only two copies are known to exist.

Given Hume's renown, it was probably inevitable that the publishers of William Collins' Detective Story Club should include him in their classic crime series, choosing to license

The Millionaire Mystery, originally published in 1901 when yellow-backs were taking their last bow. This was how their Editor introduced the reissue in 1930:

Since the publication of *The Mystery of the Hansom Cab* in 1887 [sic] Fergus Hume has written steadily and today he has to his credit a list of books which even in its length has few equals and certainly is unique so far as mainte-nance of literary standard is concerned. He is one of the pioneers of the present group of detective writers of the thriller variety and he will remain one of the best if only for such tales as *The Harlequin Opal* [1893], *The Dwarf's Chamber* [1896], *The Bishop's Secret* [1900], and the present book—*The Millionaire Mystery*.

This story is very typical of the author and for that reason alone it cannot afford to be neglected by the connoisseur of crime fiction. But as a mystery tale, its entertainment value alone makes it a book to be read. Fergus Hume has woven throughout the murder-plot a delightful love story which he introduces amid the thrills much in the way that Shakespeare introduces the hall-porter in *Macbeth*—to 'heighten' the tragedy. Perhaps the one thing about the novel, other than the actual plot itself, that you will never forget, is the character of Cicero Gramp. In his portrayal of this vagabond elocutionist, the author has rivalled Dickens himself, to whose literary style, incidentally, his bears a marked resemblance.

In reading *The Millionaire Mystery* you will be convinced that 'it is impossible not to be thrilled' by someone whose popularity at the moment may be less than one we can think of, but whose high place in Detective Fiction can never be taken from him.

PETER HAINING
2002

CHAPTER I

A MIDNIGHT SURPRISE

STEERING his course by a tapering spire notched in the eye of the sunset, a tramp slouched along the Heathton Road. From the western sky a flood of crimson light poured over the dusty white highway, which led straightly across the moor. To right and left, acres of sear coarse herbage rolled towards the distant hills, now black against the flaming horizon. In the quivering air gnats danced and flickered; the earth panted with the thirst of a lengthy drought, and the sky arched itself over the heat of a fiery furnace.

For many hours the tramp had held on steadily in the pitiless glare of the mid-June sun, and now that he saw ahead of him the spire and house-roofs and encircling trees of the village whither he was bound, a sigh of relief burst from him.

To ease his aching feet he sat down beside a mouldering millstone and wiped his beaded brow with a red bandana. He did not swear, which was singular in a tramp.

Apparently he had but recently joined the cadging profession, for about him there lingered an air of respectability and the marks of a prosperity not wholly decayed. He was stout, rubicund of countenance, and he wheezed like a sick grampus. Watery grey eyes and a strawberry nose revealed the seasoned toper; thick lips and a slack mouth the sensualist. As a begging friar of mediaeval times he would have been altogether admirable; as a modern tramp he was out of the picture.

Clothed in a broadcloth frock-coat considerably the worse for wear, he wore—oddly enough for a tramp—gaiters over his gouty-looking boots. His black gloves were darned at the finger-tips, and his battered silk hat had been ironed and brushed

1

with sedulous care. This rook-like plumage was now plentifully sprinkled with the white dust of travel. His gait, in spite of his blistered feet, was dignified, and his manners were imposing.

The road was lonely, likewise the heath. There was no one in sight, not even a returning ploughman; but the recumbent wayfarer could hear, mellowed by distance, the bells of homing cows. Beasts as they were, he envied them. They at least had a place to sleep in for the night; he was without a home, without even the necessary money to procure shelter. Luckily it was summer-time, dry and warm. Also the tramp affected the philosopher.

'This,' he remarked, eyeing a sixpence extracted from the knotted corner of his handkerchief, 'is a drink—two drinks if I take beer, which is gouty. But it is not a meal nor a bed. No! one drink, and a morsel of bread-and-cheese. But the bed! Ah!' He stared at the coin with a sigh, as though he hoped it would swell into a shilling. It did not, and he sighed again. 'Shall I have good luck in this place?' cried he. 'Heads I shall, tails I shan't.' The coin spun and fell heads. 'Ha!' said the tramp, getting on to his feet, 'this must be seen to. I fly to good fortune on willing feet,' and he resumed his trudging.

A quarter of an hour brought him to the encircling wood. He passed beyond pine and larch and elm into a cosy little village with one street. This was broken in the centre by an expanse of green turf surrounded by red-roofed houses, amongst them—as he saw from the swinging sign—a public-house, called, quaintly enough, the Good Samaritan.

'Scriptural,' said the stranger—'possibly charitable. Let us see.' He strode forward into the taproom.

In the oiliest of tones he inquired for the landlord. But in this case, it appeared, there was no landlord, for a vixenish little woman, lean as a cricket and as shrill, bounced out with the information that she, Mrs Timber, was the landlady. Her husband, she snapped out, was dead. To the tramp this hostess appeared less promising than the seductive sign, and he quailed somewhat at the sight of her. However, with a brazen assurance born of habit, he put a bold face on it, peremptorily demanding bread, cheese, and ale. The request for a bed he left in abeyance, for besides the vixenish Mrs Timber there hovered around a stalwart pot-boy, whose rolled-up sleeves revealed a biceps both admirable and formidable.

'Bread, cheese, and ale,' repeated the landlady, with a sharp glance at her guest's clerical dress, 'for this. And who may you be, sir?' she asked, with a world of sarcasm expended on the 'sir.'

'My name is Cicero Gramp. I am a professor of elocution and eloquence.'

'Ho! A play-actor?' Mrs Timber became more disdainful than ever.

'Not at all; I am not on the boards. I recite to the best families. The Bishop of Idlechester has complimented me on my—'

'Here's the bread-and-cheese,' interrupted the landlady, 'likewise the beer. Sixpence!'

Very reluctantly Mr Gramp produced his last remaining coin. She dropped it into a capacious pocket, and retired without vouchsafing him another word. Cicero, somewhat discouraged by this reception, congratulated himself that the night was fine for out-of-door slumber. He ensconced himself in a corner with his frugal supper, and listened to the chatter going on around him. It appeared to be concerned with the funeral of a local magnate. Despite the prophecy of the coin, now in Mrs Timber's pocket, Cicero failed to see how he could extract good fortune out of his present position. However, he listened; some chance word might mean money.

'Ah! 'tis a fine dry airy vault,' said a lean man who proved to be a stonemason. 'Never built a finer, I didn't, nor my mates neither. An' Muster Marlow'll have it all to 'isself.'

'Such a situation!' croaked another. 'Bang opposite the Lady Chapel! An' the view from that there vault! I don't know as any corp 'ud require a finer.'

'Mr Marlow'll be lonely by himself,' sighed a buxom woman;

'there's room for twenty coffins, an' only one in the vault. 'T'ain't natural-like.'

'Well,' chimed in the village schoolmaster, ''twill soon fill. There's Miss Marlow.'

'Dratted nonsense!' cried Mrs Timber, making a dash into the company with a tankard of beer in each hand. 'Miss Sophy'll marry Mr Thorold, won't she? An' he, as the Squire of Heathton, 'as a family vault, ain't he? She'll sleep beside him as his wife, lawfully begotten.'

'The Thorolds' vault is crowded,' objected the stonemason. 'Why, there's three-hundred-year dead folk there! A very old gentry lot, the Thorolds.'

'Older than your Marlows!' snapped Mrs Timber. 'Who was he afore he came to take the Moat House five year ago? Came from nowhere—a tree without a root.'

The schoolmaster contradicted.

'Nay, he came from Africa, I know—from Mashonaland, which is said to be the Ophir of King Solomon. And Mr Marlow was a millionaire!'

'Much good his money'll do him now,' groaned the buxom woman, who was a Dissenter. 'Ah! Dives in torment.'

'You've no call to say that, Mrs Berry. Mr Marlow wasn't a bad man.'

'He was charitable, I don't deny, an' went to church regular,' assented Mrs Berry; 'but he died awful sudden. Seems like a judgment for something he'd done.'

'He died quietly,' said the schoolmaster. 'Dr Warrender told me all about it—a kind of fit at ten o'clock last Thursday, and on Friday night he passed away as a sleeping child. He was not even sufficiently conscious to say good-bye to Miss Sophy.'

'Ah, poor girl! she's gone to the seaside with Miss Parsh to nurse her sorrow.'

'It will soon pass—soon pass,' observed the schoolmaster, waving his pipe. 'The young don't think much of death. Miss Sophy's rich, too—rich as the Queen of Sheba, and she will marry Mr Thorold in a few months. Funeral knells will give way to wedding-bells, Mrs Berry.'

'Ah!' sighed Mrs Berry, feeling she was called upon for an appropriate sentiment; 'you may say so, Mr Stack. Such is life!'

Cicero, munching his bread-and-cheese, felt that his imposing personality was being neglected, and seized upon what he deemed his opportunity.

'If this company will permit,' he said, 'I propose now to give a recitation apropos of the present melancholy event. Need I say I refer to the lamented death of Mr Marlow?'

'I'll have no godless mumming here,' said Mrs Timber firmly. 'Besides, what do you know about Mr Marlow?'

Whereupon Cicero lied lustily to impress the bumpkins, basing his fiction upon such facts as his ears had enabled him to come by.

'Marlow!' he wailed, drawing forth his red bandana for effect. 'Did I not know him as I know myself? Were we not boys together till he went to Africa?'

'Perhaps you can tell us about Mr Marlow,' said the school-master eagerly. 'None of us knows exactly who he was. He appeared here with his daughter some five years ago, and took the Moat House. He was rich, and people said he had made his riches in South Africa.'

'He did! he did!' said Cicero, deeply affected. 'Millions he was worth—millions! I came hither to see him, and I arrive to find the fond friend of my youth dead. Oh, Jonathan, my brother Jonathan!'

'His name was Richard,' said Mrs Timber suspiciously.

'I know it, I know it. I use the appellation Jonathan merely in illustration of the close friendship which was between us. I am David.'

'H'm!' snorted Mrs Timber, eyeing him closely, 'and who was Mr Marlow?'

This leading question perplexed Mr Gramp not a little, for he knew nothing about the man.

'What!' he cried, with simulated horror. 'Reveal the secrets of the dead? Never! never!'

'Secrets?' repeated the lean stonemason eagerly. 'Ah! I always thought Mr Marlow had 'em. He looked over his shoulder too often for my liking. An' there was a look on his face frequent which pointed, I may say, to a violent death.'

'Ah! say not that my friend Dick Marlow came to an untimely end.'

This outcry came from Cicero; it was answered by Mrs Timber.

'He died of a fit,' she said tartly, 'and that quietly enough, considering as Dr Warrender can testify. But now we've talked enough, an' I'm going to lock up; so get out, all of you!'

In a few minutes the taproom was cleared and the lights out. Cicero, greatly depressed, lingered in the porch, wondering how to circumvent the dragon.

'Well,' snapped that amiable beast, 'what are you waitin' for?'

'You couldn't give me a bed for the night?'

'Course I could, for a shillin'.'

'I haven't a shilling, I regret to say.'

'Then you'd best get one, or go without your bed,' replied the lady, and banged the door in his face.

Under this last indignity even Cicero's philosophy gave way, and he launched an ecclesiastic curse at the inhospitable inn.

Fortunately the weather was warm and tranquil. Not a breath of wind stirred the trees. The darkling earth was silent—silent as the watching stars. Even the sordid soul of the vagabond was stirred by the solemn majesty of the sky. He removed his battered hat and looked up.

'The heavens are telling the glory of God,' he said; but, not recollecting the rest of the text, he resumed his search for a resting-place.

It was now only between nine and ten o'clock, yet, as he wandered down the silent street, he could see no glimmer of a light in any window. His feet took him, half unconsciously as it were, by the path leading towards the tapering spire. He went on through a belt of pines which surrounded the church, and came suddenly upon the graveyard, populous with the forgotten dead—at least, he judged they were forgotten by the state of the tombstones.

On the hither side he came upon a circular chapel, with lance-shaped windows and marvellous decoration wrought in greystone on the outer walls. Some distance off rose a low wall, encircling the graveyard, and beyond the belt of pines through which he had just passed stretched the league-long herbage of the moor. He guessed this must be the Lady Chapel.

Between the building and the low wall he noticed a large tomb of white marble, surmounted by a winged angel with a trumpet. 'Dick Marlow's tomb,' he surmised. Then he proceeded to walk round it as that of his own familiar friend, for he had already half persuaded himself into some such belief.

But he realized very soon that he had not come hither for sightseeing, for his limbs ached, and his feet burned, and his eyes were heavy with sleep. He rolled along towards a secluded corner, where the round of the Lady Chapel curved into the main wall of the church. There he found a grassy nook, warm and dry. He removed his gloves with great care, placed them in his silk hat, and then took off his boots and loosened his clothes. Finally he settled himself down amid the grass, put a hand up either coat-sleeve for warmth, and was soon wrapped in a sound slumber.

He slept on undisturbed until one o'clock, when—as say out-of-door observers—the earth turns in her slumber. This vagrant, feeling as it were the stir of Nature, turned too. A lowing of cows came from the moor beyond the pines. A breath of cool air swept through the branches, and the sombre boughs swayed like the plumes of a hearse. Across the face of the sky ran a shiver. He heard distinctly what he had not noticed before, the gush of running water. He roused himself and sat up alert, and strained his hearing. What was it he heard now? He listened and strained again. Voices surely! Men's voices!

There could be no mistake. Voices he heard, though he could not catch the words they said. A tremor shook his whole body. Then, curiosity getting the better of his fear, he wriggled forward flat on his stomach until he was in such a position that he could peer round the corner of the Lady Chapel. Here he saw a sight which scared him.

Against the white wall of the mausoleum bulked two figures, one tall, the other short. The shorter carried a lantern. They stood on the threshold of the iron door, and the tall man was listening. They were nearer now, so that he could hear their talk very plainly.

'All is quiet,' said the taller man. 'No one will suspect. We'll get him away easily.'

Then Cicero heard the key grate in the lock, saw the door open and the men disappear into the tomb. He was sick with terror, and was minded to make a clean bolt of it; but with the greatest effort he controlled his fears and remained. There might be money in this adventure.

In ten minutes the men came out carrying a dark form between them, as Cicero guessed, the dead body of Richard Marlow. They set down their burden, made fast the door, and took up again the sinister load. He saw them carry it towards the low stone wall. Over this they lifted it, climbed over themselves, and disappeared into the pine-woods.

Cicero waited until he could no longer hear the rustle of their progress; then he crept cautiously forward and tried the door of the tomb. It was fast locked.

'Resurrection-men! body-snatchers!' he moaned.

He felt shaken to his very soul by the ghastliness of the whole proceeding. Then suddenly the awkwardness of his own position, if by chance anyone should find him there, rushed in upon his mind, and, without so much as another glance, he made off as quickly as he could in the opposite direction.

CHAPTER II

THE HUT ON THE HEATH

'WELL, I'm glad it's all over,' said the footman, waving a cigar stolen from the box of his master. 'Funerals don't suit me.'

'Yet we must all 'ave one of our own some day,' said the cook, who was plainly under the influence of gin; 'an' that pore Miss Sophy—me 'art bleeds for 'er!'

'An' she with 'er millions,' growled a red-faced coachman. 'Wot rot!'

'Come now, John, you know Miss Sophy was fond of her father'—this from a sprightly housemaid, who was trimming a hat.

'I dunno why,' said John. 'Master was as cold as ice, an' as silent as 'arf a dozen graves.'

The scullery-maid shuddered, and spread out her grimy hands.

'Oh, Mr John, don't talk of graves, please! I've 'ad the nightmare over 'em.'

'Don't put on airs an' make out as 'ow you've got nerves, Cammelliar,' put in the cook tearfully. 'It's me as 'as 'em—I've a bundle of 'em—real shivers. Ah, well! we're cut down like green bay-trees, to be sure. Pass that bottle, Mr Thomas.'

This discussion took place in the kitchen of the Moat House. The heiress and Miss Parsh, the housekeeper, had departed for the seaside immediately after the funeral, and in the absence of control, the domestics were making merry. To be sure, Mr Marlow's old and trusted servant, Joe Brill, had been told off to keep them in order, but just at present his grief was greater than his sense of duty. He was busy now sorting papers in the library—hence the domestic chaos.

9

It was, in truth, a cheerful kitchen, more especially at the present moment, with the noonday sun streaming in through the open casements. A vast apartment with a vast fireplace of the baronial hall kind; brown oaken walls and raftered roof; snow-white dresser and huge deal table, and a floor of shining white tiles.

There was a moment's silence after the last unanswerable observation of the cook. It was broken by a voice at the open door—a voice which boomed like the drone of a bumble-bee.

'Peace be unto this house,' said the voice richly, 'and plenty be its portion.'

The women screeched, the men swore—since the funeral their nerves had not been quite in order—and all eyes turned towards the door. There, in the hot sunshine, stood an enormously fat old man, clothed in black, and perspiring profusely. It was, in fact, none other than Cicero Gramp, come in the guise of Autolycus to pick up news and unconsidered trifles. He smiled benignly, and raised his fat hand.

'Peace, maid-servants and men-servants,' said he, after the manner of Chadband. 'There is no need for alarm. I am a stranger, and you must take me in.'

'Who the devil are you?' queried the coachman.

'We want no tramps here,' growled the footman.

'I am no tramp,' said Cicero mildly, stepping into the kitchen. 'I am a professor of elocution and eloquence, and a friend of your late master's. He went up in the world, I dropped down. Now I come to him for assistance, and I find him occupying the narrow house; yes, my friends, Dick Marlow is as low as the worms whose prey he soon will be. *Pax vobiscum!*'

'Calls master "Dick",' said the footman.

'Sez 'e's an old friend,' murmured the cook.

They looked at each other, and the thought in every mind was the same. The servants were one and all anxious to hear the genesis of their late master, who had dropped into the Moat

House, as from the skies, some five years before. Mrs Crammer, the cook, rose to the occasion with a curtsy.

'I'm sure, sir, I'm sorry the master ain't here to see you,' she said, polishing a chair with her apron. 'But as you says—or as I take it you means—'e's gone where we must all go. Take a seat, sir, and I'll tell Joe, who's in the library.'

'Joe—my old friend Joe!' said Cicero, sitting down like a mountain. 'Ah! the faithful fellow!'

This random remark brought forth information, which was Cicero's intention in making it.

'Faithful!' growled the coachman, 'an' why not? Joe Brill was paid higher nor any of us, he was; just as of living all his life with an iceberg deserved it!'

'Poor Dick *was* an iceberg!' sighed Cicero pensively. 'A cold, secretive man.'

'Ah!' said Mrs Crammer, wiping her eye, 'you may well say that. He 'ad secrets, I'm sure, and guilty ones, too!'

'We all have our skeletons, ma'am. But would you mind giving me something to eat and to drink? for I have walked a long way. I am too poor,' said Cicero, with a sweet smile, 'to ride, as in the days of my infancy, but *spero meliora*.'

'Talking about skeletons, sir,' said the footman when Mr Gramp's jaws were fully occupied, 'what about the master's?'

'Ah!' said Gramp profoundly. 'What indeed!'

'But whatever it is, it has to do with the West Indies,' said the man.

'Lor'!' exclaimed the housemaid, 'and how do you know that, Mr Thomas?'

'From observation, Jane, my dear,' Thomas smiled loftily. 'A week or two afore master had the fit as took him, I brought in a letter with the West Indy stamp. He turned white as chalk when he saw it, and tore it open afore I could get out of the room. I 'ad to fetch a glass of whisky. He was struck all of a 'eap—gaspin', faintin', and cussin' orful.'

'Did he show it to Miss Sophy?' asked Mrs Crammer.

'Not as I knows of. He kept his business to hisself,' replied Thomas.

Gramp was taking in all this with greedy ears.

'Ha!' he said, 'when you took in the letter, might you have looked at the postmark, my friend?'

With an access of colour, the footman admitted that he had been curious enough to do so.

'And the postmark was Kingston, Jamaica,' said he.

'It recalls my youth,' said Cicero. 'Ah! they were happy, happy days!'

'What was Mr Marlow, sir?'

'A planter of—of—rice,' hazarded Gramp. He knew that there were planters in the West Indies, but he was not quite sure what it was they planted. 'Rice—acres of it!'

'Well, he didn't make his money out of that, sir,' growled the coachman.

'No, he did not,' admitted the professor of elocution. 'He acquired his millions in Mashonaland—the Ophir of the Jews.'

This last piece of knowledge had been acquired from Slack, the schoolmaster.

'He was precious careful not to part with none of it,' said the footman.

'Except to Dr Warrender,' said the cook. 'The doctor was always screwing money out of him. Not that it was so much 'im as 'is wife. I can't abear that doctor's wife—a stuck-up peacock, I call her. She fairly ruined her husband in clothes. Miss Sophy didn't like her, neither.'

'Dick's child!' cried Gramp, who had by this time procured a cigar from the footman. 'Ah! is little Sophy still alive?'

He lighted the cigar and puffed luxuriously.

'Still alive!' echoed Mrs Crammer, 'and as pretty as a picture. Dark 'air, dark eyes—not a bit like 'er father.'

'No,' said Cicero, grasping the idea. 'Dick was fair when we were boys. I heard rumours that little Sophy was engaged—let me see—to a Mr Thorold.'

'Alan Thorold, Esquire,' corrected the coachman gruffly; 'one of the oldest families hereabouts, as lives at the Abbey farm. He's gone with her to the seaside.'

'To the seaside? Not to Brighton?'

'Nothin' of the sort—to Bournemouth, if you know where that is.'

'I know some things, my friend,' said Cicero mildly. 'It was Bournemouth I meant—not unlike Brighton, I think, since both names begin with a B. I know that Miss Marlow—dear little Sophy!—is staying at the Imperial Hotel, Bournemouth.'

'You're just wrong!' cried Thomas, falling into the trap; 'she is at the Soudan Hotel. I've got the address to send on letters.'

'Can I take them?' asked Gramp, rising. 'I am going to Bournemouth to see little Sophy and Mr Thorold. I shall tell them of your hospitality.'

Before the footman could reply to this generous offer, the page-boy of the establishment darted in much excited.

'Oh, here's a go!' he exclaimed. 'Dr Warrender's run away, an' the Quiet Gentleman's followed!'

'Wot d'ye mean, Billy?'

'Wot I say. The doctor ain't bin 'ome all night, nor all mornin', an' Mrs Warrender's in hysterics over him. Their 'ousemaid I met shoppin' tole me.'

The servants looked at one another. Here was more trouble, more excitement.

'And the Quiet Gentleman?' asked the cook with ghoulish interest.

'He's gone, too. Went out larst night, an' never come back. Mrs Marry thinks he's bin murdered.'

There was a babel of voices and cries, but after a moment quiet was restored. Then Cicero placed his hand on the boy's head.

'My boy,' he said pompously, 'who is the Quiet Gentleman? Let us be clear upon the point of the Quiet Gentleman.'

'Don't you know, sir?' put in the eager cook. 'He's a mystery, 'aving bin staying at Mrs Marry's cottage, she a lone widder taking in boarders.'

'I'll give a week's notice!' sobbed the scullery-maid. 'These crimes is too much for me.'

'I didn't say the Quiet Gentleman 'ad been murdered,' said Billy, the page; 'but Mrs Marry only thinks so, cos 'e ain't come 'ome.'

'As like as not he's cold and stiff in some lonely grave!' groaned Mrs Crammer hopefully.

'The Quiet Gentleman,' said Cicero, bent upon acquiring further information—'tall, yellow-bearded, with a high forehead and a bald head?'

'Well, I never, sir!' cried Jane, the housemaid. 'If you ain't describing Dr Warrender! Did you know him, sir?'

Cicero was quite equal to the occasion.

'I knew him professionally. He attended me for a relaxed throat. I was *vox et praeterea nihil* until he cured me. But what was this mysterious gentleman like? Short, eh?'

'No; tall and thin, with a stoop. Long white hair, longer beard and black eyes like gimblets,' gabbled the cook. 'I met 'im arter dark one evenin', and I declare as 'is eyes were glow-worms. Ugh! They looked me through and through. I've never bin the same woman since.'

At this moment a raucous voice came from the inner doorway.

'What the devil's all this?' was the polite question.

Cicero turned, and saw a heavily-built man surveying the company in general, and himself in particular, anything but favourably. His face was a mahogany hue, and he had a veritable tangle of whiskers and hair. The whole cut of the man was distinctly nautical, his trousers being of the dungaree, and his pea-jacket plentifully sprinkled with brass buttons. In his ears he wore rings of gold, and his clenched fists hung by his side as though eager for any emergency, and 'the sooner the better'. That was how he impressed Cicero, who, in nowise fancying the expression on his face, edged towards the door.

'Oh, Joe!' shrieked the cook, 'wot a turn you give me! an' sich news as we've 'ad!'

'News?' said Joe uneasily, his eyes still on Cicero.

'Mrs Warrender's lost her husband, and the Quiet Gentleman's disappeared mysterious!'

'Rubbish! Get to your work, all of you!'

So saying, Joe drove the frightened crowd hither and thither to their respective duties, and Cicero, somewhat to his dismay, found himself alone with the buccaneer, as he had inwardly dubbed the newcomer.

'Who the devil are you?' asked Joe, advancing.

'Fellow,' replied Cicero, getting into the doorway, 'I am a friend of your late master. Cicero Gramp is my name. I came here to see Dick Marlow, but I find he's gone aloft.'

Joe turned pale, even through his tan.

'A friend of Mr Marlow,' he repeated hoarsely. 'That's a lie! I've been with him these thirty years, and I never saw you!'

'Not in Jamaica?' inquired Cicero sweetly.

'Jamaica? What do you mean?'

'What I wrote in that letter your master received before he died.'

'Oh, you liar! I know the man who wrote it.' Joe clenched his fists more tightly and swung forward. 'You're a rank impostor, and I'll hand you over to the police, lest I smash you completely!'

Cicero saw he had made a mistake, but he did not flinch. Hardihood alone could carry him through now.

'Do,' he said. 'I'm particularly anxious to see the police, Mr Joe Brill.'

'Who are you, in Heaven's name?' shouted Joe, much agitated. 'Do you come from him?'

'Perhaps I do,' answered Cicero, wondering to whom the 'him' might now refer.

'Then go back and tell him he's too late—too late, curse him! and you too, you lubber!'

'Very good.' Cicero stepped out into the hot sunshine. 'I'll deliver your message—for a sovereign.'

Joe Brill tugged at his whiskers, and cast an uneasy glance around. Evidently, he was by no means astute, and the present situation was rather too much for him. His sole idea, for some reason best known to himself, was to get rid of Cicero. With a groan, he plunged his huge fist into his pocket and pulled out a gold coin.

'Here, take it and go to hell!' he said, throwing it to Cicero.

'Mariner, *fata obstant*,' rolled Gramp in his deep voice.

Then he strode haughtily away. He looked round as he turned the corner of the house, and saw Joe clutching his iron-grey locks, still at the kitchen door.

So with a guinea in his pocket and a certain amount of knowledge which he hoped would bring him many more, Cicero departed, considerable uplifted. At the village grocery he bought bread, meat and a bottle of whisky, then he proceeded to shake the dust of Heathton off his feet. As he stepped out on to the moor he recalled the Latin words he had used, and he shuddered.

'Why did I say that?' he murmured. 'The words came into my head somehow. Just when Joe was talking of my employer, too! Who is my employer? What has he to do with all this? I'm all in the dark! So Dr Warrender's gone, and the Quiet Gentleman too. It must have been Dr Warrender who helped to steal Marlow's body. The description tallies exactly—tall, fair beard and bald. I wonder if t'other chap was the Quiet Gentleman? And what on earth could they want with the body? Anyway, the body's gone, and, as it's a millionaire corpse, I'll have some of its money or I'm a Dutchman!'

He stopped and placed his hand to his head.

'Bournemouth, Bournemouth!' he muttered. 'Ah, that's it—the Soudan Hotel, Bournemouth!'

It was now the middle of the afternoon, and, as he plodded on, the moor glowed like a furnace. No vestige of shade was there beneath which to rest, not even a tree or a bush. Then, a short distance up the road, he espied a hut. It seemed to be in ruins. It was a shepherd's hut, no doubt. The grass roof was torn, the door was broken, though closed, and the mud walls were crumbling. Impatient of any obstacle, he shoved his back against it and burst it open. It had been fastened with a piece of rope. He fell in, headlong almost. But the gloom was grateful to him, though for the moment he could see but little.

When his eyes had become more accustomed to the half-light, the first object upon which they fell was a stiff human form stretched on the mud floor—a body with a handkerchief over the face. Yelling with terror, Cicero hurled himself out again.

'Marlow's body!' he gasped. 'They've put it here!'

With feverish haste he produced a corkscrew knife, and opened his whisky bottle. A fiery draught gave him courage. He ventured back into the hut and knelt down beside the body. Over the heart gaped an ugly wound, and the clothes were caked with blood. He gasped again.

'No fit this, but murder! Stabbed to the heart! And Joe—what does Joe know about this—and my employer? Lord!'

He snatched the handkerchief from the face, and fell back on his knees with another cry, this time of wonderment rather than of terror. He beheld the dead man's fair beard and bald head.

'Dr Warrender! And he was alive last night! This is murder indeed!'

Then his nerves gave way utterly, and he began to cry like a frightened child.

'Murder! Wilful and horrible murder!' wept the professor of elocution and eloquence.

CHAPTER III

AN ELEGANT EPISTLE

On Bournemouth cliffs, where pine-trees cluster to the edge, sat an elderly spinster, knitting a homely stocking. She wore, in spite of the heat, a handsome cashmere shawl, pinned across her spare shoulders with a portrait brooch, and that hideous variety of Early Victorian head-gear known as the mushroom hat. From under this streamed a frizzy crop of grey curls, which framed a rosy, wrinkled face, brightened by twinkling eyes. These, sparkling as those of sweet seventeen, proved that their owner was still young in heart. This quaint survival of the last century knitted as assiduously as was possible under the circumstances, for at a discreet distance were two young people, towards whom she acted the part of chaperon. Doubtless such an office is somewhat out-of-date nowadays; but Miss Victoria Parsh would rather have died than have left a young girl alone in the company of a young man.

Yet she knew well enough that this young man was altogether above reproach, and, moreover, engaged by parental consent to the pretty girl to whom he was talking so earnestly. And no one could deny that Sophy Marlow was indeed charming. There was somewhat of the Andalusian about her. Not very tall, shaped delicately as a nymph, she well deserved Alan Thorold's name. He called her the 'Midnight Fairy', and, indeed, she looked like a brunette Titania. Her complexion was dark, and faintly flushed with red; her mouth and nose were exquisitely shaped, while her eyes were wells of liquid light—glorious Spanish orbs. About her, too, was that peculiar charm of personality which defies description.

Alan her lover was not tall, but uncommonly well-built and

18

muscular, as fair as Sophy was dark—of that golden Saxon race which came before the Dane. Not that he could be called handsome. He was simply a clean, clear-skinned, well-groomed young Englishman, such as can be seen everywhere. Of a strong character, he exercised great control over his somewhat frivolous betrothed.

Miss Vicky, as the little spinster was usually called, cast romantic glances at the dark head and the fair one so close to one another. As a rule she would have been shocked at such a sight, but she knew how keenly Sophy grieved for the death of her father, and was only too willing that the girl should be comforted. And Miss Vicky occasionally touched the brooch, which contained the portrait of a red-coated officer. She also had lived in Arcady, but her Lieutenant had been shot in the Indian Mutiny, and Miss Vicky had left Arcady after a short sojourn, for a longer one in the work-a-day world. At once, she had lost her lover and her small income, and, like many another lonely woman, had had to turn to and work. But the memory of that short romance kept her heart young, hence her sympathy with this young couple.

'Poor dear father!' sighed Sophy, looking at the sea below, dotted with white sails. 'I can hardly believe he is gone. Only two weeks ago and he was so well, and now—oh! I was so fond of him! We were so happy together! He was cold to everyone else, but kindly to me! How could he have died so suddenly, Alan?'

'Well, of course, dear, a fit is always sudden. But try and bear up, Sophy dear. Don't give way like this. Be comforted.'

She looked up wistfully to the blue sky.

'At all events, he is at peace now,' she said, her lip quivering. 'I know he was often very unhappy, poor father! He used to sit for hours frowning and perplexed, as if there was something terrible on his mind.'

Alan's face was turned away now, and his brow was wrinkled. He seemed absorbed in thought, as though striving to elucidate some problem suggested by her words.

Wrapped up in her own sorrow, the girl did not notice his momentary preoccupation, but continued:

'He never said good-bye to me. Dr Warrender said he was insensible for so long before death that it was useless my seeing him. He kept me out of the room, so I only saw him—afterwards. I'll never forgive the doctor for it. It was cruel!'

She sobbed hysterically.

'Sophy,' said Alan suddenly, 'had your father any enemies?'

She looked round at him in astonishment.

'I don't know. I don't think so. Why should he? He was the kindest man in the world.'

'I am sure he was,' replied the young man warmly; 'but even the kindest may have enemies.'

'He might have made enemies in Africa,' she said gravely. 'It was there he made his money, and I suppose there are people mean enough to hate a man who is successful, especially if his success results in a fortune of some two millions. Father used to say he despised most people. That was why he lived so quietly at the Moat House.'

'It was particularly quiet till you came, Sophy.'

'I'm sure it was,' she replied, with the glimmer of a smile. 'Still, although *he* had not me, you had your profession.'

'Ah! my poor profession! I always regret having given it up.'

'Why did you?'

'You know, Sophy. I have told you a dozen times. I wanted to be a surgeon, but my father always objected to a Thorold being of service to his fellow-creatures. I could never understand why. The estate was not entailed, and by my father's will I was to lose it, or give up all hope of becoming a doctor. For my mother's sake I surrendered. But I would choose to be a struggling surgeon in London any day, if it were not for you, Sophy dear.'

'Horrid!' ejaculated Miss Marlow, elevating her nose. 'How can you enjoy cutting up people? But don't let us talk of these things; they remind me of poor dear father.'

'My dear, you really should not be so morbid. Death is only natural. It is not as though you had been with him all your life, instead of merely three years.'

'I know; but I loved him none the less for that. I often wonder why he was away so long.'

'He was making his fortune. He could not have taken you into the rough life he was leading in Africa. You were quite happy in your convent.'

'Quite,' she agreed, with conviction. 'I was sorry to leave it. The dear sisters were like mothers to me. I never knew my own mother. She died in Jamaica, father said, when I was only ten years old. He could not bear to remain in the West Indies after she died, so he brought me to England. While I was in the convent I saw him only now and again until I had finished my education. Then he took the Moat House—that was five years ago, and two years after that I came to live with him. That is all our history, Alan. But Joe Brill might know if he had any enemies.'

'Yes, he might. He lived thirty years with your father, didn't he? But he can keep his own counsel—no one better.'

'You are good at it too, Alan. Where were you last night? You did not come to see me.'

He moved uneasily. He had his own reasons for not wishing to give a direct answer.

'I went for a long walk—to—to—to think out one or two things. When I got back it was too late to see you.'

'What troubled you, Alan? You have looked very worried lately. I am sure you are in some trouble. Tell me, dear; I must share all your troubles.'

'My dearest, I am in no trouble'—he kissed her hand—'but I am your trustee, you know and it is no sinecure to have the management of two millions.'

'It's too much money,' she said. 'Let us dispose of some of it, then you need not be worried. Can I do what I like with it?'

'Most of it—there are certain legacies. I will tell you about them later.'

'I am afraid the estate will be troublesome to us, Alan. It's strange we should have so much money when we don't care about it. Now, there is Dr Warrender, working his life out for that silly extravagant wife of his!'

'He is very much in love with her, nevertheless.'

'I suppose that's why he works so hard. But she's a horrid woman, and cares not a snap of her fingers for him—not to speak of love! Love! why, she doesn't know the meaning of the word. We do!' And, bending over, Sophy kissed him.

Then promptly there came from Miss Parsh the reminder that it was time for tea.

'Very well, Vicky, I dare say Alan would like you to give him a cup,' replied Sophy.

'Frivolous as ever, Sophia! I give up a hope of forming your character—now!'

'Alan is doing that,' replied the girl.

In spite of her sorrow, Sophy became fairly cheerful on the way back to the hotel. Not so Alan. He was silent and thoughtful, and evidently meditating about the responsibilities of the Marlow estate. As they walked along the parade with their chaperon close behind, they came upon a crowd surrounding a fat man dressed in dingy black. He was reciting a poem, and his voice boomed out like a great organ. As they passed, Alan noticed that he darted a swift glance at them, and eyed Miss Marlow in a particularly curious manner. The recitation was just finished, and the hat was being sent round. Sophy, always kind-hearted, dropped in a shilling. The man chuckled.

'Thank you, lady,' said he; 'the first of many, I hope.'

Alan frowned, and drew his fiancée away. He took little heed of the remark at the time; but it occurred to him later when circumstances had arisen which laid more stress on its meaning.

Miss Vicky presided over the tea—a gentle feminine employment in which she excelled. She did most of the talking; for Sophy was silent, and Alan inclined to monosyllables. The good lady announced that she was anxious to return to Heathton.

'The house weighs on my mind,' said she, lifting her cup with the little finger curved. 'The servants are not to be trusted. I fear Mrs Crammer is addicted to ardent spirits. Thomas and Jane pay too much attention to one another. I feel a conviction that, during my absence, the bonds of authority will have loosened.'

'Joe,' said Alan, setting down his cup; 'Joe is a great disciplinarian.'

'On board a ship, no doubt,' assented Miss Vicky; 'but a rough sailor cannot possibly know how to control a household. Joseph is a fine, manly fellow, but boisterous—very boisterous. It needs my eye to make domestic matters go smoothly. When will you be ready to return, Sophy, my dear?'

'In a week—but Alan has suggested that we should go abroad.'

'What! and leave the servants to wilful waste and extravagance? My love!'—Miss Vicky raised her two mittened hands—'think of the bills!'

'There is plenty of money, Vicky.'

'No need there should be plenty of waste. No; if we go abroad, we must either shut up the house or let it.'

'To the Quiet Gentleman?' said Sophy, with a laugh.

Alan looked up suddenly.

'No, not to him. He is a mysterious person,' said Miss Vicky. 'I do not like such people, though I dare say it is only village gossip which credits him with a strange story.'

'Just so,' put in Alan. 'Don't trouble about him.'

Miss Vicky was still discussing the possibility of a trip abroad, when the waiter entered with a note for Sophy.

'It was delivered three hours ago,' said the man apologetically, 'and I quite forgot to bring it up. So many visitors, miss,' he added, with a sickly smile.

Sophy took the letter. The envelope was a thick creamy one, and the writing of the address elegant in the extreme.

'Who delivered it?' she asked.

'A fat man, miss, with a red face, and dressed in black.'

Alan's expression grew somewhat anxious.

'Surely that describes the man we saw reciting?'

'So it does.' Sophy eyed the letter dubiously. 'Had he a loud voice, Simmonds?'

'As big as a bell, miss, and he spoke beautiful: but he wasn't gentry, for all that,' finished Simmonds with conviction.

'You can go,' said Alan. Then he turned to Sophy, who was opening the envelope. 'Let me read that letter first,' he said.

'Why, Alan? There is no need. It is only a begging letter. Come and read it with me.'

He gave way, and looked over her shoulder at the elaborate writing.

'Miss' (it began),

'The undersigned, if handsomely remunerated, can give valuable information regarding the removal of the body of the late Richard Marlow from its dwelling in Heathton Churchyard. *Verbum dat sapienti!* Forward £100 to the undersigned at Dixon's Rents, Lambeth, and the information will be forthcoming. If the minions of the law are invoked the undersigned with vanish, and his information lost.

'Faithfully yours, Miss Sophia Marlow,

'CICERO GRAMP.'

As she comprehended the meaning of this extraordinary letter, Sophy became paler and paler. The intelligence that her father's body had been stolen was too much for her, and she fainted.

Thorold called loudly to Miss Vicky.

'Look after her,' he said, stuffing the letter into his pocket. 'I shall be back soon.'

'But what—what—?' began Miss Vicky.

She spoke to thin air. Alan was running at top speed along the parade in search of the fat man.

But all search was vain. Cicero, the astute, had vanished.

CHAPTER IV

ANOTHER SURPRISE

HEATHTON was only an hour's run by rail from Bournemouth, so that it was easy enough to get back on the same evening. On his return from his futile search for Cicero, Alan determined to go at once to the Moat House. He found Sophy recovered from her faint, and on hearing of his decision, she insisted upon accompanying him. She had told Miss Vicky the contents of the mysterious letter, and that lady agreed that they should leave as soon as their boxes could be packed.

'Don't talk to me, Alan!' cried Sophy, when her lover objected to this sudden move. 'It would drive me mad to stay here doing nothing, with that on my mind.'

'But, my dear girl, it may not be true.'

'If it is not, why should that man have written? Did you see him?'

'No. He has left the parade, and no one seems to know anything about him. It is quite likely that when he saw us returning to the hotel he cleared out. By this time I dare say he is on his way to London.'

'Did you see the police?' she asked anxiously.

'No,' said Alan, taking out the letter which had caused all this trouble; 'it would not be wise. Remember what he says here: If the police are called in he will vanish, and we shall lose the information he seems willing to supply.'

'I don't think that, Mr Thorold,' said Miss Vicky. 'This man evidently wants money, and is willing to tell the truth for the matter of a hundred pounds.'

'On account,' remarked Thorold grimly; 'as plain a case of blackmail as I ever heard of. Well, I suppose it is best to wait until we can communicate with this—what does he call himself?—Cicero Gramp, at Dixon's Rents, Lambeth. He can be arrested there, if necessary. What I want to do now is to find out if his story is true. To do this I must go at once to Heathton, see the Rector, and get the coffin opened.'

'I will come,' insisted Sophy. 'Oh, it is terrible to think that poor father was not allowed to rest quietly even in his grave.'

'Of course, it may not be true,' urged Alan again. 'I don't see how this tramp could have got to know of it.'

'Perhaps he helped to violate the secrets of the tomb?' suggested Miss Vicky.

'In that case he would hardly put himself within reach of the law,' Alan said, after a pause. 'Besides, if the vault had been broken into we should have heard of it from Joe.'

'Why should it be broken into, Alan? The key—'

'I have one key, and the Rector has the other. My key is in my desk at the Abbey Farm, and no doubt Phelps has his safe enough.'

'Your key may have been stolen.'

'It might have been,' admitted Alan. 'That is one reason why I am so anxious to get back tonight. We must find out also if the coffin is empty.'

'Yes, yes; let us go at once!' Sophy cried feverishly. 'I shall never rest until I learn the truth. Come, Vicky, let us pack. When can we leave, Alan?'

Thorold glanced at his watch.

'In half an hour,' he said. 'We can catch the half-past six train. Can you be ready?'

'Yes, yes!' cried she, and rushed out of the room.

Miss Vicky was about to follow, but Alan detained her.

'Give her a sedative or something,' he said, 'or she will be ill.'

'I will at once. Have a carriage at the door in a quarter of an hour, Mr Thorold. We can be ready by then. I suppose it is best she should go?'

'Much better than to leave her here. We must set her mind at rest. At this rate she will work herself into a fever.'

'But if this story should really be true?'

'I don't believe it for a moment,' replied Alan. But he was evidently uneasy, and could not disguise the feeling. 'Wait till we get to Heathton—wait,' and he hastily left the room.

Miss Vicky was surprised at his agitation, for hitherto she had credited Alan with a will strong enough to conceal his emotions. The old lady hurried away to the packing, and shook her head as she went.

Shortly they were settled in a first-class carriage on the way to Heathton. Sophy was suffering acutely, but did all in her power to hide her feelings, and, contrary to Alan's expectations, hardly a word was spoken about the strange letter, and the greater part of the journey was passed in silence. At Heathton he put Sophy and Miss Vicky into a fly.

'Drive at once to the Moat House,' he said. 'Tomorrow we shall consider what is to be done.'

'And you, Alan?'

'I am going to see Mr Phelps. He, if anyone, will know what value to put upon that letter. Try and sleep, Sophy. I shall see you in the morning.'

'Sleep?' echoed the poor girl, in a tone of anguish. 'I feel as though I should never sleep again!'

When they had driven away, Alan him took the nearest way to the Rectory. It was some way from the station, but Alan was a vigorous walker, and soon covered the distance. He arrived at the door with a beating heart and dry lips, feeling, he knew not why, that he was about to hear bad news. The grey-haired butler ushered him into his master's presence, and immediately the young man felt that his fears were confirmed. Phelps looked worried.

He was a plump little man, neat in his dress and cheerful in manner. He was a bachelor, and somewhat of a cynic. Alan had known him all his life, and could have found no better adviser in the dilemma in which he now found himself. Phelps came forward with outstretched hands.

'My dear boy, I am indeed glad! What good fairy sent you here? A glass of port? You look pale. I am delighted to see you. If you had not come I should have had to send for you.'

'What do you wish to see me about, sir? asked Alan.

'About the disappearance of these two people.'

'What two people?' asked the young man, suddenly alert. 'You forget that I have been away from Heathton for the last three days.'

'Of course, of course. Well, one is Brown, the stranger who stayed with Mrs Marry.'

'The Quiet Gentleman?'

'Yes. I heard them call him so in the village. A very doubtful character. He never came to church,' said the Rector sadly. 'However, it seems he has disappeared. Two nights ago—in fact, upon the evening of the day upon which poor Marlow's funeral took place, he left his lodgings for a walk. Since then,' added the Rector impressively, 'he has not returned.'

'In plain words, he has taken French leave,' said Thorold, filling his glass.

'Oh, I should not say that, Alan. He paid his weekly account the day before he vanished. He left his baggage behind him. No, I don't think he intended to run away. Mrs Marry says he was a good lodger, although she knew very little about him. However, he has gone, and his box remains. No one saw him after he left the village about eight o'clock. He was last seen by Giles Hale passing the church in the direction of the moor. Today we searched the moor, but could find no trace of him. Most mysterious,' finished the Rector, and took some port.

'Who is the other man?' asked Alan abruptly.

'Ah! Now you must be prepared for a shock, Alan. Dr Warrender!'

Thorold bounded out of his seat.

'Is he lost too?'

'Strangely enough, he is,' answered Phelps gravely. 'On the night of the funeral he went out at nine o'clock in the evening to see a patient. He never came back.'

'Who was the patient?'

'That is the strangest part of it. Brown, the Quiet Gentleman, was the patient. Mrs Warrender, who, as you may guess, is quite distracted, says that her husband told her so. Mrs Marry declares that the doctor called after nine, and found Brown was absent.'

'What happened then?' demanded Alan, who had been listening eagerly to this tale.

'Dr Warrender, according to Mrs Marry, asked in what direction her lodger had gone. She could not tell him, so, saying he would call again in an hour or so, he went. And, of course, he never returned.'

'Did Brown send for him?'

'Mrs Marry could not say. Certainly no message was sent through her.'

'Was Brown ill?'

'Not at all, according to his landlady. We have been searching for both Brown and Warrender, but have found no traces of either.'

'Humph!' said Thorold, after a pause. 'I wonder if they met and went away together?'

'My dear lad, where would they go to?' objected the Rector.

'I don't know; I can't say. The whole business is most mysterious.' Alan stopped, and looked sharply at Mr Phelps. 'Have you the key of the Marlow vault in your possession?'

'Yes, of course, locked in my safe. Your question is most extraordinary.'

The other smiled grimly.

'My explanation is more extraordinary still.' He took out Mr Gramp's letter and handed it to the Rector. 'What do you think of that, sir?'

'Most elegant calligraphy,' said the good man. 'Why, bless

me!' He read on hurriedly, and finally dropped the letter with a bewildered air. 'Bless me, Alan!' he stammered. 'What—what—what—'

Thorold picked it up and smoothed it out on the table.

'You see, this man says the body has been stolen. Do you know if the door of the vault has been broken open?'

'No, no, certainly not!' cried the Rector, rising fussily. 'Come to my study, Alan; we must see if it is all right. It must be,' he added emphatically. 'The key of the safe is on my watch-chain. No one can open it. Oh dear! Bless me!'

He bustled out of the room, followed by Alan.

A search into the interior of the safe resulted in the production of the key.

'You see,' cried Phelps, waving it triumphantly, 'it is safe. The door could not have been opened with this. Now your key.'

'My key is in my desk at the Abbey Farm—locked up also,' said the young man hastily. 'I'll see about it tonight. In the meantime, sir, bring that key with you, and we will go into the vault.'

'What for?' demanded the Rector sharply. 'Why should we go there?'

'Can't you understand?' said Alan impatiently. 'I want to find out if this letter is true or false—if the body of Mr Marlow has been removed.'

'But I—I—can't!' gasped the Rector. 'I must apply to the Bishop for—'

'Nonsense, sir! We are not going to exhume the body. It's not like digging up a grave. All that is necessary is to look at the coffin resting in its niche. We can tell from the screws and general appearance if it has been tampered with.'

The clergyman sat down and wiped his bald head.

'I don't like it,' he said. 'I don't like it at all. Still, I don't suppose a look at the coffin can harm anyone. We'll go, Alan, we'll go; but I must take Jarks.'

'The sexton?'

'Yes. I want a witness—two witnesses; you are one, Jarks the other. It is a gruesome task that we have before us.' He shuddered again. 'I don't like it. Profanation!'

'If this letter is to be believed, the profanation has already been committed.'

'Cicero Gramp,' repeated Mr Phelps as they went out. 'Who is he?'

'A fat man—a tramp—a reciter. I saw him at Bournemouth. He delivered that letter at the hotel himself; the waiter described him, and as the creature is a perfect Falstaff, I recalled his face—I had seen him on the parade. I went at once to see if I could find him, but he was gone.'

'A fat man,' said the Rector. 'Humph! He was at the Good Samaritan the other night. I'll tell you about him later.'

The two trudged along in silence and knocked up Jarks, the sexton, on the way. They had no difficulty in rousing him. He came down at once with a lantern, and was much surprised to learn the errand of Rector and Squire.

'Want to have a look at Muster Marlow's vault,' said he in creaking tones. 'Well, it ain't a bad night for a visit, I do say. But quiet comp'ny, Muster Phelps and Muster Thorold, very quiet. What do ye want to see Muster Marlow for?'

'We want to see if his body is in the vault,' said Alan.

'Why, for sure it's there, sir. Muster Marlow don't go visiting.'

'I had a letter at Bournemouth, Jarks, to say the body had been stolen.'

Jarks stared.

'It ain't true!' he cried in a voice cracked with passion. 'It's casting mud on my 'arning my bread. I've bin sexton here fifty year, man and boy—I never had no corp as was stolen. They all lies comfortable arter my tucking them in. Only Gabriel's trump will wake 'em.'

By this time they were round the Lady Chapel, and within sight of the tomb. Phelps, too much agitated to speak, beckoned to Jarks to hold up the lantern, which he did, grumbling and muttering the while.

'I've buried hundreds of corps,' he growled, 'and not one of 'em's goed away. What 'ud they go for? I make 'em comfortable, I do.'

'Hold the light steady, Jarks,' said the Rector, whose own hand was just as unsteady. He could hardly get the key into the lock.

At last the door was open, and headed by Jarks, with the lantern, they entered. The cold, earthy smell, the charnel-house feeling shook the nerves of both men. Jarks, accustomed as he was to the presence of the dead, hobbled along without showing any emotion other than wrath, and triumphantly swung the lantern towards a niche wherein reposed a coffin.

'Ain't he there quite comfortable?' wheezed he. 'Don't I tell you they never goes from here? It's a lovely vault; no corp 'ud need a finer.'

'Wait a bit!' said Alan, stepping forward. 'Turn the light along the top of the coffin, Jarks. Hullo! the lid's loose!'

'An' unscrewed!' gasped the sexton. 'He's bin getting out.'

'Unscrewed—loose!' gasped the Rector in his turn. The poor man felt deadly sick. 'There must be some mistake.'

'No mistake,' said Alan, slipping back the lid. 'The body has been stolen.'

'No 't'ain't!' cried Jarks, showering the light on the interior of the coffin. 'There he is, quiet an'—why,' the old man broke off with a cry, 'the corp ain't in his winding-sheet!'

Phelps looked, Alan looked. The light shone on the face of the dead.

Phelps groaned.

'Merciful God!' he groaned, 'it is Dr Warrender's body!'

CHAPTER V

A NINE DAYS' WONDER

THERE was sensation enough and to spare in Heathton next morning. Jarks lost no time in spreading the news. He spent the greater part of the day in the taproom of the Good Samaritan, accepting tankards of beer and relating details of the discovery. Mrs Timber kept him as long as she could; for Jarks, possessed of intelligence regarding the loss of Mr Marlow's body, attracted customers. These, thirsty for news or drink, or both, flocked like sheep into the inn.

'To think that a corp of mine should be gone!' creaked he in his aged voice. 'Man and boy, I niver heard tell of such things—niver! Why Muster Marlow should go beats me—ay, that it does!'

'It doesn't beat me,' cried Mrs Timber in her most acidulated voice. 'I know who took the body.'

'That you don't!' contradicted Jarks incoherently; 'fur passon, he don't know, so I don't know as how you'd know, Mrs Timber.'

'It was that fat play-actor out of this very house,' snapped the landlady.

'And how can you prove that, Mrs Timber?' asked the sexton contemptuously.

'Why, he had no money for a bed, and he had to sleep in the open. I dare say he slept in the churchyard, and stole the body to sell it back again, it being well known as Miss Sophy's a Queen of Sheba for riches.'

'All very well,' said Slack the schoolmaster; 'but if he took away Mr Marlow's body, how did he put Dr Warrender's in its place? And how could he without the key of the vault?'

'No,' said the stonemason, 'he couldn't get into that there vault without a key. I built him myself, me and my mates. If that fat man put the doctor there, he must have killed him. There's a hole in his heart as you could put your fist in. It's murder!' cried the man, dashing his hand on the table, 'sacrilege and murder!'

It took a good many tankards of Mrs Timber's strong ale to wash down the sinister word 'murder'. Every point of the matter was discussed, but no one could arrive at any decision. Slack voiced the general sentiment when he rose to go.

'We must wait for the police,' said Slack.

But Alan Thorold was of the contrary opinion. He did not wish to wait for the police, or to have anything to do with the police. The difficulty was that he could not get the Rector to take this view, and the next morning Mr Phelps sent the village constable for the inspector at Burchester, the big market town twenty miles away across the heath. Meantime, at an early hour, Alan presented himself at the Moat House. He broke the news as gently as he could. Both Sophy and Miss Vicky were horrified.

'To think of such things taking place in a Christian graveyard!' cried the little woman, wringing her hands. 'Sacrilege and murder! It makes one believe in the existence of atheists and anarchists, and such-like dreadful people—it does, indeed!'

Contrary to Thorold's expectation, Sophy proved to be the more composed of the two. She neither wept nor fainted, but, very pale and very still, listened to all that he had to say. When he had finished, she had only one question to ask.

'Who did it?' she demanded in the calmest voice.

'I can't say—I don't know,' stammered Alan, taken aback by her attitude generally. 'We must find out. If your father had enemies—but even an enemy would have had no object in doing this.'

'What about the man in Bournemouth?'

'Cicero Gramp? I intend to go up to London tomorrow and see him. If he can tell the truth, it will be well worth the money he demands.'

'So I think, Alan. Can't you go today?'

He shook his head.

'There is so much to do here, Sophy. The Rector has gone to break the news of her husband's death to Mrs Warrender. And he has sent over to Burchester for the police. The inspector—Blair is his name—will be here at noon. I did not want the police brought into the matter, but Mr Phelps insisted.'

'Why did you not want to consult the police?'

'I am afraid if this vagabond gets wind that the law has intervened he may give us the slip. However, I shall go up to Dixon's Rents first thing in the morning, before the case gets into the papers.'

'Do you think this man Gramp has anything to do with the murder, and with the removing of poor father's body?'

'No, I don't,' replied Alan promptly. 'He would not dare to give evidence if he were. I hear that he was turned out of the Good Samaritan on the night of the funeral. It is likely enough that he saw the removal of the body, and possibly the murder. Naturally, such a creature as that wants to sell his information. He is a blackmailer, this man, but I don't credit him with murder or body-snatching.'

'Body-snatching!' cried Miss Vicky, who was dabbing her red eyes with eau-de-Cologne. 'Oh, the terrible word!'

'Alan,' said Sophy, after a pause, 'do you believe the man who took my father's body killed Dr Warrender?'

'I do. Warrender was out on that night, and might have come across the man carrying away the body, and the murder might have arisen out of that.'

'How do you know Dr Warrender was out?' cross-examined Sophy.

'Mrs Warrender told the Rector so. Warrender went to see the Quiet Gentleman, but not finding him in, said that he would return. He never did, and now we know the reason.'

'Why don't you make certain whether he saw the Quiet Gentleman?'

'Brown? That's impossible; he also has disappeared.'

'Who was he?'

'I don't know,' said Alan gloomily.

'Does anyone know?'

'Not to my knowledge. Perhaps the police may find out. Sophy, what is the matter?'

For the girl was clapping her hands and laughing hysterically.

'It was Brown who took my father's body and killed the doctor!' she cried. 'I am certain of it!'

'Why are you certain?'

'I feel it. I can't say why.'

'But your father did not know this man. I never heard him allude to the Quiet Gentleman.'

'I dare say not,' returned Sophy doggedly; 'but if the man had nothing to do with it, why should he disappear? And Dr Warrender went to see him. Oh! I am sure he is the guilty person. He might be an enemy of father's.'

'Sophia, your father did not know him,' put in Miss Vicky, who was listening open-mouthed to all this.

'Oh, I am not so sure of that!' cried the girl impatiently. 'If he did, Joe will know. Ring the bell for him.'

'Did Joe know the Quiet Gentleman?' Alan asked when he had rung.

'I do not think that Joseph did,' said Miss Vicky. 'He told me that he tried several times to speak to him, but got no reply.'

'I don't wonder at that,' replied the young man drily; 'the man was dumb.'

'Dumb?' echoed the ladies.

'Didn't you know? Ah, well, perhaps not. I didn't know myself until the Rector told me last night. Yes, he was dumb—

that was why the village called him the Quiet Gentleman. Oh, here is Joe!'

'Joe,' said Sophy, going directly to the point, 'have you heard about—?'

'Yes, miss,' said Joe, interrupting to save her mentioning so painful a subject, 'I know, and if I find the swab as did it, I'll kill him.'

Joe said this in a quietly savage way, which made Miss Vicky shudder.

'Have you any idea who carried off the body, Joe?'

'No, sir, I have not—but,' added the man grimly, 'I'm going to look for him.'

The old maid shuddered again at the expression in his blood-shot eyes.

'"Vengeance is mine. I will repay, saith the Lord",' she put in severely.

'All werry good,' said Mr Brill, 'but I guess the Lord needs an instrument to carry out that text.' He spat on his hands and added slowly, 'I'm that instrument!'

'Had my father any enemies that you know of, Joe?'

'No, miss, not that I knowed of. He had rows, as a man should, had the Cap'n, but I don't know any swab as 'ud have stolen his corpse.'

'And murdered Dr Warrender,' said Alan, who was watching the man.

'As you say, sir,' replied the sailor calmly, 'and murdered Dr Warrender. No, I can't rightly call anyone to mind.'

'Did you know the Quiet Gentleman, Joe?'

'I did not, miss. Brown he called hisself—leastways, Mrs Marry told me so, for Brown had no tongue. I tried to pass the time o' day, meeting him friendly like on the road, but he only put his hand to his mouth and shook his white head. I don't know nothing about him.'

'Do you know a tramp named Cicero Gramp?' asked Alan, after a pause.

'Well, I did in a way.' Joe drew his huge hand across his mouth, and seemed to be considering his reply. 'In this way, sir. He comed here to the kitchen and put 'em all wrong with his lies. I kicked him out—leastways, I giv 'im something to take 'imself orf.'

'What did he come here for?'

Joe clenched his teeth and frowned dreadfully.

'I wish I knowed, I'd ha' broken his cocoanut!' said he. 'He was a liar, miss, savin' your presence. Said 'e knowed your father, the Cap'n, which,' said Joe slowly, 'was a d—d lie—beggin' your pardon, miss.'

'Said he knew my father?' echoed Sophy anxiously. 'What did he know about him?'

'Nothin',' replied Joe firmly. 'Make your mind easy, miss—nothin'.'

It seemed to Alan as though the old sailor wished to intimate that there really was something in Marlow's past which might be known, but that the tramp was ignorant of it. He evidently wanted to reassure the girl, yet Alan was well aware that Sophy knew practically nothing of her father's life. He resolved to try the effect of a surprise.

'Joe,' said he slowly, 'it was this tramp who told me the body had been stolen.'

Joe's hard, shiny hat, which he had been twisting nervously in his hands, fell to the ground. His face was a dark crimson when he stooped to pick it up, and he stammered:

'Hi, sir! that—that lubber. How did he know?'

'That I have to find out. He offers to sell the information for a hundred pounds.'

Joe rubbed his hands and looked ferocious.

'What I want to know, sir, is, where is the swab?'

'In London. I'm going up to see him tomorrow.'

'This afternoon,' put in Sophy sharply. 'You are going this afternoon, Alan.'

'Certainly, my dear,' Alan said promptly; 'I'll go this afternoon—if the police don't want me.'

'The police!' gasped Joe, shifting nervously from one leg to the other.

'Yes.' Alan darted a keen glance at him. 'Mr Phelps has sent for the police to investigate this murder of Dr Warrender.'

'Well, I hope they'll find him, sir,' said Joe, recovering his stolidity, 'for I make no doubt that the swab as killed the doctor carried off the Cap'n's body.'

'So I think, Joe, and I am going to London to find out from Cicero Gramp.'

'You'll find he'll tell you that the Quiet Gentleman killed Dr Warrender,' put in Sophy.

The old sailor choked, and looked at her with absolute terror. 'How do you know that, miss?' he asked.

'I only think so. The Quiet Gentleman has disappeared. Probably he killed the doctor, and then took my father's body.'

'It might be so, miss. If I find him—'

Joe repeated his former savage declaration, and Miss Vicky duly shuddered.

'Then you can't help us in any way, Joe?' said Alan, eyeing him thoughtfully.

'No, sir, I can't. I don't know who carried off the Cap'n, and I don't know who stabbed the doctor. If I did, I'd kill him. When you find him, sir, let me know.'

After which speech the old sailor again pulled his forelock, scraped his foot, and rolled out of the room. He appeared somewhat relieved to get away.

Alan did not quite know what to make of Joe. The man was so nervous that it seemed as though he knew something and was afraid of committing himself. On the other hand, this sailor was devoted to Sophy, and had been in Marlow's service for thirty years. It was only reasonable to conclude, therefore, that he would wish her to benefit by any knowledge he might possess. On the whole, Alan was perplexed, but he kept it to himself, determining, nevertheless, to keep an eye on Joe. When the door was closed, Sophy turned to Alan.

'Alan,' she said slowly, 'I love you dearly, as you know, and I wish to become your wife. But I swear by the memory of my father that until you find out who has done this wicked thing and bring the man to justice, I will not marry you!'

'Sophy!' cried Thorold entreatingly.

'I mean what I say,' repeated the girl, in a low, fierce voice. 'We must avenge my father. When the wretch is caught and hanged, then I'll marry you, Alan.'

'Sophia, a marriage under such circumstances—'

'Miss Parsh,' cried Sophy, turning on the meek old maid, 'do you think I can sit down tamely under this insult to the dead? My father's body has been carried off. It must be found again before I marry—before I can think of marriage, Alan.'

'Sophy is right,' cried Thorold, drawing the girl to him and kissing her. 'She is right, Miss Parsh. I swear also that I will devote my life to solving this mystery. Your father's body shall be brought back, Sophy, and the murderer of Dr Warrender shall hang. Good-bye, dear. Today I go to London. The first step towards the discovery of this crime will be to see Cicero Gramp. He may supply the clue.'

'Yes, yes. Bribe him; pay him anything, so long as you get at the truth.'

Alan kissed the girl again, and then left the room. Before he started, he intended to see the Rector and the local inspector of police. As he stepped out on to the road, he noticed Phelps coming along in the hot sunshine. The little parson was puffing and blowing and wiping his forehead.

'Alan! Alan!' he called out in short gasps as he came within speaking distance. 'She's gone! She's gone to—'

'She! Gone! Who's gone? Where?'

'Why, Mrs Warrender! She's disappeared. Oh, dear me; how terrible all this is! Whew!'

CHAPTER VI

THE MISSING KEY

So excited was the little parson that Alan feared lest he should take a fit. The Good Samaritan was no great distance away, so thither he led him, into Mrs Timber's private parlour.

'Now, sir,' said Alan, when his old tutor seemed somewhat more composed, 'tell me all about Mrs Warrender.'

But before Mr Phelps could reply, the vixenish landlady made her appearance. She was highly honoured at seeing the Rector within her doors, and curtsied a hint for orders. And, in truth, the little clergyman, undone with excitement, was quite ready to stimulate his jaded nerves.

'Eh, Mrs Timber?' he said. 'Yes; you might get us a little Cognac, I think. Old; the best you have, Mrs Timber, and a jug of fresh-drawn water from the well, please. Alan?'

'I'll join you,' said young Thorold promptly.

He, too, felt that he was in nowise beyond reach of a little stimulant.

Silent for once in her life, Mrs Timber brought of her best, which, be it said, was passing good. Mr Phelps lost no time in brewing his measure and drank it down with gusto.

'That's good, Alan, my boy; very good,' said he, setting down the tumbler with a sigh of relief. 'God forgive me, I fear to think what my good brethren would say did they see their Rector in a public-house! though to be sure the Good Samaritan is a most respectable hostelry. But, Alan, why did you bring me here?'

'Indeed, sir, I feared you would be ill out there in the blazing sun. I did only what I thought wise. But about Mrs Warrender—you say she has disappeared?'

'Eh, yes.' Mr Phelps wiped his bald head vigorously. 'I went

41

to break the news to her after you had gone to see Sophy, and I found she had left for London.'

'London? Why London?'

'That is just what I wanted to know, my dear Alan. It seems she received last night a letter which threw her into a state of great excitement. She was bad enough that way, as it was, the servant said; but this letter, it appears, drove her into a perfect frenzy.'

'Do you know what was in the letter?'

'I asked that—oh, trust me, Alan, to be precise about details— but the servant said she did not know. Mrs Warrender put it in her pocket. That spoke volumes from the servant's point of view. All night long, it appears, she was walking about the room using the most fearful language—God forgive her!—and this morning at eight o'clock she started off to catch the 9.30 express at the Junction.'

'And is she coming back?'

'That I don't know, my boy.'

Mr Phelps looked round cautiously and lowered his voice to a whisper.

'She took her jewels with her.'

'Her jewels?'

'Yes; she had a quantity of jewellery. She put all the money she could get from her husband into clothes and diamonds—a most extravagant woman, Alan. Well, she's gone, that's certain, jewels and all. She left no address, and said no word about returning. What do you think of it?'

'Upon my word, sir, I don't know what to think. The whole place has gone mad, it seems to me; the entire village is topsy-turvy. Marlow's body stolen, Warrender murdered, and his body placed in poor Marlow's coffin; and now here is Mrs Warrender cleared out significantly with her jewels; and the Quiet Gentleman—'

'Brown, the dumb man? What about him? I know he, too, has vanished; but what else?'

'I'm going to tell you, sir. The key of the vault—'

'Not your key, Alan?'

'Yes, my key, Mr Phelps; the Quiet Gentleman has it!'

'God bless me—that is, God forgive me, Alan, are you mad too?'

'No, sir, not yet; though I admit I'm fairly on the way, with all this. Tell me, do you know who this so-called Quiet Gentleman really is?'

'No, Alan, I don't. I spoke to him, but found he was dumb. Now he too is gone.'

'Yes, with Marlow's body on his hands, and Warrender's death on his soul!'

'You don't mean that! Are you sure?'

Mr Phelps was greatly agitated.

'I go only by circumstantial evidence, it is true. You know, of course, the funeral of Mr Marlow took place in the morning?'

'Yes, yes; and at two o'clock you took Sophy and Miss Parsh to Bournemouth.'

'I did. Well, about five o'clock, Brown—we'll call him that instead of the Quiet Gentleman, though I don't believe it really is his name—well, about that time Brown walked over to Abbey Farm. He brought a letter purporting to come from me to my housekeeper, Mrs Hester.'

'From you, Alan?'

'Yes, the letter was forged,' said Alan with emphasis. 'It directed Mrs Hester to allow Brown to remain at the farm until I returned. It was in my handwriting, and signed with my name. She knew nothing about Brown, save that he was staying at Mrs Marry's, and she thought it somewhat strange he should come to stop at the farm during my absence. But as the instructions in the letter were quite plain, and she knew my handwriting well—that shows how expert the forgery was—she gave Brown the run of the place. In the meantime she wrote to me at Bournemouth asking me if all was right, and enclosed the forged letter. Here it is!'

As he saw the handwriting, Mr Phelps started.

'Upon my word, Alan, I don't wonder Mrs Hester was deceived, especially when you consider her sight is not good! Why, I myself with my eyes should certainly take it for yours.' (Mr Phelps wore pince-nez, but nevertheless resented any aspersion on his optical powers.) 'But why on earth didn't she telegraph to you?'

'Well, you know how old-fashioned and conservative she is, sir. She makes out through the Scriptures—how, I cannot tell you—that the telegraph is a sinful institution. Therefore it is not to be wondered at that she trusted to the post. I got her letter only this morning as, of course, it followed me on from Bournemouth. Nevertheless, I knew about the loss of the key last night.'

'Ah! the loss of the key. Yes, go on, Alan.'

'Very well. Brown, being allowed to remain in my house, proceeded to make himself quite at home in the library. Mrs Hester, writing her letter—no easy task for her—took no further heed of him. He was in the room for quite an hour, and amused himself, it appears, in breaking open my desk. Having forced several of the drawers, he found at last the one he wanted—the one containing the key of the vault. Then he made all things beautifully smooth, so that Mrs Hester should not see they had been tampered with, and leaving a message that he would return to dinner, went out ostensibly for a walk. He returned, it appears, to his lodging, and left there again about nine o'clock in the evening. Since then nothing has been seen or heard of him.'

'God bless me, Alan! are you sure he has the key?'

'Positive. I looked in my desk last night and it was not there. But everything was done so nicely that I am strongly of the opinion that Mr Brown has served his apprenticeship as a cracksman, and that under a pretty good master too. No one but he could have stolen that key. Besides, the forged letter shows plainly that he came to the farm with no honest intentions.

But what I can't understand,' continued Alan, biting his moustache, 'is how the man came to know where the key was.'

'Extraordinary—yes, that is extraordinary. Undoubtedly he it was who stole the body and gained access to the vault with your key. But the murder of Dr Warrender—'

'He committed that too; I am convinced of it. Warrender called to see him, found he was out, and I have no doubt followed him. He probably saw Brown remove the body, and of course interfered, upon which the villain made short work of him. That is my theory, sir.'

'And a very sound one, too, in many respects,' said the Rector. 'But Brown could not have removed the body alone. He must have had an accomplice.'

'True; and it is for that very reason I am going to town this afternoon. Cicero Gramp may be able to supply some information on that point. It is quite possible he slept in the churchyard and saw the whole business—murder and all.'

'Alan! Alan!' cried Mr Phelps, horrified. 'Do you believe this murder was committed on the sacred soil of the churchyard, in God's own acre, Alan? No one, surely, could be so vile!'

'I do, sir; and at the door of the vault. Brown, as you say yourself, cleverly concealed the body in Marlow's coffin. He had no time to screw it down again, apparently. He must have had a pretty tough job to cut through that lead. He had to trust to chance, of course, that the vault would not be visited until he had got a safe distance away with his booty. And, indeed, but for Gramp's letter, no one would ever have thought of going there. In fact, this Brown is a most ingenious and dangerous criminal.'

'He is; indeed he is. But what could he possibly want the body for?'

'Ha! that's just it! I fancy this is a case of blackmail. If you remember, a millionaire's body was stolen in America some few years ago, and only restored to the family on payment by them of a very large sum of money.'

'Oh, that is what you think he is after?'

'Yes, I do. It is highly probable, I think, that in a few weeks, or perhaps even in less time, we shall receive a letter demanding some thousands for the return of the body.'

'But surely the police—'

'Oh, Mr Brown will look after all that. You may depend upon it he'll make himself quite safe before he goes that far. So talented a gentleman as he would not be likely to omit all necessary precautions of that kind.'

'Humph!' muttered Mr Phelps, considering, 'and of Mrs Warrender's suspicious flight, what think you?'

'I confess I don't know quite what to make of that. I have no great opinion of her as a woman; still, I should hardly credit her with being in league with this ruffian.'

'No, indeed; for that, she must needs be the worst of women,' said Mr Phelps with warmth. 'Why, Alan, poor Warrender was simply crazy about her. He worked day and night to provide her with the finery she craved for. Besides, she seemed really fond of him.'

'Who was she?' asked Alan bluntly.

'Well, I shouldn't like to say it to everyone, Alan, but Mrs Warrender had been an actress.'

'An actress! Under what name?'

'That I cannot tell you. I called there one day and I heard her reciting Shakespeare. Her elocution seemed to me so fine that I complimented her upon it. Then she told me that she had been on the stage, and had retired when she married Warrender.'

'That's very strange! I always thought she had somewhat of a professional manner about her.'

'And her hair, Alan! *Flava coma*—yellow hair; not that I mean, for one moment, she was what the Romans referred to by these words. Well, my boy, what is to be done now?'

'I am going up to London in an hour's time.' Alan glanced at his watch while speaking.

'But you'll miss seeing Blair, the inspector,' remonstrated Mr Phelps.

'I'll see him when I return: you can explain the case as well as I, sir. I shall bring Gramp back with me if I can manage it.'

'And Mrs Warrender—shall I tell Blair about her?'

'I fear you must. But let him be circumspect. It is not necessary to take any steps against her until we are tolerably sure of the reason for her sudden flight. When do they hold the inquest on Warrender?'

'Tomorrow.'

'Well, I'll be back tonight and tell you what I've done.' And Alan rose to go.

'One moment, my dear boy. What about Sophy?'

'I've seen her, and, of course, I was judicious in what I told her. She knows nothing about the loss of the key and my suspicions of Brown, although, funnily enough, she herself suspects him.'

'Bless me! On what grounds can she do that?'

'Oh, on the purely feminine grounds that she suspects him. She declares she will not marry me until her father's body is discovered.'

'Very right; very proper. I quite agree with her. You should start your married life with an absolutely clean sheet, Alan.'

The young man nodded, and as he left the inn he delivered himself of one warning.

'Whatever you do, keep your eye on Joe Brill,' he said significantly.

'Why—why? What for?'

'Because I fancy he knows a good deal more than he is inclined to tell,' replied Alan.

Then, without further comment, he drove off, leaving the Rector considerably bewildered at this abrupt interpolation of a fresh name into the persons of the drama.

Meanwhile, Alan caught his train, and in due time, or a very fair approach to it, arrived in London. He took a hasty lunch at Waterloo, and drove to Westminster Bridge. Here he dismissed his cab, and set about inquiring for Dixon's Rents. The slum—its name was highly suggestive of its being such—appeared to be well known. The first constable he asked was both familiar with and communicative about it.

'It's within easy distance of Lambeth Palace, sir,' he said. 'A bit rough by night, but you'll be all right there in the daytime. Ask any constable near by the Palace, sir, and he'll put you right. Thank you, sir.'

Alan left the officer of the law well pleased with his unlooked-for half-crown, and walked on towards the Palace. The second constable could not leave his beat, but the bestowal of another half-crown elicited from him the practical suggestion that a certain young shoeblack of repute should act as guide. The shoeblack was quite near at hand, and very shortly was enrolled as guide for the occasion. Together he and Alan started off, leaving the constable well content, though withal a trifle mystified, not to say curious.

The shoeblack led the way, and Alan followed closely. They turned away from the river into a mass of houses, where the streets became more and more squalid, and the population more and more ragged and unkempt. At length, after many twistings and turnings, they arrived at the entrance to a narrow cul-de-sac, and he was informed that this was his destination. He rewarded and dismissed the shoeblack, and proceeded down the dirty lane. Almost the first person he saw was a tall woman standing at the entrance of the court, closely veiled. She seemed to be hesitating whether she would come on or not. Then, suddenly, she threw up her veil. As she did so Alan uttered an exclamation of surprise.

It was Mrs Warrender!

CHAPTER VII

IN DIXON'S RENTS

AT the sound of Alan's voice Mrs Warrender started like a guilty thing. He was astonished beyond measure at finding her in the same unsavoury neighbourhood as himself, bound, for all he knew, on the same errand. At all events, it was surely more than a coincidence that she should be on the threshold of Gramp's dwelling, so to speak.

'Mrs Warrender,' he said, gravely lifting his hat, 'this is indeed a surprise. Of course, you know what has happened at Heathton?'

'I know all,' answered the woman, in a rich, low voice. 'Jarks, the sexton, told my servant this morning what has happened to poor Julian, and that his body has been found in the Marlow vault.'

'Are you sure you did not know of it last night?' asked Alan quietly.

'Mr Thorold!'

The colour rushed to her face.

'I mean that the letter which disturbed you so much might have hinted at the murder.'

'A letter? How do you know I got a letter last night?'

'The Rector called to break the news to you this morning, and your servant told him that you already knew it; also that you had left for London—with your jewels, Mrs Warrender,' added Alan significantly.

'And you followed me!' cried the woman savagely. 'Do you intend to accuse me of my husband's murder?'

'I certainly do not; and I did not follow you. I am here on the same errand as yourself.'

She looked terrified.

'How do you know what my errand is?'

'Because I can put two and two together, Mrs Warrender. I also received a letter—at least, Miss Marlow did, and from the same man—the man who lives here.'

'Cicero Gramp?'

'That is the name. You see, I was right. Does he intend to blackmail you also, and did you bring your jewels to satisfy his demands?'

She looked down the court. They were comparatively alone. A few ragged children were playing about, and some slatternly women were watching them from doorways. A man or two, brutalized by drink, hovered in the distance. But a smart constable, who passed and repassed the entrance of the cul-de-sac, casting inquisitive glances at Alan and his companion, kept these birds of prey from any nearer approach. Finding that they were out of earshot, Mrs Warrender produced a letter and handed it to Alan. It was written on the same thick, creamy paper, and in the same elegant handwriting as had been the communication to Sophy. He read it in silence. As he had expected, it informed Mrs Warrender that her husband was dead, and that Cicero Gramp, on payment of two hundred pounds, could inform her where the body could be found. His price had evidently gone up. But what struck Alan most was the nature of the information now offered. Cicero declared that he could tell the widow where her husband's body was to be found. The body had already been discovered in the Marlow vault. Ergo, Cicero Gramp knew it was there. If so, had he seen the murder committed and the body taken into the vault? It seemed probable. Indeed, it seemed likely that he could solve the whole mystery; but, strangely enough, the prospect did not seem to afford Mr Thorold much satisfaction. He handed back the letter with a dissatisfied smile.

'I think you have wasted your time coming up,' he said. 'Jarks, no doubt, told your servant that the doctor's body had already been discovered. Why, then, come up to pay blackmail?'

'I want to find out who killed Julian,' she said.

'Then you are on your way to see this man?'

'Yes.' She shuddered. 'But this terrible place. I am afraid.'

'Then why come here? I am going to see Mr Gramp on Miss Marlow's behalf. If you like, I will represent you also.'

'No, thank you; I must see him myself.'

'Very well. I suppose you are not staying in town?'

'Yes, at the Norfolk Hotel. I shall remain until tomorrow, so as to sell my jewels and bribe this man.'

'There will be no need to sell your jewels,' said Alan soothingly. 'I will be responsible for the blackmail. Have you the jewels with you?'

'No, I dared not bring them. He might have robbed me. They are in my bedroom at the hotel.'

'Then go back at once and look after them. I will bring this man there in, let us say, an hour.'

'Thank you, Mr Thorold,' she said. 'I accept your offer. I am really afraid to go down that slum.'

He gazed after her fine figure as she walked hurriedly away. Somehow that haughty air and resolute gait did not fit in well with her expression of fear. It was curious. He felt there was something strange about Mrs Warrender. However, she had been open enough with him, so he did not choose to think badly of her.

The man he sought was not easy to find. Mr Gramp had his own reasons for keeping clear of the police. The whole alley was known by the name of Dixon's Rents, and Thorold had no idea in which of the houses to ask for him. He questioned a stunted street arab with wolfish eyes, emphasizing his request with a sixpence.

'Oh, Cicero!' yelped the lad, biting the coin. 'Yuss, he's round about. Dunno! Y'ain't a 'tec?'

'What's that?'

'A de-tec-tive,' drawled the boy. 'Cicero ain't wanted, is he?'

'Not by me. Is Cicero generally—er—wanted?' inquired Alan delicately.

The urchin closed one eye rapidly, and grinned with many teeth. But, instead of replying he took to shouting hoarsely for 'Mother Ginger'. The surrounding population popped out of their burrows like so many rabbits, and for the next few minutes 'Mother Ginger' was asked for vigorously. Alan looked round at the ragged, blear-eyed slum-dwellers, but could see nothing of the lady in question. Suddenly his arm was twitched, and he turned to find a dwarf no higher than his waist trying to attract his attention. Mother Ginger, for it was she, had a huge head of red hair, fantastically decked with ribbons of many colours. Her dress, too, was rainbow-hued, like Joseph's coat. She had carpet slippers on her huge feet, and white woollen gloves on her large hands. Her face was as large as a frying-pan and of a pallid hue, with expression-less blue eyes and a big mouth. Alan saw in her a female Quasimodo.

'Wot is it?' she inquired. Evidently Mother Ginger was vain of her finery and of the attention she attracted. 'Is it Mr Gramp you want, m'dimber-cove?'

'Yes. Can you take me to him?' asked Thorold, wincing at the penny-whistle quality of her voice. 'Is he at home?'

'P'r'aps he is, p'r'aps he ain't,' retorted Mother Ginger, with a fascinating leer. 'Wot d'ye want with him?'

'This will explain.' And Alan put Cicero's letter into her hand. 'Give him that.'

She nodded, croaked like a bull-frog, and vanished amongst the crowd. Mr Thorold found himself the centre of attraction and the object of remark.

This somewhat unpleasant position was put an end to by the appearance of Mother Ginger, who clawed Alan, and drew him into a house at the end of the court. The tatterdemalions gave a yell of disappointment at the escape of their prey, and their prey congratulated himself that he had not made his visit at night. He felt that he might have fared badly in this modern Court of Miracles. However, it appeared that he was safe under the protection of Mother Ginger. With the activity of a monkey, she conducted him up a dirty staircase and into a bare room furnished with a bed, a chair, and a table. Here Alan was greeted by a bulky creature in a gorgeous red dressing-gown, old and greasy, but still pretentious. He had no difficulty in recognizing the man whom he had seen reciting on the parade at Bournemouth.

'I welcome you, Mr Thorold,' said Cicero in his best Turveydrop style. 'Mother Ginger, depart.'

To get rid of the woman, Mr Thorold placed a shilling in her concave claw, upon which she executed a kind of war-dance, and vanished with a yelp of delight. Left alone with the pompous vagabond, the young man took the only chair, and faced his host, who was sitting majestically on the bed, his red dressing-gown wrapped round him in regal style.

'So you are Cicero Gramp?' began Alan. 'I have seen you—'

'At Bournemouth,' interrupted the professor of elocution and eloquence. 'True, I was there for the benefit of my health.'

'And to blackmail Miss Marlow.'

'Blackmail—a painful word, Mr Thorold.'

'How do you know my name?'

'It is part of my business to know all names,' was the answer—'*ex nihilo nihil fit*, if you understand the tongue of my namesake. If I did not know what I desire to know, my income would be small indeed. I visited the salubrious village of Heathton, and learned there that Miss Marlow and Mr Thorold, to whom she was engaged, were recreating themselves at the seaside with an inferior companion. Bournemouth was the seaside, and I went there. On seeing a young lady with a spinster and a gentleman in attendance, I noted Miss Marlow, Mr Thorold, and Miss Parsh.'

'And made yourself scarce?'

'I did,' admitted Cicero frankly. 'I departed as soon as you were out of sight, knowing that my letter would be delivered, and that you might call in the police.'

'Ah, a guilty conscience!'

'Far from it.' Cicero flung open his dressing-gown and struck his chest. 'Here purity and innocence and peace are enthroned. I did not wish to be taken by the minions of the law, lest they should wrest from me for nothing what I should prefer to sell for a few pounds. Besides, I wished to see you in my own house. A poor establishment,' said Mr Gramp, looking round the meagre room, 'but mine own.'

He bowed gracefully, as if for applause.

'Come, Mr Gramp,' said Alan diplomatically, 'let us get to business. What do you know about this matter?'

'About the hundred pounds?' asked the man with an appearance of great simplicity.

'I'll pay you that, more or less, when I know what your information is worth.'

'More or less won't do, Mr Thorold. I want, from Miss Marlow or from you, one hundred pounds.'

'I know, and two hundred from Mrs Warrender.'

'Ah!'—Cicero did not move a muscle—'she has told you that I can give you information about the body of her husband?'

'Yes, and she has come to town to see you. However, I have intercepted her, and she is waiting to see you in a place I know of. You must come with me, Mr Gramp.'

But Cicero shook his head uneasily.

'An Englishman's house is his castle,' he said. 'This is my house, my keep, my donjon. *Quod erat demonstrandum!*'

'Oh, confound your dictionary Latin!' cried Alan impatiently. 'You are afraid of the police?'

'Far from it, Mr Thorold. I have nothing to fear from them. For one hundred pounds I lay bare my heart.'

'I'll give you fifty pounds on condition you tell me all you know. From Mrs Warrender you won't receive a penny.'

'Then she shall never know where lies the body of her late lamented partner.'

'She knows that already,' said Alan coolly.

'Ha!'—Cicero gave a dramatic start—'you seek to deceive me!'

'Indeed, I do nothing of the sort; I found the body myself.'

'Where, may I ask?' said Gramp, his thoughts going back to the hut on the heath.

'In the Marlow vault, in the coffin of the dead man who was carried away.'

Cicero's jaw fell. He was truly surprised.

'How the devil did it get there from the hut?' he said.

'The hut—what hut?'

'I want my money before I tell you that, Mr Thorold.'

Alan took five ten-pound notes out of his pocket.

'Here is fifty pounds,' he said; 'it will be yours if you tell me all you know, and come with me to see Mrs Warrender.'

'Aha!' Cicero's eyes glittered, and his fingers longed to clutch the money. Such wealth had not been his for many a long day. 'And the police?'

'I thought you did not fear them?' was the reply.

'I don't, for I have done nothing to put myself in the power of the law. But I am afraid, as this body has been found, that you will have me arrested, and so I shall lose the money.'

'If you are innocent of the murder and the sacrilege, you won't be arrested, Gramp. And the money I will give you after we have seen Mrs Warrender.'

'On your word of honour as a gentleman?'

'Yes, on my word of honour. If you can throw light on this mystery, and bring home these crimes to the person who has committed them, I am quite willing to pay you.'

'I don't know about bringing home the crimes, Mr Thorold,' said Cicero, rising, 'but I will tell you all I know in the presence of Mrs Warrender. Permit me to assume my visiting garb. Where is the lady?'

'At the Norfolk Hotel.'

'I know it. Many a glass which cheers have I drained there. *Dulce desipere in loco.* You don't know Horace, perhaps?'

'I suspect you don't,' said Alan, annoyed by this hedge-Latin. 'Hurry up!'

'Fifty pounds, Mr Thorold.'

'After our interview with Mrs Warrender,' amended the other significantly.

'Command my services,' said Cicero, and rapidly put on his frock-coat, battered hat and gloves.

After he had brushed his greasy broadcloth, and dusted his large boots with the red bandana, he announced that he was ready.

The oddly-assorted pair proceeded to the Norfolk Hotel through the Lambeth slums. Cicero seemed to be very well known and very popular. He exchanged greetings with shady acquaintances, patted ragged children on the head, and arrived at the hotel swelling with pride. He felt that he had shown Alan he was a man of consequence. Arrived at their destination, they were shown by a slipshod waiter into a shabby sitting-room on the first floor where they found Mrs Warrender. She rose, and on seeing Cicero, gave a shriek of surprise.

'Bill!' she cried with a gasp.

'Clara Maria!' exclaimed the so-called Cicero, 'my beloved sister! What a surprise!'

CHAPTER VIII

AN IMPORTANT INTERVIEW

'WELL, I never!' gasped the widow, who, womanlike, was the first to find her tongue. 'Is it really you, Billy?—but I might have guessed it, from your writing. Yet it never entered my head!' She stopped and grew suddenly furious. 'My husband, you wretch!—have you killed him?'

'No, Clara Maria, no! I came here to give information about his poor body. I did not expect to find my sister—the celebrated Miss de Crespigny—in the person of Mrs Warrender!'

'What is all this about?' demanded Alan quietly. 'Is this your brother, Mrs Warrender?'

'To my shame, sir, I confess this—this creature'—Mrs Warrender brought out the word with a hiss—'this degraded beast, is my brother.'

'Oh, Clara Maria, how can you—'

'Hold your tongue!' interrupted the lady angrily. 'You were always a drunkard and a scoundrel! Now you've come to black-mailing! Two hundred pounds from me, you wretch! Not one sixpence!'

'I have already,' said her brother majestically, 'arranged pecuniary matters with my friend Mr Thorold. But I wonder at you, Clara Maria, I really do, considering how we parted. Is this the greeting of flesh and blood?' cried Mr Gramp in a soaring voice, and standing on tiptoe. 'Is this what human nature is made of? The late Sir Isaac Newton was a prophet indeed when he made that remark.'

'Mountebank!' hissed Mrs Warrender, curling her handsome lip.

'We were both mountebanks at one time, Mr Thorold,' he

said, turning to Alan, who, in spite of his anxiety, was watching the scene with unconcealed amusement. 'My sister was the celebrated Miss de Crespigny; I, the once noted actor, Vavasour Belgrave—'

'And his real name is Billy Spinks!' put in Mrs Warrender scornfully.

'William Spinks,' corrected Mr Gramp, as it may be convenient to call him. 'Billy is merely an endearing term to which, alas! your lips have long been strangers. But you needn't talk,' said Cicero, becoming angry, and therewith a trifle vulgar; 'your name is Clara Maria Spinks!'

'And a very good name, too,' retorted the lady. 'Cut the scene short, Billy.'

'That is my advice also,' put in Alan, who was growing weary. 'I do not want to know any more about your relationship. That you are brother and sister is nothing to me.'

'I hope, Mr Thorold, that you won't reveal my degraded connection in Heathton,' cried Mrs Warrender, much agitated. 'It would ruin me. With great difficulty I attained a position by marrying my poor dear Julian, and I don't want to fall back into the mud where this worm writhes.' She darted a vicious glance at Cicero.

'Be content, Mrs Warrender; your secret is safe with me.'

'Denying her own flesh and blood!' moaned Gramp, and sat down.

Speech and attitude were most effective, and Mrs Warrender, with a spark of her old theatrical humour, played back.

'Yes, I deny you,' she cried, rising quickly and stretching out a denunciatory hand. 'You were always a brute and a disgrace to me. Look at that creature, Mr Thorold! He is my brother. Our parents were on the stage—barnstormers they were—and played in the provinces for bite and sup. They put us on the stage, and when they died, left a little money to Billy there. He was to bring me up. How did he fulfil his trust? By making me work for him. As an actor, even in the meanest parts, he was a failure. I am not much of an actress myself, although I was well known as Miss de Crespigny, and billed all over London. It was my figure and my looks that did it. I appeared in burlesque ten or twelve years ago, and I had wealth at my feet.'

'I have heard of you,' said Alan, recalling his college days and certain photographs of the most beautiful burlesque actress in London. He wondered he had not recognized her long before. Mrs Warrender, shaking with passion, went on as though she had not heard him.

'Wealth was at my feet,' went on the widow—'wealth and dishonour. He,' she cried, and pointed the finger of scorn at the unabashed Cicero, 'he lived on me! He would have me stoop to dishonour for his sake! Then I lost my voice. The creature treated me basely. I left him; I ran away to the States of America, and appeared in ballets for my looks alone. In New Orleans I met Julian Warrender—he was old, but he was madly in love with me—and I married him for a home. We came to England five years ago, and settled at Heathton. I always did my best to be a good wife, although I dare say I was extravagant. Diamonds! yes, I have diamonds, and I made Julian buy me all he could. And why?—to provide against the days of poverty which I knew would come. They have come—my husband is dead. God help me!' Her voice rose to a scream. 'Murdered!' she cried.

'This,' interpolated Gramp, addressing no one in particular, 'is very painful.'

'You beast! Why do you come into my life again? I wanted to know about my poor husband's death, and I brought up my jewels to bribe the man who called himself Cicero Gramp into confessing who had murdered him. I find that my own brother is the blackmailer. You would extort money from me, you wretch! Never! never! never! I disown you—I cast you out! William Spinks, blackguard you were! Cicero Gramp, scoundrel, thief, blackmailer, and, for all I know, murderer, you are!

Away with you—away!' and Mrs Warrender, very white in face and very exhausted in body, sat down.

'Very good,' said her brother, rising; 'I go.'

'Without your fifty pounds?' asked Alan, sneering.

'I forgot that,' he said, smiling blandly.

'Don't give him a penny, Mr Thorold!' cried the woman with vehemence.

'I promised him the money, and he shall have it,' replied Alan coldly. 'I have heard your story, Mrs Warrender, and it is safe with me. No one in Heathton shall know. Your brother will not speak of it either.'

'How do you know that?' asked Cicero, with an evil look.

'Because you shall not have the fifty pounds until I have your promise to hold your tongue about your relationship to Mrs Warrender while you are in Heathton.'

'I am not going to Heathton,' growled Gramp like a sulky bear.

'Yes, you are. You are coming to tell your story to Inspector Blair. If you don't, not only will you lose your fifty pounds, but I will have you arrested as a suspicious character.'

'You promised that the police should not touch me.'

'I promised nothing of the sort. Now, tell me what you saw of these crimes—for there are two: sacrilege and murder—and then come to Heathton. Behave well, keep Mrs Warrender's secret, and you shall have fifty pounds and your freedom. Otherwise—' Alan held up his finger.

'Oh, Mr Thorold!' cried the widow, wringing her hands, 'if this horrible man comes to Heathton, I am lost!'

'Indeed no! He will hold his tongue. Won't you?'

'You seem very sure of it,' said the professor of eloquence.

'Of course I am. You see, Mr Gramp, I have the handling of the late Mr Marlow's money, and I can buy your silence.'

'Not for fifty pounds.'

'We shall see about that. It's either fifty pounds or the police. Choose!'

Cicero folded his arms, and bowed his head.

'I will take the money,' he said, 'and I will hold my tongue—while I am at Heathton giving my evidence. Afterwards—' he looked at his sister.

'Afterwards,' said Alan smoothly, 'we will make other arrangements. Now tell your story.'

'And tell the truth!' put in Mrs Warrender sharply.

'Clara Maria!' Cicero was about to break forth in furious speech, but he restrained himself. '*Hodie mihi eras tibi!*' said Mr Gramp, with a strange look at Alan—'if you understand Latin.'

'I think I am able to follow you, my friend. You mean 'Today to me, tomorrow to thee,' which would be all right if it was I who quoted the saying. But this time it is not your day, and as to your tomorrow, it may never come.'

'We shall see about that,' said Cicero savagely and pointedly.

Alan felt an unpleasant thrill run through him, for the man's look was evil beyond telling. But he betrayed nothing of this, and signed to Gramp to continue.

Quite understanding the position, Cicero reverted to his grand theatrical manner. He rose from his chair, rested one hand on the back of it, and thrust the other into his breast. As from a rostrum he delivered his speech, and dwelt upon his own words with the gusto of a modern Micawber.

'Mr Thorold and Clara Maria,' he began in deep tones, 'a few days ago circumstances connected with money turned me weary and hungry from the seaport of Southampton. I went—let us be plain—I went on the tramp, and in the course of my peregrinations I drew near Heathton, a salubrious village, notorious at the present moment for the crimes which have been committed there. I spun a coin, my only sixpence, to decide if an intrusion into that village would bring me good or evil fortune. The coin said good, so to Heathton I went. As I shall shortly pocket fifty quid—a vulgar term, but eloquent, Clara Maria, so don't frown—I dare not say that my only sixpence told me a lie. That sixpence bought me a meal in the Heathton public-house. Where is that meal or sixpence now? *Eheu! Fuit Ilium.*'

'Go on,' said Alan curtly, for the orator paused.

'At the Good Samaritan I heard much about Mr Marlow and the funeral, and learned a few facts which were of use to me afterwards.'

'When you thrust yourself into the kitchen at the Moat House, I presume?'

'You are correct, Mr Thorold. I did good business there; and I learned, from the irresponsible chatter of the domestics, a few other facts which may also prove valuable.'

He looked directly at Alan as he said this.

'Go on! go on!' said Thorold again. But he felt uneasy.

'I was turned out of the Good Samaritan by a hard-hearted landlady called—appropriately, I confess—Mrs Timber. As the night was fine, I slept in the churchyard, opposite the tomb of Mr Marlow. Soon after midnight I was awakened by voices. I looked out, and saw two men, one tall, the other short.'

'Who were they?' Alan asked anxiously.

'One I knew later; the other one I am still in doubt about, as I did not see his face.'

'But the names?'

'You shall hear the names, Clara Maria, when I am ready, not before. These men went into the tomb, remained there for some time, and came out with the body. They lifted it over the low wall of the churchyard, and went, I think, across the moor.'

'You followed?' cried Alan breathlessly.

'No. I was afraid I might get into trouble, so I ran in the opposite direction. I slept the rest of the night in a hayrick far from the churchyard. Next day I sought the Moat House kitchen, and listened to the talk of the servants. Then I went away with the idea of seeing Miss Marlow at Bournemouth, as the servants said she was there with Mr Thorold. On the moor I saw a hut. I went into it to eat a frugal meal. In it I found'—Cicero paused to give his words due effect—'a corpse.'

'Whose corpse?'

'That of the man who had assisted to steal the body, Clara Maria. Your husband, Dr Warrender!'

'You liar!' shrieked the widow, making a bound at him. 'Oh, you liar!'

Alan flung himself between these affectionate relatives, or it might have fared badly with Cicero.

'Hold hard, Mrs Warrender!' he said, holding her back; 'let us listen.'

'Listen to his lies! Do you hear that he says my husband stole Mr Marlow's body?'

'So he did,' said Cicero doggedly. 'I'm telling you what I shall tell to the police. The tall man was Dr Warrender. I saw his face in the lantern-light. Who the short man was I do not know.'

'How did you recognize Dr Warrender?' demanded Alan, when Mrs Warrender had sat down again.

'I didn't know him at the time; but I had his description from the servants.'

'Tall, yellow beard, bald head?' said Thorold rapidly.

'Yes, that was the man who assisted to remove the body, and that is the description of the corpse I found in the hut.'

'My husband's body was found in the vault, you liar!' cried the widow.

'Was it, Clara Maria? Well, all I can say is I don't know how it got there. I left it in the hut myself.'

'Why did you not give information to the police?'

'What! And get locked up on suspicion of murder? No, thank you, Mr Thorold. I ran away from that corpse as I would have done from the devil.'

'Whose child you are,' said his sister bitterly.

'Don't miscall your own father, Clara Maria. Well, sir, I went on to Bournemouth, and wrote two letters, one to Miss Marlow, and one to my sister, although I did not know she was my sister then. Had I known I had a relative in Heathton,' said Cicero with pathos, 'I should have asked for a bed.'

'And your sister, Billy Spinks, would have set the dogs on you.'

'I am sure you would, Clara Maria. You were always one for sentimental scenes.'

'Tell me, Gramp, is this all you know of these crimes?' put in Alan.

'All, Mr Thorold. I think, sir, it is worth fifty pounds.'

'Humph! We'll see what the police say. You have no objection, I suppose, to come with me to Heathton and repeat this story?'

'Having a clear conscience,' said Cicero, with a superior smile, 'I can safely say that I have not. But the fifty, Mr Thorold?'

'Will be paid after you have told Blair this story.'

'If you are so poor,' put in Mrs Warrender, 'where did you get money to buy that writing-paper? It was costly paper.'

'It was,' admitted Mr Gramp with pride—'it was, Clara Maria. I always do things in style. If you remember, I got a prize at school for letter-writing.'

'Where did you get the money?'

'From a nautical man called Joe Brill—a sovereign.'

'A sovereign from Joe Brill?' cried Alan, starting. 'Why?'

'Ah! you may ask,' said Cicero. 'In my opinion it was hush-money.'

'Hush-money! What do you mean, man?'

'Mean! I mean that I believe Joe Brill was the short man I saw that night. Yes, Mr Thorold, Joe stole the corpse, and Joe killed foully, with a knife, my respected brother-in-law. *Hinc illae lachrymae!*'

CHAPTER IX

INVESTIGATION

WHILST Alan Thorold was dealing with Cicero and his sister in London, Inspector Blair was co-operating with the Rector in obtaining evidence relating to the murder. The inspector was a dry, dour, silent man, born in England, but of Scotch descent. He was cautious to a fault, and never expressed an opinion without having well considered what he was going to say. It was now a common sight in Heathton for his long, lean figure and the Rector's short, plump one to be seen constantly together.

He was now in the Rectory dining-room with a good glass of port beside him, and Mr Phelps, standing on the hearth-rug, was supplying him with all the details he had collected in connection with the mystery. The case was getting so much more interesting than Blair, the sad and silent, had expected that he was becoming, for him, quite vivacious. He asked the Rector one question after another.

'Mr Thorold has gone to Dixon's Rents, sir?'

'Yes, Mr Inspector; I expect he'll have some news for us when he returns tonight.'

'He seems a clever young gentleman,' Blair said musingly. 'I dare say he will bring this man Gramp with him.'

'Do you think that Gramp can point out the guilty person?'

'That, sir, I am not prepared to say offhand. If convenient, I should like to take a look round.'

'Certainly. Where shall we go, Mr Inspector?' and Mr Phelps rose briskly.

'To the vault, if you please, sir. Afterwards we will call on Mrs Marry.'

The Rector paused at the door.

'I told you all Mrs Marry had to say about Brown.'

'Quite so, sir. But I wish to have a look at the rooms occupied by the man. Also, I think it would be as well to examine his luggage.'

'Can you do that without a warrant?'

'I'll take the risk,' said Blair coolly. 'An examination may not be quite legal under the circumstances, but as Brown undoubtedly procured the key of the vault by that forged letter, I am entitled to look upon him as a suspicious character. Should he come back, sir—of which I have my doubts—I can account for my action.'

'Humph! I think you are right. Come, then, and look at the vault.'

To the vault they went, and found Jarks showing the outside of it to a crowd of morbid sightseers. Indeed, the tragedy had drawn people from far and near to Heathton, and the usually quiet place buzzed like a hive. Mrs Timber was making her fortune, and blessed the day she had turned Cicero the tramp out of her house. To him alone did Mrs Timber ascribe the theft of the body. As to his connection with the murder of Dr Warrender, she was not so certain.

'Come, come!' cried Mr Phelps, in his fussy manner, on finding Jarks haranguing the crowd. 'This is most ridiculous— most out of place. Jarks, I am astonished at your desecrating the graveyard in this way.'

'No desecration, reverend sir,' said Jarks, in his rusty voice, 'I wos only showing 'em where I laid Muster Marlow by, comfortable. Go—'

'Go away—go away, all of you!'

'Come on to the right!' shouted Jarks. 'I'll show 'ee where a soocide as they brought in crazy is tucked away. A lovely grave with a good view, an' as nice a stone as I iver seed. In my young days he'd have been buried in cross-roads with a stake, but they do trate 'em kindly nowadays. Ah yis. This way to the soocide, neighbours!' And Jarks headed the crowd to the other side of the graveyard. The keen, cold eye of Inspector Blair cleared them out more quickly than Jarks' invitation.

'Dear me! most indiscreet of Jarks!' said the Rector, opening the door of the vault. 'Come in, Mr Inspector. Here's a candle. Tut, tut! I've burnt my fingers. Deuce take—Hum—God forgive me for bad language! This is the niche, Mr Inspector; yonder the coffin—a very handsome one. The lead is cut, you perceive. Ah, poor soul! And we meant it to last till the Great Day.'

While the Rector ran on in this fashion, Blair the silent examined the empty coffin. He noted that the lead casing had been cut with a sharp instrument, and very neatly done—so neatly that the inspector became thoughtful.

'That wasn't done by a man in a hurry,' he mused. But he said nothing, and merely turned to Mr Phelps with a question: 'Who screwed down the coffin?'

'Who?—bless me, let me think! Yes, yes. Dr Warrender—poor soul!—and Joe Brill. Faithful fellow, Joe! Would see the last of his master.'

'Wasn't the undertaker present?'

'Crank? Well, yes, he was. But I am sorry to say, Mr Inspector'—here the face of the Rector became severe—'that on that day Crank was intoxicated.'

'H'm! Who made him drunk?'

'Himself, I suppose,' rejoined Mr Phelps, a trifle tartly. 'Crank requires no one to tempt him.'

'Few men do, sir,' said Blair, and again examined the coffin. He passed his long, delicate hand over every inch of it, particularly fingering the lid; then he looked round the niche where it rested, peered into the others, and considered well all that he saw, while Mr Phelps chattered. 'Quite so,' said the detective at length; 'let us go outside.'

He examined the graveyard as carefully as he had done the vault. In the angle formed by the Lady Chapel he found the long grass crushed down, and part of it torn up to make a pillow.

'Humph! a squatting-place,' said Blair, who had read a good deal about prehistoric man. 'A tramp has been sleeping here.'

'A tramp!' repeated the Rector. 'Of course that was Cicero Gramp, who wrote the letter.'

'No doubt. I dare say he saw the whole business.' Blair continued his researches, and came to a halt at the wall which divided churchyard from pine-wood. He pointed to a loose stone which had been knocked off. 'Did you observe this before, sir?'

'No,' replied Mr Phelps, raising his pince-nez. 'But that's nothing. You see, the wall has been put together without mortar—simply stones piled one on top of the other. A high wind, now—'

'I don't think a high wind knocked this stone off. You will notice, sir, that it has fallen on the other side. Excuse me,' and Blair, active as a deer, leaped over the wall and disappeared into the pine-belt. Phelps rubbed his nose, not understanding these Red Indian methods. In ten minutes the inspector returned. 'I can't find the trail,' said he, 'but from the evidence of that wall, I suspect the body was carried over it.'

'Where to, Mr Inspector?'

'Probably to a cart waiting on the highroad, which runs across the moor. But, of course, I'm in the dark as to that. Let me see the keyhole of the vault-door.' He went back and had a good look at it. There were no scratches to be seen. 'Humph!' said the inspector; 'this was opened quietly enough, and by a man who knew what he was about. There was no hurry or fumbling in putting in the key.'

'Ah!' said the Rector, looking wise. 'What key? Not this one?'

'No, Mr Phelps, I don't suspect you. Probably the key was that stolen from Mr Thorold's desk by the Quiet Gentleman.'

'You speak as though you were not quite sure.'

'There might have been a third key,' Blair said cautiously.

'If so, why should Brown have stolen Thorold's key?'

'That's one of the things I have to find out. Let us call on Mrs Marry.'

Mrs Marry was a voluble, buxom woman with rosy cheeks, and a great amount of curiosity as to matters which did not concern her. But, clever as she was, it seemed that she had nothing to tell about Mr Brown. With many curtsies and much talk she conducted Rector and inspector into a gimcrack parlour full of gaudy furniture, Berlin wool mats, antimacassars, and wax flowers.

'When Jeremiah died,' explained the widow with pride, 'I spent the nest-egg he left me on that elegant set of chairs and sofa, also on the curtains, table, and glass lustres, which are considered very fine. It was my intent, gentlemen, as a lone widder, to take in single gentlemen, and they likes something to tickle the eye.'

'A most inviting room, Mrs Marry,' said the Rector, perching himself carefully on a fragile chair, all varnish and design, but entirely wanting in solidity; 'but Mr Brown—'

'Ah, sir, he's gone where we must all go;' and Mrs Marry wiped away an imaginary tear.

But her remark called forth a question from Blair, who had been making a close examination of the room:

'How do you know he is dead?'

'Bless the man! wouldn't he be back if he wasn't? I'm sure he was comfortable enough, and my cooking is above blame, thank Heaven! If anyone—'

'Mr Brown went out at nine o'clock?' said Blair, cutting her short.

'I won't deceive you, Mr Policeman, he did. He stayed in most of the day, and went out in the afternoon. At six he came back for his bite and sup, and at nine he went out again to take the air. He said so, at least, and I ain't set eyes on him since.'

'He said so?' remarked Mr Phelps.

'On his fingers, of course. He was dumb, sir, but not deaf, and he conversed on his fingers wonderful. I can talk myself that way,' said Mrs Marry gravely, 'having a niece as is deaf and dumb in an asylum. I expect it was my knowing the language as brought Mr Brown here to lodge.'

'Where did he come from?'

'London town, he gave me to understand, sir. But he didn't talk much—on his fingers—about himself. He was very quiet, ate and drank, read books—'

'What kind of books?'

'Novels, sir—yellow novels, in a foreign tongue. Here, sir, is the rosewood bookcase. He also wrote a great deal, but what I don't know. I thought he had ideas of becoming a writing person himself.'

Blair opened the bookcase, and one by one examined a dozen or so French novels ranged on the lower shelf. They were all by good authors, the usual paper-covered cheap editions—nothing strange about them. No name was written in any one of them. He shut up the bookcase with a look of disappointment.

'Was your lodger a Frenchman?' he asked.

'Lor', sir, I dunno! He talked English with his fingers. I've seen him reading the newspapers.'

'He did not look like a foreigner,' remarked the Rector.

'Ah! I quite forgot you knew the man, Mr Phelps. Can you describe his looks?'

'He was not very tall, had long white hair and a beard, ruddy cheeks, and dark eyes. He was usually dressed in a grey suit, and walked with a stout stick.'

'Gout in his feet,' put in Mrs Marry, not at all pleased at being left out in the cold. 'He wore cloth boots for his gout—walked very badly, did Mr Brown.'

'Strange!' murmured Blair, again looking round the room. 'How could an old man helpless through gout in the feet carry off a dead body? Humph!'

'He carried off no dead body!' cried Mrs Marry, crimson with wrath, 'if it's Mr Marlow's corpse you're talking of. I believe Mr Brown's bin murdered like the doctor.'

'Why do you believe so?'

'Because I've made up my mind to believe it,' said Mrs Marry fiercely. 'And I'd like to see the man as would change my mind.'

'So should I,' remarked Blair. 'Well, Mrs Marry, show me Mr Brown's room. I must examine his luggage.'

'There's only one box, and that's locked.'

'I'll take the liberty of opening it.'

'But you can't. I'm an honest woman. What'll Mr Brown say when he comes back and finds his things gone? Besides, there's a trifle of rent, and—'

'Hold your tongue!' said the inspector, with a glance which quelled her. 'I will take nothing away. You forget who I am, Mrs Marry. Show me the bedroom.' And the landlady, thinking better of it, obeyed without further argument.

The box was there—a common, brown-painted travelling-box. There was no name on it, and it proved to be locked. The inspector asked for a chisel, and forced it open. Within he found three suits of grey clothes, some linen and socks, together with a pair of cloth boots—nothing else. No name on the shirts, no tailor's tag on the clothes. Evidently nothing of Mr Brown's identity was to be learned from his belongings.

'The man from nowhere,' said Phelps, gazing blankly around him.

But Inspector Blair was not yet satisfied. He searched both sitting-room and bedroom, questioned Mrs Marry, looked at some torn pieces of paper in the fireplace, and—found nothing. Rector and inspector walked out of the cottage as wise as when they had entered it. So far their search had been a failure.

All that afternoon Blair hunted the village for evidence. He heard how Warrender had called at Mrs Marry's house, how he had left there to follow the Quiet Gentleman, who had been seen by the peasant going in the direction of the moor. Blair recalled the loose stone dropped from the churchyard wall, and his own theory that the corpse had been taken to a cart on the road. He sent out the police, and had the heath searched, even to the hut where the corpse had been, but all with no result. And as yet he was ignorant of what Cicero knew.

Tired and baffled, he returned to Heathton to the inn. Here

he found a messenger from Mr Phelps, asking him to call at the Rectory. He hurried there, and was met by Alan Thorold, who presented Cicero and Mrs Warrender. Then the tramp told the story of all that he had seen. Blair rubbed his chin.

'Can the doctor have helped Brown to do it?' he said half aloud.

'No, he did not!' cried Mrs Warrender angrily. 'My husband was as good a man as ever lived. Why should he steal a corpse?'

'Humph! Why indeed!'

Blair recollected something he had seen in the vault of which he cared not to speak until he could be more certain. So he held his peace.

'Even if the late lamented Dr Warrender did violate the sanctity of the tomb,' said Cicero softly, 'who killed the late lamented Dr Warrender?'

'Perhaps the shorter man who helped him,' said the Rector. 'That was—'

'Hold your tongue just now,' whispered Alan, for Cicero was about to mention Joe Brill's name; 'we'll come to that later. Who's that?'

It proved to be Mrs Marry, who came in with part of a torn envelope in her hand. On the envelope was an obliterated stamp, but the writing had been torn off.

'I found this in Mr Brown's room,' she said, 'on the floor by the edge of the carpet. How it escaped my dusting I don't know.'

Blair looked at this piece of evidence.

'Jamaica stamp,' he said.

'Strange!' cried the Rector. 'I know Marlow was at one time in Jamaica.'

'And my husband, Dr Warrender, came from Jamaica,' said the widow.

There was silence. They looked at one another. But no one had any explanation to offer.

CHAPTER X

ANOTHER DISAPPEARANCE

In the course of his investigations Mr Blair had examined the servants at the Moat House. From the footman he heard of the West Indian letter, and of the effect it had produced upon Mr Marlow. Search had been made for that letter as likely to throw some light on the mystery, but without success. Evidently Mr Marlow had thought it important enough to destroy. His secret, whatever it might have been, had gone to the grave with him. It was a strange coincidence that the man Brown should also have a correspondent in Jamaica. He it was who had stolen the key of the vault from Alan's desk. Again, Dr Warrender—who, as his wife told Alan, had been in Jamaica—had been murdered. Between these three men, then—Marlow, Brown and Warrender—there was evidently some connecting-link. Had there not been, Warrender would not have assisted to remove the body of the millionaire, and Brown, by stealing the key, would not have helped him.

'There is no doubt in my mind that Brown was the short man seen by Gramp,' Blair said to Alan. 'And he was followed from Mrs Marry's by Dr Warrender, who was bound on the same errand.'

'You mean the theft of the body?'

'I think so. Brown had the key and Gramp saw them remove the corpse.'

'He saw Warrender,' corrected Alan, 'not Brown.'

'I judge the other was Brown, from the theft of the key and the fact that Warrender called to see him, and then followed. Again, both men have disappeared—at least, one has. The other is dead.'

'And who murdered him?'

'Brown,' said the inspector, with conviction. 'I am sure of it.'

'How can you be sure?'

'Because something unforeseen happened—the murder, probably. In the ordinary course of things, I take it, Brown would have come back to fetch his luggage, and would have gone away in a manner less likely to arouse suspicion. Probably he and Warrender had a quarrel when they put the corpse in the cart. Brown killed the doctor, and then drove away.'

'But, Blair,' argued Alan, 'you forget that the doctor's body was seen in the hut. Even if Brown had dragged it there—which, I admit, he might have done—I don't see how he could have brought it back again to the vault.'

'I do, Mr Thorold. It was Brown who had the key. Most likely he put the dead body in a place of safety, then came back the following night, to hide it away in the safest place he knew of—to wit, the vault. If you recollect, no alarm as to the loss of Marlow's body was given, or was likely to be given. Warrender's dead body would not have been searched for in the vault. It is, at least, highly improbable that the vault would have been opened.'

'That is true,' assented Alan. 'But that Cicero by chance saw the affair, I dare say we should have remained in ignorance of the business for many a long day. No one would have gone to the vault. A very clever man, this Brown.'

'Very clever. But for the accident of Cicero having slept in the churchyard, he would have got off scot-free. As it is, I don't see how we can hunt him down. His gout, his dumbness, his white hair and beard may have been assumed. The fact of the linen left at Mrs Marry's being unmarked is proof enough that he was disguised.'

'Perhaps,' said Alan doubtfully. 'What I can't make out is how he knew I had the key of the vault in my desk.'

'Did you mention it to anyone?'

'Only to Mr Phelps.'

'Where?'

'In the churchyard after the funeral. We were all round the vault and the service was just over. Phelps locked the door with his key and asked me where mine was. I said, "In my desk in the library."'

'Was Brown present at the funeral?'

'Yes, I think I caught a glimpse of him.'

'Was there a crowd round the vault door when it was closed?'

'There was; but I didn't notice Brown on that occasion.'

Blair nodded.

'Very probably. You were too much taken up with the business in hand. Yet, I'll swear Brown was in the crowd, and heard you say where the key was. The clever scoundrel made use of the information that same afternoon.'

'I believe you are right,' said Alan, clenching his fist. 'Oh, I do wish we could find the villain! But what object could he have had in stealing the body?'

'I can guess. Mr Marlow was a millionaire.'

'Well, in a small way, yes.'

'In a way quite big enough to pay a handsome ransom, Mr Thorold.' The inspector smiled. 'Depend upon it, we shall hear from this so-called Brown. He will ask a good few thousands for the return of the corpse. Oh, it is not the first time this game has been played.'

'Well, if Brown writes, we'll have him arrested for the murder.'

'Humph!' said Blair, shaking his head, 'that is easier said than done. He has been too clever for us so far, he may prove too clever in the matter of obtaining the reward of his wickedness. Well, Mr Thorold, the inquest takes place tomorrow, but I haven't got much evidence for the jury.'

He was right. All his talk had been built up upon theory, and on the slenderest of circumstantial evidence. The fact that Brown, the mysterious, had stolen the key—and even that was not absolutely proved—did not show that he had stolen the body. Cicero could not swear to his identity, and, even presuming that he had committed the sacrilege, there was no evidence that it was he who had murdered Warrender.

And so the inquest on the body of the ill-fated doctor was held, the theft of the millionaire's corpse being merely a side-issue. Can it be wondered that the jury were puzzled? All that could be scraped together by Blair was put before them. Cicero related his midnight experience; Mrs Warrender told how her husband went out to see a patient; Mrs Marry how the doctor called at her house, and afterwards followed Brown. Finally, Alan and his housekeeper gave evidence as to the loss of the key, and the forged letter was produced. Out of this sparse detail little could be made, and after some deliberation, the jury brought in the only verdict possible under the circumstances:

'The deceased has been murdered by some person or persons unknown.'

'Most unsatisfactory,' said Blair grimly; 'but there is no more to be said.'

'What can you do now?' asked Alan. 'Shall you give up the case?'

'That depends upon you, sir, or, rather, upon Miss Marlow.'

'In what way?'

'In the money way, Mr Thorold. I'm a poor man, and must attend to my duties. All the same, if Miss Marlow will offer a reward, I will do my utmost to find out who stole her father's body and who murdered the doctor.'

'Why couple the two crimes?'

'Because, sir, in my opinion, Brown committed both. Give a reward, Mr Thorold, and I'll do my best; otherwise, as I have other urgent matters on hand, I must drop the business. But I don't deny,' continued the inspector, stroking his chin, 'that if I were a moneyed man I'd work at this business for the sheer love of it. It is a kind of criminal mystery which does not happen every day.'

'The reward shall be offered,' said Alan. 'Miss Marlow will be guided by me.'

Needless to say, Sophy was guided by him. Indeed, so eager was she that the remains of her father should be recovered that, had not Alan suggested it, she would have offered a reward herself. Also, she was anxious to assist Mrs Warrender, who in spite of her vulgarity and somewhat covetous disposition, was really a well-meaning woman.

The result of this was that two rewards were offered—one thousand for the detection of the person who had stolen the body, and a like sum for any information likely to lead to the arrest of Warrender's murderer. So here were two thousand pounds going a-begging, and hundreds of people hoped to have a chance of gaining the money. The case was so strange and mysterious that it had attracted not a little attention, and the fact that the missing body was that of a millionaire added to the interest excited by the fact of its disappearance. The London papers were full of leaders and letters suggesting solutions of the mystery. The provincial press took up the cry, and throughout the three kingdoms everyone was talking of the case. It was even said that Miss Marlow, the present possessor of all this wealth, would marry the person who secured the thief and the murderer.

'I won't marry you, Alan dear, until my father's body is back in the vault,' said Sophy; 'but at the same time, I won't marry anyone else.'

'But suppose I fail to find the body, Sophy?'

'Then I must remain a spinster for the rest of my life.'

'In that case you condemn me to be a crusty old bachelor.'

'Never mind. We can still be friends and lovers.'

'I'd rather we were man and wife,' sighed Alan.

But he did not believe that she would cling to this idea of perpetual spinsterhood for any length of time. As for Miss Vicky, she thought Sophy mad to have thought of such a thing, and took her roundly to task.

'A woman ought to marry,' she said, breaking through the barriers of her ordinary primness. 'Do you think, if my darling had lived, I should now be a wretched old maid? No, indeed! It would have been my delight to have been an obedient and loving wife to Edward.'

'I'm sure I wish he had lived!' cried Sophy, embracing her; 'and I won't have you call yourself crabbed. You are the sweetest, dearest woman in the world!'

'So poor Edward thought,' sighed Miss Vicky, fingering the precious brooch which always decorated some portion of her small person. 'Alas the day! How often he told me so! But he died for his country on the field of glory,' she cried, with a thrill of pride; 'and in spite of my lonely old age, I don't grudge his precious blood. Noble—noble Edward!' and she wept.

'Don't cry any more, Vicky.'

'It's your obstinacy I'm crying at, Sophia. If your poor dear pa's remains are not found within a certain time, marry Mr Thorold and be happy.'

'I can't—I won't. How can I be happy knowing poor father isn't at rest?'

'His soul is at rest—the earthly tabernacle is nothing. Come, Sophia, don't break with your life's happiness!'

'Alan and I understand one another, Vicky. I dare say we shall marry some day. But the body must be found.'

'Lord grant it!' ejaculated Miss Vicky piously, and said no more. For she found that the more she argued the more obstinate Sophy grew.

Amongst those who had hopes of gaining the reward was Cicero. He had come out of the ordeal of a public examination unscathed, and was now in the possession of his well-earned fifty pounds. Being anxious to remain in Heathton for the purpose of prosecuting his inquiries, he magnanimously forgave Mrs Timber, and took up his quarters at the Good Samaritan. Now that he had money and paid his bill regularly, the good lady considered it politic to treat him with more civility, although, after the manner of women, she felt constrained to remind him, every now and again, of his former poverty. But these remarks did not affect Mr Gramp in the least. He regarded her no more than if she had been a fly, and sailed about the village in a suit of new broadcloth and the best of tall hats, airing his eloquence. He became an attraction at the inn, and discoursed there every evening in fine style.

Mrs Warrender was much averse to his staying on at Heathton. She lived in constant dread lest the relationship between them should be discovered. But Cicero never mentioned it—nor did he ever mention her. Still, she felt doubtful, and one evening, on the plea that she wished to hear more of what he knew about her husband's murder, she sent for him. He arrived to find her in a low evening dress, glittering with diamonds, and looking very handsome—so handsome, indeed, that even he could not refrain from giving vent to his admiration.

'Upon my word, you are a Juno, Clara Maria!' he said, when they were alone. 'There is money in you yet!'

'I know what you mean, Billy,' replied the doctor's widow coldly, 'but I'm not going on the stage again in burlesque or anything else.'

'How are you going to live?' he asked with brutal candour.

'That's my business,' retorted Mrs Warrender. 'I have enough to live on, even without selling my jewels. Perhaps I shall marry again.'

'I'm sure you will, Clara Maria. You always were a determined woman.'

'Hold your tongue, and tell me how much longer do you intend to disgrace me here?'

'How can I tell you, if I am to hold my tongue?' said Cicero coolly. 'As to staying here, I'm not disgracing you that I know of. No one knows you are my ungrateful sister.'

'Billy, if I wasn't a lady, I'd—Ungrateful, indeed, you brute! Go away at once!'

'No, Clara Maria, not till I find out who killed my brother-in-law. I never knew him,' said Cicero, wiping away a tear; 'but as his nearest relative, I must avenge him.'

'That won't do, Billy,' said his sister sourly; 'you only want the reward.'

'Both rewards, Clara Maria. With two thousand pounds I could be a gentleman for the rest of my life.'

'That you will never be.'

'I would do nothing—'

'You never have, you lazy vagabond!'

'Don't interrupt and insult me, Clara Maria, but work with me.'

'Work with you?' gasped Mrs Warrender. 'At what?'

'At this case, Clara Maria. I believe that the secret of this mystery is to be found in the island of Jamaica—in the past life of Mr Marlow. Now, your husband knew the late lamented millionaire in Jamaica, and he might have left some papers relative to the acquaintance. If so, let me see them, and I'll get on the track of the assassin. We will share the reward.'

'My husband did leave papers,' Mrs Warrender said thoughtfully, 'but I won't show them to you, Billy. You'd take all the money. No, I'll read his papers myself, and if I can find anything likely to reveal the name of the person who stole the body and murdered Julian, I shall tell Mr Thorold.'

'You won't get the reward!' cried Cicero in an agony.

'Oh yes, I will; I'm as clever as you are, Billy. Thank you for the idea!'

'You won't work with me?'

'No,' said she firmly, 'I won't; I know you of old, and I want you to keep out of my way. Leave this village and I'll give you twenty pounds.'

'What! when there is a chance to make two thousand? No, Clara Maria.'

'Then earn the reward yourself. There's Joe Brill, he might tell you what you want to know,' mocked Mrs Warrender. 'My husband said he was with Marlow for thirty years.'

'I wish I could ask Joe Brill,' said Cicero gloomily. 'Ever since he tipped me the sovereign I have suspected Joe Brill; but he's gone!'

'Gone! Gone where?'

'I don't know. I only heard the news tonight. He's gone away without a word, and vanished!' And Cicero groaned.

CHAPTER XI

THE STRANGER

THAT Joe Brill had disappeared from Heathton was perfectly true. So far Cicero was correct; but in stating that the man had vanished without a sign he was wrong. News—to be precise, gossip—travels more quickly in a village than in a town; it also gets more quickly distorted. For the intimacy of villagers is such that they are readier than less acquainted folk to take away from, or add to, any talk about those whose everyday life they know so well.

Joe Brill had left a letter for Sophy, who, in much alarm, consulted Miss Parsh. The consultation was overheard by the footman, who told the servants without mentioning the letter, about which he was not very clear himself, having caught only scraps of the conversation. The kitchen discussed the news, and retailed it to the baker, who, with the assistance of his wife, a noted gossip, spread it broadcast over the village. Thus, in the evening, it came to Cicero's greedy ears; and so it was that he came to tell his sister that Joe Brill had disappeared without a sign. Sophy knew better.

'Isn't it dreadful?' she said to Miss Vicky. 'Joe is very cruel to leave me like this in my trouble. He knows that I look upon him as one of my best friends. To be thirty years with father, and then to leave me! Oh, dear Vicky, what does it mean?'

For answer, Miss Vicky read the letter aloud. It was badly written, and badly spelled; but it was short and to the point. Amended it ran as follows:

'HONOURED MISS,

'I am called away on business which may turn out well for you. When I'll come back, miss, I don't know; but

82

wait in hope. Stand by and nail your colours to the mast. Don't trust no one but Mr Thorold. Your prayers, honoured miss, are requested for your humble servant,

'JOSEPH BRILL.'

'Most extraordinary!' said Miss Vicky, and laid down the letter to gaze blankly at Sophy.

'I shall go mad with all this worry!' cried the poor girl, taking the letter. 'Oh, dear Vicky, everything has gone wrong since father died.'

'Hush! Don't talk of it, Sophia. Your pa's remains have gone, but his soul is above. Dr Warrender has been buried, and the verdict of twelve intelligent men has been given. We must think no more of these matters. But Joseph's letter—'

'Is more of a mystery than all the rest put together,' finished Sophy. 'Just listen to the nonsense Joe writes: "I'm called away on business." What business, Vicky?—and how can it turn out well for me? He doesn't know when he'll come back; that means he won't come back at all. "Wait in hope." Hope of what, for goodness' sake, Vicky? And Alan—of course, I'll trust no one but Alan. How absurd to put that in! Then he finishes by asking my prayers, just as though he were going to die. Vicky, is Joe mad?'

'No; Joseph is too clear-headed a man to lose his wits. It's my opinion, Sophia, that he's gone to search for your poor papa's remains.'

This was Alan's opinion also when he read the letter, and heard of Joe's disappearance. He questioned the servants, but they could give no details. The page, who slept in the same room, declared that he woke at six o'clock to find Joe's bed empty; but this did not alarm him, as Joe was always the first in the house to be up. So Alan went to the railway-station, and learnt there that the old sailor, carrying some things tied up in a handkerchief, had taken the 6.30 train to the junction. A wire to the junction station-master, who knew Joe, elicited the reply that he had gone on to London by the express. Beyond this it was hopeless to attempt to trace him; for at Waterloo Station Joe had vanished into the crowd, and was lost. Alan told the lamenting Sophy that nothing could now be done but wait for his return.

'But will he return?' demanded the girl tearfully.

'I think so. I agree with Miss Vicky: Joe has gone to search for your father's body.'

'But he has no idea where it is. If he did, he would surely have told me or you, Alan, knowing how anxious we are!'

'He may have a clue, and may want to follow it up himself. And I believe, Sophy, that Joe knows more about the matter than we think. Do you remember that he gave Cicero a sovereign to leave the Moat House?'

'What of that?'

'Only that a sovereign was a large sum for a servant like Joe to give. He thought, no doubt, that Cicero knew too much, and he wanted to get him away before he could be questioned. It was his guilty conscience which made him so generous.'

'Guilty conscience, Alan? What had Joe done?'

'Nothing, so far as I know,' replied Thorold readily. 'But I am convinced there is something in your father's past life, Sophy, which would account for the violation of the vault. Joe knows it, but for some reason he won't tell. I questioned him about the ridiculous sum he gave to Cicero, but I could get no satisfactory explanation out of him—nor could Blair.'

'You don't think he was the short man with Dr Warrender on that night, Alan?' asked the girl somewhat tremulously.

'No, I do not; I asked the boy who sleeps in the same room. He said that Joe went to bed as usual, and that he never heard him go out. Besides, Sophy, I am certain the accomplice of Warrender was Brown.'

'The Quiet Gentleman?'

'Yes; he had the key of the vault. And also, by the evidence of the stamp, he had something to do with Jamaica. Perhaps he knew your father there.'

'Perhaps he did. Joe would know.'

'Joe will not speak, and, at all events, he has gone. We must wait until he comes back.'

'Are you not going to make any more search for the body, Alan?'

'My dearest, I have not the slightest idea where to begin. The case has baffled the police, and it baffles me. I have made inquiries all round the country, and I can find no one who saw Brown with your father's dead body, or, indeed, anything else which might have aroused suspicion. There is only one hope that we may get it back.'

'The reward?'

'No; although Blair, and, I believe, Cicero, intend to work for that. The hope lies in the chance that Brown, whoever he is, may have taken away the body for blackmail. In that case we may get a letter demanding money—probably a large sum. We must pay it, and have your father's remains brought back.'

'And the murder, Alan?'

'Ah! that is a difficult part. When Brown stole the body he did not intend to commit murder; that came about in some unforeseen way. The danger that he may be arrested for the murder may keep Brown from applying for blackmail, always supposing, Sophy, that such is his object.'

'In that case we may never recover poor father.'

'I am afraid not. However, we must live in hope.'

This conversation ended in the usual unsatisfactory way. On the face of it there was nothing to be done, for Alan could obtain no clue. Brown, if Brown were indeed the guilty person, had managed so cleverly that he had completely cut his trail. Even the offer of the reward brought forth no fresh information. The mystery was more a mystery than ever.

In his capacity of trustee, Alan had looked through the papers of the dead man. He found no documents or letters whatever relating to his life in Jamaica, yet there were plenty dealing with his doings in South Africa. Twenty years before he had left

Kingston with the child Sophy. He brought her to England, and placed her in the Hampstead convent. Then he sailed for the Cape, and had made his fortune there. Fifteen years after he returned, to buy the Moat House, and settled. Sophy came to live with him, and he had passed a quiet, peaceful time until his sudden death. So far all was clear; but the Jamaica life still remained a mystery. When he died he was over sixty. What had he done with himself during the forty years he had lived in the West Indies? Joe could have told; but Joe, as mysterious as his master, had disappeared, and even if he had remained, Alan could have got nothing out of him. The old sailor, as had been proved both by Thorold and the inspector, was as dumb as an oyster.

'Did Marlow ever mention Jamaica?' Alan asked Mr Phelps, when next they met.

'Once or twice, in a casual sort of way. He said he had sailed a good deal amongst the islands.'

'And Joe was a sailor. I wonder if Marlow went in for trading there?'

'It's not impossible,' said the Rector; 'but that fact, even if we knew it to be true, could throw no light on the disappearance of his body.'

'I don't know. I have a good mind to go to Jamaica—to Kingston—to make inquiries. The West Indian Island area is not so very large. If Marlow had been a trader there twenty years ago, he would still be remembered amongst them. I might come across someone who knew of his past life.'

'You might,' assented Phelps, with an amount of sarcasm surprising in so mild a man, 'if Marlow were his real name.'

The two were sitting over their wine in the twilight amid the glimmer of shaded candles. This last remark of the Rector's so surprised Alan, that he turned suddenly, and knocked his glass off the table. After he had apologized for the accident, and after the debris had been collected by the scandalized butler, the Squire asked Mr Phelps what he meant.

'It is hard to say what I mean.' The Rector sipped his port meditatively. 'Marlow was always a mystery to me. Undeniably a millionaire and a gentleman, Alan, and while here a man of clean life. And I have met people in London'—the worthy parson dabbled a little in shares—'who knew him in South Africa. He was highly respected there, and he made his millions honestly, so far as millions can be made honestly in these gambling days. But I always felt that there was some mystery about the man. It was Warrender who gave me the clue.'

'Ah! Warrender came with Marlow to Heathton.'

'Yes, but there was no mystery about that. Warrender told me that he had met Marlow at Kingston, Jamaica. Afterwards the doctor settled in New Orleans. There he met his wife, who was on the stage. He did not do very well, so Mrs Warrender urged him to return to England. He did so, and met Marlow by chance in London, where they renewed their acquaintance. Sorry to see that Warrender was so unfortunate, Marlow brought him down here, where he did very well.'

'I don't think he did well enough to have supplied Mrs Warrender with her diamonds, sir.'

'Alan, don't speak evil of the dead. She did not get the diamonds from Marlow, but legitimately, my dear boy, from her husband.'

'And where did he get them? His practice must have brought him in little enough.'

'No, I won't say that. The fact, I think, is that there was some understanding between the two men, and that Marlow gave Warrender money.'

'He must have given him a good deal, then. Those jewels represent a lot. Seems like a kind of blackmail, sir.'

'On that point, Alan, I would prefer not to give an opinion.'

'And Warrender helped to steal the body of his patron,' mused Alan. 'Strange. But about this idea of a false name.'

'Well, it was at dinner one evening. The ladies had retired, and I was alone with Marlow and Warrender, talking over our wine, just as you and I might be now, Alan. The doctor had taken a little too much, and on one occasion he addressed the other man as Beauchamp. Marlow flashed one fierce glance at him, which sobered him at once. I made no remark on the incident at the time, but it stuck in my memory.'

'Then you think that Mr Marlow was called Beauchamp in Jamaica?'

'Warrender's slip gave me that impression,' said the Rector cautiously.

'How very strange!' murmured Alan, toying with his glass. 'Do you know the will? Of course, I am trustee.'

'Sophy's trustee—why, yes. All the money goes to her, doesn't it?'

'Most of it. There are legacies to myself, Joe Brill, and Miss Parsh. Sophy gets the rest, on conditions.'

'What conditions?'

'One is that she marries me, the other that she pays two thousand a year to a man called Herbert Beauchamp.'

It was the Rector's turn to be startled.

'Bless me, the same name!'

'It would appear so. Perhaps this Herbert Beauchamp is a relative of the so-called Marlow. The money is to be paid into the Occidental Bank of London for transmission to him.'

'Where is he?'

'I don't know. But now that you have told me so much, I shall take the first instalment myself to the Occidental Bank and make inquiries about the man. The manager may be able in some measure to account for all this.'

'I hope so, I hope so,' cried the bewildered Rector, 'for the mysteries seem to me to deepen.'

'Meanwhile,' went on Alan calmly, 'I shall see Mrs Warrender. She may know something that will be useful to us.'

'I don't think so,' the Rector said doubtfully. 'Bless me, why should she? It was long afterwards that she met the doctor in New Orleans.'

'Well, he might have told her about Marlow. At all events, I'll see her. You know,' added Alan, curling his lip, 'Mrs Warrender is fond of money, and amenable to bribery.'

Thorold was usually correct in his forecasts of what would happen, but this time he was quite wrong. The widow received him kindly, and told him absolutely nothing. Acting on the advice given her by Cicero, she had been searching through the papers of her late husband. She had not found what she sought, but she had found quite enough to show that there was a mystery in Mr Marlow's past life—a mystery which was sufficiently important to be worth money. It was the intention of this astute woman to play her own game, a game which had for stake a goodly portion of Sophy's millions, and she had no desire for a partner. To Cicero and to his wish to join her she soon gave the go-by. And when Alan came upon the scene, she gave him to understand that she knew nothing. Her intention was to prepare her bombshell alone, and when it was ready, to explode it in Sophy's presence. That her knowledge would be profitable to her from a financial point of view she felt pretty secure, for the same blood ran in the veins of Clara Maria Warrender and of Cicero Gramp.

'I wish I could help you, Mr Thorold,' she said; 'but I knew nothing of Mr Marlow. My husband never spoke to me about his life in Jamaica.'

'Did he leave any papers?'

'Lots of rubbish, but nothing that could enlighten us as to Mr Marlow's past.'

'Can I see them?'

'Oh, I am so sorry, but I burnt them.'

He did not believe her, and went away with the conviction that she was playing a deep game. Meanwhile a new personage had come upon the scene—a man who told an astonishing story, and who made a no less astonishing claim—a slight, dark, bright-eyed man, accurately dressed, but foreign looking. He presented his card at the Moat House, with a request to see Miss Marlow.

'Captain Lestrange!' exclaimed Sophy. 'Who is he, Thomas?'

'Looks like a foreigner, miss. Shall I show him in?'

'Yes,' she said; and the visitor was announced almost immediately.

He started theatrically when he saw the girl. Sophy, annoyed by his manner, drew back.

'Captain Lestrange?' she queried coldly.

'Captain Lestrange,' was the reply, 'and your father.'

CHAPTER XII

A STRANGE STORY

SOPHY neither screamed nor fainted at this extraordinary announcement; indeed, it appeared to her so very ridiculous that she felt more inclined to laugh. However, she controlled her feelings, and spoke very quietly—so quietly that the visitor was somewhat disconcerted.

'Why do you make this strange assertion?' she asked, looking again at his card.

'Because it is true.'

'What proof can you give me of its truth?'

'Three proofs, Sophy, if I may call—'

'You may not!' interrupted the girl, flushing. 'I am Miss Marlow.'

'For the present,' assented the man, with an ironical smile. 'Soon you will be Miss Lestrange. Three proofs, then, I have. Firstly, I can tell you the story of how I lost you; secondly, there is the resemblance between us; and, thirdly, I have the certificate of your birth. Oh, it is easily proved, I can assure you.'

She shivered. He spoke very positively. What if his claim could be substantiated? She looked at him; she glanced into a near mirror, and she saw with dismay that there *was* a strong resemblance. Like herself, Lestrange, as he called himself, was slight in build, small in stature. He also had dark hair and brilliant eyes; the contour of his face, the chiselling of his features, resembled her own. Finally, he had that Spanish look which she knew she herself possessed. So far as outward appearances went, she might well have been the daughter of this rakish-looking stranger. He smiled. From her furtive glance into the mirror he guessed her thoughts.

'You see the glass proclaims the truth,' said he. 'Think of your supposed father, Richard Marlow—tall, fair, blue-eyed, Saxon in looks! Like myself, you have the Spanish look and possess all the grace and colour of Andalusia. I always thought you would grow up beautiful. Your dear mother was the loveliest woman in Jamaica.'

She did not answer, but the colour ebbed from her cheeks, the courage from her heart. It was true enough that she in no way resembled Mr Marlow. This man might be her father, after all. Yet he repelled her; the glance of his glittering eyes gave her a feeling of repulsion. He was a bad man, of that she felt certain. But her father? She fought against her doubts, and with a courage born of despair she prepared to defend herself until help arrived. Her thoughts flew to Alan; he was the champion she desired.

'I expect my guardian, Mr Thorold, in a quarter of an hour,' she said in a hard voice. 'You will be good enough to relate your story to him. I prefer to hear it when he is present.'

'You don't believe me?'

'No, I do not. Mr Marlow treated me as his daughter, and I feel myself to be his daughter. Do you expect me to believe you, to rush into your arms without proof?'

'I have shown you one proof.'

'A chance resemblance counts for nothing. What about the certificate?'

He produced a pocketbook, and took out a piece of paper.

'This is a copy of the entry in the register of the Church of St Thomas at Kingston. You will find it all correct, Marie.'

'Marie! What do you mean?'

'That paper will inform you,' said Lestrange coolly.

Sophy read the certificate. Truly, it seemed regular enough. It stated that on the 24th of June, 18—, was born at Kingston, in the island of Jamaica, Marie Annette Celestine Lestrange. The names of the parents were Achille Lestrange and Zelia, his wife. Sophy could not suppress a start. The 24th of June was her birthday; the date of the year was also correct. She was twenty-one years of age now. She turned to him.

'You are Achille Lestrange?'

'Your father—yes.'

'I don't admit that, monsieur.'

'Why do you call me "monsieur"?'

'You are French, are you not?'

'French by descent, if you will, but I am a British subject. Also, I am a Roman Catholic. You are of the same faith?'

'Yes, I am of the true Faith.'

'I am glad of that,' said Lestrange indolently; he was as indolent as graceful, and reminded Sophy of a full-fed tiger. 'I am pleased to hear that Marlow allowed you to retain your faith since he took from you your father and your name.'

'Do you know that my father is dead?'

'Pardon me, he is alive, and sitting before you.'

Sophy ignored his remark.

'Do you know that Mr Marlow is dead?' she asked again.

'Ah! now you speak as you should. Yes, I heard something about his death. The fact is, I have only just landed from a Royal Mail steamer at Southampton—two days ago, in fact— so I know very little. But I have heard of the disappearance of his body. It is town talk in London. One cannot open a newspaper without coming across theories of how it happened.'

'And the murder of Dr Warrender? Do you know of that also?'

'Of course. The two things go together, as I understand. Marlow's body is lost; Warrender was stabbed. How unfortunate that two people I knew should be out of the way when I come to claim you!'

'Did you know Dr Warrender?' asked Sophy quickly.

'As I know myself,' was the answer. 'Twenty years ago, when you were a child, a mere infant, he practised in the town of Falmouth, Jamaica. He left after certain events which happened there, and, I believe, practised again in New Orleans. He married there, too, it was said.'

'Yes; his wife lives at Heathton.'

'Ah! I shall be glad to see her. Has the man who murdered her husband been discovered?'

'No; he cannot be found.'

'Nor ever will be, I suspect,' said Captain Lestrange coolly. 'From what I read, the whole criminal business was conducted in the most skilful manner. I wonder why they stole poor Dick's body.'

'Poor Dick!' retorted the girl indignantly. 'Are you speaking of my father?'

'Of the man who passed as your father—yes, Marie, I am.'

'Pray don't call me Marie! I am Sophia Marlow.'

'As you please. Temper again! Oh, how you remind me of Zelia!'

She was confounded at the cool assurance of the man. Nothing seemed to ruffle his temper or banish his eternal smile. He was more hateful to her than ever. Never would she acknowledge herself his daughter, even should he prove his claim! She was of age, and her own mistress. The will of Richard Marlow left the money, not to 'my daughter' but to 'Sophia Marlow', so there was no possibility of the money being taken from her. Then she thought of Alan. He would stand between her and this man. And even as this thought came into her mind, the door opened, and Thorold came forward eagerly to meet her; but, on perceiving the stranger, he stopped short. Lestrange rose and bowed in a foreign fashion.

'Oh, Alan!' cried Sophy, 'I am so glad you have come! I was waiting for you.'

'And I also,' remarked Lestrange.

'Who is this gentleman, Sophy?' demanded Alan.

'He calls himself Captain Lestrange. Here is his card.'

'Captain in the army of the Peruvian Republic,' said the man, 'and this young lady's father!'

'Confound you!—what—what—!'

'Oh yes, Alan. He says he is my father—that my true father stole me from him. Here is the certificate of my birth, he says.'

'And here'—Lestrange pointed to Sophy—'here is my second self. Can you deny the resemblance? By the way, who are you?'

The inquiry was made with graceful insolence, and was meant to provoke the young man into losing his temper. But in this it failed.

'I am Alan Thorold,' he said quietly, 'the Squire of Heathton, and I am engaged to marry Miss Marlow—'

'Pardon—Mademoiselle Lestrange,' interpolated the Captain, and resumed his seat. 'I claim this young lady as my daughter.'

'Good,' said Thorold coldly. 'Your proofs?'

'The resemblance between us, the certificate of her birth, and the story of how I lost my dear Marie twenty years ago.'

'The resemblance I admit, but that goes for nothing. As to the certificate, it is that of Marie Lestrange, and not of Sophy Marlow.'

'Is not the birthday of Miss Marlow, as you will call her, on the 24th of June—'

'Yes,' said Sophy, before Alan could stop her. 'The day and the year are both correct. I am twenty-one, and I was born on the 24th of June, 18—.'

'Very good; and at Kingston?'

'At Kingston,' admitted the girl; 'but, for all that, I am not your daughter.'

'I agree with Miss Marlow,' said Mr Thorold. 'Let us hear your story. That it will convince me I do not promise.'

'Ah!' cried the foreigner, with an ironical smile. 'None so blind as those who won't see. What a pity that Marlow and Warrender are both dead!'

'Oh, you know that?'

'As I had the honour of telling Miss Marlow'—Lestrange put so sneering an accent on the name that Alan felt inclined to kick him—'I know that. I landed in England from Jamaica only two days ago. But, as you know, everyone is talking of the mystery, and by this time I know the case as well as you do.'

Alan winced, and Sophy glanced at him apprehensively. Would her champion fail her? Would this man prove his claim? She was in deadly terror lest he should. But Alan had no intention of yielding.

'Go on,' he said again. 'Miss Marlow and I will hear your story.'

'Very good. I am glad to see that you have the British instinct of fair play. I will be as brief as possible, and you can ask me any questions you wish. My name is Achille Lestrange, the man who is mentioned in that certificate. I am—or, rather, I was—a Captain in the Peruvian Army. I retired after the war between that country and Chile. However, I have ample means to live on, and I retain my military rank, out of sheer vanity, if you will.'

'All this,' said Alan, 'is beside the point.'

'It is necessary to explain my position. More than twenty years ago I was married at Kingston to Zelia Durand. We had one child—a little girl—the same who now sits beside you.'

'I won't hear of it!' cried Sophy angrily.

'We shall see,' he went on cheerfully. 'You may change your mind when I have got to the end of my story. I regret to say that Mrs Lestrange—I do not call her Madame,' explained the Captain, 'because I am truly English in speech and manner—well, Mrs Lestrange had a bad temper. We did not get on well together. And, besides, I was jealous'—his eyes flashed fire—'yes, I was jealous of Herbert Beauchamp.'

'Herbert Beauchamp!' Alan thought of Marlow's will and of the legacy. How did this man come to know the name?

CHAPTER XIII

A STRANGE STORY—*continued*

CAPTAIN LESTRANGE recovered from his momentary emotion, and raised his eyebrows at Alan's involuntary exclamation.

'I beg your pardon, Mr Thorold.'

'Nothing,' said the other hastily. 'I fancied the name was familiar.'

'Ah! You may have heard Marlow mention it.'

'No. He never spoke of his past life.'

'He had good reason to be reticent, as you shall hear.'

But here Sophy burst out: 'Be good enough to continue your story without vilifying my father.'

'Your father!' sneered the Captain.

'The story—the story!' cried Alan.

'I continue,' said Lestrange, with a nod. 'As I say, I was jealous of Beauchamp, for before our marriage he had been an admirer of my Zelia's. And, as a matter of fact, she was a singularly attractive woman. You might guess as much,' added he blandly, 'seeing that her grace and beauty are reproduced in her daughter. But to continue: Zelia had many admirers, three of whom she distinguished above the others—myself, Herbert Beauchamp, and my cousin, Jean Lestrange. I was the lucky man who won her. Jean ceased to pay any attention to her after the marriage, but Beauchamp was persistent. I remonstrated with him—we nearly had a duel—but to no purpose; and I am sorry to say that Zelia encouraged him.'

'Proceed with your story, and leave my mother alone,' cried Sophy.

Alan started, for he remembered with a pang that Sophy had told him her mother's name was Zelia; but he kept silent, and a terrible dread came over him that this man would prove his statements after all.

Meanwhile the narrator went on pleasantly.

'Beauchamp,' he said, fingering his moustache, 'was a sugar-planter—at least, he was supposed to be one. He had a plantation some miles from the town of Falmouth, which is on the other side of Jamaica. It was there that Dr Warrender practised. He was a bachelor in those days, and he was considered rather a wild fellow. Probably for that reason he was a bosom friend of Beauchamp's.'

'Do you mean to infer that Beauchamp was wild?'

'Well, not exactly. I must be honest. He was adventuresome rather than wild. He was fond of yachting, and had a smart sailing boat in which he used to cruise amongst the islands. Warrender frequently went with him. Beauchamp was a very handsome man, and extremely popular with women. I know that to my cost,' he added bitterly, 'when he set his affections on Zelia. She was my wife—she was the mother of my child—yet she eloped with him.'

'I—I—don't believe it,' said Sophy in a suffocating voice.

'If it were not true, my child, you would not be sitting there under the false name of Sophia Marlow.'

'One moment,' put in Alan, clasping the girl's hand, 'you have yet to prove that Miss Marlow is Marie Lestrange.'

'If you would not interrupt so often, I could do so,' said the man insolently. 'As I say, Zelia ran away with Beauchamp. He brought his yacht to Kingston when I was absent, and sailed off with her. She carried with her my child—my adorable Marie.' Here Lestrange fixed an affectionate look on Sophy. 'I returned to find my home dishonoured,' he went on, 'my life wrecked. Jean came to console me. He also had heard of Beauchamp's treachery, and that the boat had sailed for Falmouth. We followed—'

Here Lestrange broke down. Whether his emotion was genuine or not, Alan could not say. He looked at Sophy, and she at him. Having fought down his emotion, the Captain resumed his seat and his story:

'Jean and I arrived at Falmouth. There we heard that Zelia was very ill, and that Beauchamp had taken her to his plantation. Dr Warrender, our informant said, was in attendance. The whole town knew that she was my wife, that she had dishonoured me, and that I was on my may to settle accounts with the man who had wrecked my happiness. My cousin and I rode out to Beauchamp's plantation, for it was within a few miles of Falmouth, as I said. The night was dark and stormy—we arrived in pouring rain, and by the wailing of the negroes we knew that death was in the house. Yes'—he grew dramatic—'Zelia was dead; torture, remorse, sorrow, had brought about her punishment!'

'You are very ready to condemn her,' said Alan.

'She had dishonoured me!' cried the man, waxing melodramatic. 'It was well that she should die. I rushed away to her room, where she lay calm in death, and Jean remained to arrange matters with Beauchamp. I challenged him to a duel. Jean was my second. But Beauchamp refused to fight, and—he murdered Jean.'

'Murdered your cousin?' queried Alan sceptically.

'Yes. I was praying beside my wife's bed. I heard cries for help, and when I came out I found Jean dead, stabbed to the heart by Beauchamp. The scoundrel had fled—he had taken my child with him.'

'Why should he have encumbered himself with the child?'

'To wring my heart!' replied Lestrange savagely. 'He knew that I loved my little Marie. He carried her away. I would have followed, but all my troubles and the shock of Zelia's death brought on an attack of fever. I rose from my bed weeks later to hear that Beauchamp had vanished. On the night he committed the double crimes of murder and kidnapping he went on board his yacht at Falmouth, and was never heard of again. I searched for him everywhere, but without success.'

'What about his estate?' asked Alan.

'There he has been cunning. It seemed that he had long since planned to elope with Zelia, and that some weeks before he had sold his land. He took the money with him, and the child. Had Zelia been alive she would have gone too. As months and years went by, I gave up hope, and I believed that the yacht had foundered.'

Suddenly Sophy got up, much agitated.

'I can listen to this no longer,' she said. 'You are telling lies.'

'Her mother's temper,' muttered Lestrange. 'Zelia's masterly way of crushing argument.'

'Don't call her my mother!' cried Sophy. 'I won't have it. I am not the child that was taken away by Beauchamp. I never knew anyone of that name.'

'Probably not,' replied Lestrange smoothly. 'There were reasons for its being kept from you. But Mr Thorold—'

'Mr Thorold is waiting to hear the end of the story,' said that gentleman coolly. 'I have yet to hear who Beauchamp is and how you traced him.'

'This is mere evasion.' The Captain was losing his temper somewhat. 'You know who the man is as well as I do.'

'I am waiting to hear how you connect the two.'

'What two?' asked Miss Marlow.

But in her own heart she knew the answer. Yet, like a loyal soul, she kept true to the memory of the dead.

Lestrange took no notice of her.

'You are either very dull or very cunning,' he said addressing Alan pointedly. 'The latter, I think. How did I find Beauchamp again? In a curious way. I saw an illustrated paper in Jamaica, which gave a portrait of the famous South African millionaire, Richard Marlow. The face had on its right cheek a jagged scar. Jean gave that scar to Beauchamp with his diamond ring. No doubt it was the drawing of blood which led to the murder.'

'Then you assert that Marlow was none other than Herbert Beauchamp?'

'I do. Also that Sophia Marlow is my child whom he carried away. I have mourned her for twenty years. By the accident of the illustrated paper I have traced her. At Southampton I heard of Marlow's death, so I knew that he had escaped punishment on earth. But at least I have found my dear child Marie.'

'I am not your child!' she cried. 'I will never acknowledge you as my father.'

'In that case'—Lestrange rose to his feet and looked very stern—'I must appeal to the law.'

Alan laughed.

'The law can't help you,' he said. 'Sophy is over age and her own mistress. Even if you can prove your case, you cannot force her to go with you.'

'Natural affection—'

'Don't talk to me about natural affection!' cried the girl. 'I know nothing about you. Nothing in the world will make me go with you!'

'But if I tell my story to the world?' cried Lestrange, hinting a threat.

'Tell it, by all means,' said Thorold, putting his arm round Sophy. 'You can hurt only the memory of the dead. Even if Marlow, as you assert, killed your cousin, he is dead, and beyond your reach.'

'Are you so sure he is dead?' sneered the man.

'Of course we are sure,' cried Sophy indignantly. 'Didn't I see him dead in his coffin?'

'Well,' said Lestrange, preparing to go, 'it is most extraordinary to me that he should have died so suddenly and so conveniently. His body, too, has been stolen. That also is convenient.'

'Do you mean that he is alive?'

'Yes. He feigned death to escape me.'

'How could he have known that you were coming?'

'I don't know,' was the answer, 'but I shall find out. It shall be my business to search for the body of Richard Marlow.'

'Do,' said Thorold calmly. 'And when you find it you will gain the reward of a thousand pounds.'

'I shall gain more than that, Mr Thorold. My daughter—'

'Never! Never! Leave this house, sir, and don't come near me again!'

The man moved towards the door. He had picked up the certificate and put it in his pocket.

'You turn your own father out into the street,' he said. 'Very good. I shall take my own means of punishing you for your want of filial respect. It is to the bad influence of Mr Thorold that I owe this reception. Be assured, Mr Thorold, that I shall not forget it. To revert to the tongue of my progenitors, I shall say *Au revoir* but not "Adieu". We shall meet again.'

And clapping on his hat with a jaunty air, Captain Lestrange walked out of the room.

When the door had closed after him, Sophy turned to Alan.

'Do you think this story is true?' she asked.

'I must admit that there appears to be some truth in it,' was the reply. 'The certificate is correct as to your age, your birthday, and your birthplace, and the name of your mother also is correct.'

'Then, am I that man's daughter?'

'Not necessarily. He may have assumed the name. He may— oh, I don't know what to think! But even if he proves his case, you won't go with him?'

'Never! never! How can we find out the truth?'

'Joe might know. I wish he would come back. I wonder if, after all, your father can be alive—Marlow, I mean.'

'How can that be? We both saw him dead. Dr Warrender gave a certificate of the death. Why do you ask?'

'Well, it is strange. In his will a sum of two thousand a year is left to be paid to a man called Herbert Beauchamp, through the Occidental Bank.'

'And he says that my father was Herbert Beauchamp.'

'I know. Can your father have feigned death to avoid him?'

'Impossible. He did not know Captain Lestrange was coming.'

'Well,' said Alan slowly, 'there was that West Indian letter which agitated him so much. It might have been a warning. However, it is no use theorizing. I'll go to the Occidental Bank, and find out Herbert Beauchamp.'

'You won't find that he is my own father, Alan; I am sure of that. He may be a relative. No, no! He is not a murderer! He is dead—quite dead! I don't believe a word of the story.'

Alan sighed.

'Time alone can prove its truth or falsehood, Sophy,' he said.

CHAPTER XIV

THE ENMITY OF CAPTAIN LESTRANGE

THAT same evening the Rector was coming in to dine with Alan. The young man was glad that he had asked him, for he was anxious to consult his old friend about the strange tale he had heard, and about the steps which should be taken to prove its truth or falsity. He stayed with Sophy till it was nearly six o'clock. Miss Parsh had not been called into counsel. She was too timid, they thought, and too likely to lose her head. Moreover, Alan felt that she would give the girl overmuch sympathy and make her nervous. So he did all the bracing he could, advised her not to take the old lady into her confidence, and rode home to the Abbey Farm in the cool twilight.

As he passed the Good Samaritan, Mrs Timber came flying out in a flutter of excitement.

'Sir! sir! Mr Thorold!' she called. And then, as he checked his horse: 'Is the gentleman all right? He's a furriner, and I never did hold as they could pay honest.'

'What are you talking about, Mrs Timber?' asked the young man, utterly bewildered.

'Why, of the gentleman you sent to me, sir.'

'I sent no gentleman. Stay! Do you mean Captain Lestrange?'

'Yes, sir, that's his name—a nasty French name. He said you recommended my house. I'm sure I'm very much obliged, Mr Thorold.' Here Mrs Timber dropped her best curtsy and smiled a sour smile. 'But I arsk again, sir, is he good pay?'

Alan was amazed at the Captain's impudence in making him stand sponsor for his respectability.

'I don't know anything about the gentleman, Mrs Timber,' he said, giving his horse the spur. 'He is a stranger to me.'

'Oh, is he?' muttered the landlady to herself as Alan galloped off. 'Well, he don't get nothing out of me till I sees the colour of his money. The idea of giving Mr Thorold's name when he had no right to! Ah! I doubt he's a robber of the widder and the orphan. But I'll show him!'

And Mrs Timber, full of wrath, went into her hotel to have it out with her new lodger.

Alan rode fast and hard in the waning light, between the flowering hedgerows—rode to get away from his thoughts. The advent of Lestrange with his cut-and-dried story, with his accusation of the dead, and his claim to be Sophy's father, was ominous of evil. Alan had his own uncomfortable feelings, but of these he decided to tell no one, not even Phelps, although Phelps was his very good friend. In taking this resolution, Alan made a very serious mistake—a mistake which he found out when it was too late to remedy his injudicious silence.

He had just time to dress for dinner before his guest arrived. Knowing that Mr Phelps was dainty in his eating, Mrs Hester had prepared a meal such as the good Rector loved. Alan's wine was of the best, and he did not stint it, so Mr Phelps addressed himself to the solemn business of dinner, with the conviction that he would enjoy himself; and Alan kept his news to himself until they were in the smoking-room. Then, when his guest was sipping aromatic black coffee and inhaling the fragrance of an excellent cigar, the young Squire felt compelled to speak, and exploded his bombshell without further notice.

'Mr Phelps, I have unpleasant news,' he said, filling his pipe.

The clergyman looked piteously at the excellent cigar, and took another sip of the coffee.

'Oh, Alan, my boy, must you?'

'You can judge for yourself,' replied Alan, unable to suppress a smile. 'Sophy had a visitor today.'

'Indeed! Anyone connected with these mysteries which so perplex us?'

'In one way, yes; in another, no. He is a Captain Lestrange.'

'Lestrange! Lestrange!' repeated the Rector. 'I don't know the name. Who is he?'

'Sophy's father!' said Alan simply, and lighted up, while Mr Phelps remonstrated:

'My dear Alan, if this is a jest—'

'It is no jest, sir, but, I fear, a grim reality. This man comes from Jamaica.'

'Dear me! Marlow came from Jamaica. Does he know—'

'He knows all Marlow's past life.'

'The dev—ahem! God forgive me for swearing. And who was Marlow?'

'According to Lestrange, a murderer.'

Phelps dropped his cigar and stared at his old pupil.

'Alan, are you mad?'

'No. At the present moment I am particularly sane. This man says that Marlow was a murderer, and he himself claims to be Sophy's father. Take some green Chartreuse, Mr Phelps, and I'll tell you all about it.'

The Rector's nerves had received such a shock at the abrupt way in which Alan had told his news that he very willingly poured himself out a liqueur. Then he relighted his cigar, and signed to the young man to proceed.

'If I must hear it!' sighed he. 'Such a pity, too, when I was so comfortable. Ah! Man is born to trouble. Go on, my dear lad!'

'You will find it really interesting,' said Thorold encouragingly, and told his story in as concise a way as he could. The narrative was interrupted frequently by the Rector. When it was ended he was too much astonished to make any remark, and the other had to stir up his intelligence. 'What do you think of it, sir?'

'Really—bless me!—I hardly know. Do you believe it, Alan?'

'There are so many things in it which I know to be true, that I can't help thinking the man is honest, in so far as his story goes,' said Alan gloomily. 'Whether Sophy is really his child I can't say. She is certainly very like him, and the certificate appears to be genuine. Again, Mr Phelps, you heard Warrender call Marlow "Beauchamp", and, as I told you, a sum of two thousand a year is by Marlow's will to be paid to a Herbert Beauchamp. What if he should be Marlow himself?'

'I can't—I won't believe it!' cried the Rector, rubbing his bald head. 'The man is as dead as a doornail—you saw the corpse yourself, Alan. The body was put in a leaden casing, hermetically sealed, and that in a tightly-screwed-down oaken coffin. Even if Marlow had been in a trance—if that is what you mean—he could not have survived that! He would have died of suffocation—he would have been asphyxiated. Bless my soul! I don't believe it for one moment.'

'But how do you account for the income left to Herbert Beauchamp?'

'He must be a relative,' said the Rector.

'But the same Christian name, Mr Phelps? Still, of course, that is not impossible—he might be a relative. I will see the manager of the bank, and insist upon knowing the address of this man.'

'Supposing he won't give it?'

'Then I shall call in the police. I must get to the bottom of this affair. Why should that body have been stolen?'

'Perhaps Lestrange can tell you, Alan.' The little parson jumped up in a state of wild excitement. 'What if he should be the Quiet Gentleman—Brown?'

'Impossible—he landed at Southampton only two days ago.'

'Oh! so he says, but you must find out if it is true.'

'I will examine the passenger-list of the last steamer.'

'It is strange,' said the Rector—'strange that Marlow—let us call him Marlow—should have died so opportunely. If you remember, he was much worried by a West Indian letter he received a week before his death.'

'Yes; I believe that was written to warn him against Lestrange.

To escape being arrested on a charge of murder, he—he—well, what did he do?'

'He didn't feign death, at all events,' said Mr Phelps. 'Bless me, Alan! I know the feel and the look of a corpse. I've seen dozens! Besides, you studied for medicine—your knowledge must tell you—'

'Yes, I could have sworn he was, as you say, dead as a door-nail. Of course'—Alan cast about in his mind for some hypothesis—'that is—the shock of impending danger hinted at in that letter might have killed him. He died in a fit, sir, and died very suddenly.'

'Humph! You didn't attend him?'

'I—a layman! My dear sir, Warrender attended him.'

'And Warrender was his bosom friend in Jamaica. Alan, Warrender must have recognized him as Beauchamp—must have known Sophy was not his daughter—must have known that he had been accused of murder in Jamaica.'

'Quite so,' said Alan composedly, 'and so Mrs Warrender's diamonds are accounted for. He blackmailed Marlow. I can see it plainly.'

'Then the murder of—of Warrender?' whispered the Rector, with a look of terror.

'Ah! we are still in the dark about that. Marlow, being dead, could not have killed him. Humph! I wonder if Lestrange is the Quiet Gentleman after all!'

'Alan!' said Phelps suddenly. 'Joe Brill!'

'What about him?'

'Do you think he is guilty? He was devoted to his master. Warrender possessed his master's secret, and Joe might have killed him, and have run away to escape arrest.'

Alan shook his head.

'There was no suspicion against Joe,' he said. 'Why should he have run away?'

'His guilty conscience, perhaps.'

'A man who had nerve enough to commit such a murder

and take the corpse of his victim back to the vault wouldn't have any conscience to speak of. Besides, the boy who slept in Joe's room says he was not out on that night.'

'No, no—of course not,' said the Rector. 'Then it can't be Joe. Well, I give it up!'

'I don't,' said Alan grimly. 'I go to London tomorrow to solve the mystery.'

This he did. He left next morning and was away for three days, leaving Mr Phelps to console and protect Sophy from any annoyance on the part of Lestrange, who remained in the village. The Captain propitiated Mrs Timber by the payment of a week's board and lodging in advance, and this was enough to convince the landlady that he was a most estimable person.

Naturally enough, he and Cicero Gramp came into contact, and, equally naturally, Cicero did his best to find out what business the Captain had in Heathton. But this was no easy task, for Lestrange was guarded in speech, and did not at first encourage his advances, judging very truly that Mr Gramp was a scoundrel, and could be dangerous. But finally he decided that the gentleman in broadcloth, if properly handled, could be converted into a useful tool, and he determined to make use of him in that capacity. The intimacy began one night when Cicero, having taken more than was good for him, allowed his tongue to wag more freely than usual. Lestrange thus became aware that it could dispense useful knowledge.

'I tell you what it is, my noble Captain,' said Cicero, with drunken gravity, 'you are a clever man—I am another. Why shouldn't we get that reward by working together?'

'Really, my friend, I hardly see what I can do. I am a stranger here.'

'That's why we ought to work together. You are not in these parts for nothing. The gossip of servants—ah!' Gramp looked significantly at Lestrange. 'Oh, I heard how you were turned out of the Moat House.'

'What do you mean, my dear friend?' asked the Captain, in silky tones.

'Oh! that you've got some game on—so have I. Let us work together.'

'Pooh! pooh! You are talking nonsense.'

'Nonsense which may mean money. See here, I know that you were kicked out of the Moat House. Ah! the gossip of menials.'

'Pardon me, but I was not kicked out.'

'You were. Young Thorold did it. He wants all the money, and he'll get it by marrying that girl—if I let him.'

'If you let him? What do you mean?'

'Mean? Why, that I hate young Thorold, and that I want a few thousands!'

'Oh! and how do you intend to get them?'

'Never you mind. If we work together—but, then, we don't. *Cedant arma togae*—which means, you're a soldier, I'm a lawyer—so that's all right. Good-night.'

And he staggered off, leaving Lestrange with much food for meditation.

The outcome of this was that next morning the Captain met Cicero half-way, and later in the day Sophy received a note from Lestrange asking to see her. If she would not consent, he added, Mr Thorold would be placed in a position of great danger.

After some reflection Sophy sent for Mr Phelps, and they decided to see the scamp. So on a Saturday morning Captain Lestrange was received in the library of the Rectory.

'Well, sir,' said Phelps, 'and what have you to say about Mr Thorold?'

'Only this,' was the reply: 'that he is a scoundrel!'

'Indeed!' the Rector stopped Sophy's exclamations. 'On what grounds?'

'On the grounds that it was he who stole the body of Richard Marlow!'

CHAPTER XV

TROUBLE

THE Rector and Sophy looked at one another, and then at Lestrange, smiling and confident. They knew Alan too well to credit so monstrous an accusation for one moment. Indeed, the idea appeared so ridiculous to Sophy that she laughed outright.

Lestrange frowned.

'You laugh now,' he said. 'You will weep later. What I say is true. Thorold stole the body of your father—your supposed father!' he sneered, 'for, say what you like, you are my child.'

'I don't acknowledge the relationship,' retorted the girl with spirit, 'and I never will. Mr Marlow was my father. I shall always think of him as such. As to your accusation of Mr Thorold, it is merely another trick to cause me trouble. I suppose you will say next that he murdered Dr Warrender?'

'I say nothing of the sort,' replied the Captain, nettled by her open contempt, 'yet he may have done so, for all I know. But I state only what I can prove.'

'You cannot prove this ridiculous charge!' cried the Rector. 'Mr Thorold is incapable of such a crime.'

'Ah!' drawled the other coolly, 'you see, Mr Thorold is scientific, and does not look upon his deed as a crime.'

'What do you mean by that?' asked Mr Phelps sharply.

'I mean that Mr Thorold was once a medical student—at least, I have been told as much.'

'It is true, quite true,' said Sophy, opening her eyes, for in her innocence she did not see what the man meant. But the Rector did, and winced. He anticipated the accuser.

111

'You mean that Mr Thorold stole the body for scientific purposes?'

'For dissection—yes. Mr Thorold is, I understand, an enthusiast in surgery. Marlow—or, rather, I should say, Beauchamp—died of an obscure disease, and Warrender and Thorold removed the body to hold a post-mortem on it. They were the men seen by Cicero Gramp—you see, I know all about it. They probably carried the body to the moor hut to dissect it. Whether they quarrelled or not, I do not know, nor do I know if it was Thorold who killed the doctor. All I say is, that those two stole the body.'

'Oh, indeed!' remarked Mr Phelps ironically, 'and Thorold put the remains of Dr Warrender back in the vault, I suppose? And what did he do with Marlow's body?'

'I don't know. Buried it on the moor, very likely.'

'Mr Thorold had not the key of the vault,' cried Sophy indignantly. 'It had been stolen by the Quiet Gentleman.'

'So I understand,' retorted Lestrange sharply. 'And who says so? Mr Thorold himself. Believe me, sir,' he turned to the Rector, 'that key was never stolen. Thorold had it in his pocket. He lied about that for his own safety.'

'I don't believe it,' said Mr Phelps decisively. 'Thorold was at Bournemouth on the night the crime was committed.'

'I know he was!' cried Sophy, with emphasis. 'He was with me and Miss Parsh.'

'You are wrong, both of you. He came back to Heathton on that night, and returned to Bournemouth before dawn. I understand it is only an hour's journey from here.'

'It is not true,' insisted Sophy uneasily. 'I saw Mr Thorold at eight o'clock that night at the Soudan Hotel.'

'I dare say. But at ten o'clock he was at Heathton.'

'How can you prove that?'

'If you will permit me,' said Lestrange, and rising, he left the room.

Before Mr Phelps and Sophy could exchange a remark, he was back again with a man who had evidently been waiting.

'Jarks!' cried the Rector, much annoyed. 'And what has Jarks to do with this preposterous story?'

'If you ask him he will tell you,' said Lestrange politely, and resumed his seat.

The Rector looked indignantly at his sexton, who, as a minor official in the church, should have quailed before his superior. But there was no quailing or cringing about Jarks. The old fellow was as malicious as a magpie, and as garrulous. Looking more rusty than ever, he stood twisting his greasy old hat, and shifting from one leg to the other.

'Oh, I seed Muster Alan; yes, I seed un. On the night o' the funeral I were in the yard, a lookin' at 'em as I'd tucked away, an' I clapped eyes on Muster Alan. He wor' lookin' at the vault where I'd put away the last of 'em, he wor.'

'About what time was that?' asked Mr Phelps, with severity.

'Well, it might be about ten, Muster Phelps, sir.'

'And what were you doing out of bed at that hour?'

'Lookin' at 'em,' retorted Jarks, wiping his mouth. 'Lor' bless you, Muster Phelps, all in the yard's m'own handiwork save some of the old uns. I like to see 'em all quiet an' humble in their narrow homes. Ay, an' I seed Muster Alan, an' he sez, "I've come to look round, Jarks, an' you needn't say as I've bin about. Here's money for ye." Ay, he did say that, an' guv me money. Course I said nothin' as there isn't no law agin folk walkin' round to see how them as has passed away is gettin' along.'

'How long was Mr Thorold with you?'

'It might be about five minutes, sir. He went to ketch a train at the half-hour to go back to Miss Sophy—hopin' I sees you well, miss!' with a pull of his forelock to the girl, who was standing pale and trembling at this disastrous confirmation.

'Why didn't you tell me this, Jarks?'

'Lor' bless you, Miss Sophy, 'twas little use vexin' you. 'Sides, when I found Muster Marlow was gone, arter bein' put away comfortable-like in the vault, I did say to Muster Alan arterwards as it wasn't friendly-like of him to upset my handiwork. But

Muster Alan he says as he had nowt to do with the takin' of him, an' how he got out of the vault, being screwed and soldered down, was more than he knew. So he being the Squire, Miss Sophy, it wasn't my place to say nothin'. I knows the station of life I've bin called to.'

'It was your duty to come to me,' said the Rector severely.

'Naw, naw!' Jarks shook his head. "'T'ain't no good makin' bad blood, Muster Phelps. Muster Alan wor in the yard, but he didn't take the last of 'em away.'

'I say he did!' put in Lestrange, with emphasis.

'Ay, ay! You thinks you knows a lot. But I tell you, you don't. If it wasn't that I let slip to that fat un while mazed wi' drink, as I seed Muster Alan, you'd niver have know'd naught. Naw! But when the wine's in Jarks he talks foolish-like. Ay, he babbles as a babe does Jarks!'

'Who is this fat man he speaks of?' asked Sophy.

'My other witness,' replied Lestrange promptly. 'You can go, Jarks. Send in Cicero.'

The sexton nodded, wiped his mouth, and backed to the door with a final excuse.

'As I wor sayin', Muster Phelps, 'twouldn't be right to blame Jarks for holdin' the tongue o' he, Muster Alan wantin' it so. But the red wine—which is to say, beer an' such like—maketh the heart of Jarks glad, as sez Holy Scripture. An' I'll go now, wishin' you an' Miss Sophy happiness an' long life.'

After which apologetic speech the old sinner creaked out of the room pulling his forelock.

'You see,' said Lestrange, with a triumphant look at the other two, 'Thorold was in Heathton, and in the churchyard on that night.'

'It would seem so; but that does not prove he took away the body,' put in Sophy.

'My second witness can prove that. Come in, Cicero.'

The fat man, resplendent in new clothes, rolled into the room.

'*Pax vobiscum*,' said he.

The Rector turned an angry glance on him.

'This is not the time for playing the fool,' he said cuttingly. 'You are a cunning rogue, but some day you will overreach yourself. Now, then, out with your lie.'

'Lie! I scorn to pervert the truth, reverend sir. I shall tell the truth *in puris naturalibus.*'

'I hope not,' threw in the Rector, laughing, in spite of himself, at this abuse of quotation.

'Which means, reverend sir,' went on the old scoundrel coolly, 'that in the hut on the heath I found the corpse of Dr Warrender.'

'But not the body of my father,' said Sophy.

'No, but I saw that taken away from the vault. Undoubtedly, Miss Marlow, the body was carried to the hut for the purpose of dissection by Mr Thorold. He was foolish enough to leave behind him evidence of his iniquitous purposes. Behold!' and Cicero produced a lancet in his most dramatic manner. '*Nota bene,*' said he grandly.

Phelps bent forward and took the instrument in his hand. It had an ivory handle, on which were carved two letters, 'A.T.'

'You found this in the hut?' he asked.

'I did, reverend sir. It must have been dropped by Mr Thorold. If not, how did it come there? I pause for a reply.'

'Why did you not tell Mr Thorold about this?' demanded Sophy.

'I bided my time—'

'To blackmail him!' she cried, with scorn.

'A harsh word, Miss Sophia. Certainly I would have demanded a small payment from Mr Thorold, had I shown him that. But Mr Thorold insulted me, it matters not how. *Nemo me impune lacessit*, Miss Sophia, and I determined to punish the young man. My military friend was good enough to enter into partnership with me for the purpose of clearing up this matter, hence I told him of my discovery. There is no more to be said.'

'Save this,' put in Lestrange, who appeared to be getting somewhat weary of Cicero's cumbersome diction, 'that here is the proof that it was Thorold who carried off the body. Do you believe now in his guilt?'

'I reserve my opinion,' said the Rector, who could not but acknowledge to himself that things looked black for Alan.

'I don't!' cried Sophy, rising. 'If fifty men, with fifty lancets, came to tell me this story, I would not believe a word against Mr Thorold. He can explain. I believe in him firmly, and, to prove my belief, I shall marry him as soon as I can.'

'You'll do nothing of the sort!' cried Lestrange, losing his temper. 'I am your father, and I command you to come with me.'

'And I am my own mistress, and I refuse,' she said quietly. 'You can't frighten me. I don't believe your stories.'

'Nor do I,' said the Rector. 'When Mr Thorold comes back, he will, no doubt, be able to explain his presence in Heathton on that night, and also the loss of his lancet.'

'He shall explain it to the police!' cried Lestrange, in a threatening manner.

'No, no,' said Cicero, apprehensive at this mention of his natural enemies; 'let us take counsel together. Cannot this matter be adjusted, so that Mr Thorold may escape the reward of his iniquitous proceedings?'

Sophy looked at him with a satirical smile. Then she turned to address Lestrange as the senior partner in this firm of scoundrels.

'How much do you want?' she asked.

The Captain winced. He did not like the question to be put quite so crudely.

'I do not understand,' he said.

'I think you do. How much do you require to hold your tongue?'

'Say five thousand,' whispered Mr Gramp.

But Lestrange shook him off, and marched to the door very upright and indignant.

'I will let you know my price—'

'Ah!' said Sophy scornfully.

'When I have seen the police,' finished he, and marched out.

Cicero had to follow, but he turned at the door and winked.

'He will not go to the police,' said he, in a hurried voice. 'Might I suggest five—'

'Be off, you scoundrel!' cried the Rector indignantly, and thrust him out.

Then he resumed his seat, and looked at Sophy.

'Well?' said he.

'Alan can explain,' said she decisively.

'But if Lestrange goes to the police?'

'He won't,' she said. 'Cicero will stop that. Meanwhile I wait for Alan.'

They talked on for a long time, but could come to no conclusion. Undoubtedly Alan had been near the vault on that night, had been in the hut, and had said nothing of these things to anyone. It certainly looked suspicious, but Sophy insisted that her lover could and would explain. In spite of appearances, she had faith in Alan's honesty and in Alan's honour.

That same evening she dined with the Rector, without even Miss Vicky in attendance.

Towards the end of the meal, Alan walked in unexpectedly. He looked somewhat downcast, but there was no sign of fear in his bearing. After greetings had been exchanged he sat down with them. Neither the Rector nor Sophy was anxious to inform him of the accusation which had been brought against him.

'How went the business?' asked Mr Phelps.

'Badly—for us,' was the reply. 'Lestrange certainly arrived by the boat he said he came by. I saw his name, Achille Lestrange, on the passenger-list of the *Negress*.'

'Ah! the devil speaks true sometimes!' said the Rector. 'And what about Beauchamp?'

'Yes, yes!' cried Sophy. 'Did you find him? Did you see him?'

'No,' replied Alan quietly, 'but I heard of him. Beauchamp is dead!'

CHAPTER XVI

ALAN'S DEFENCE

'DEAD!' repeated Sophy, after a pause. 'Then was this Mr Beauchamp really my father or a relative?'

'I think he was Mr Marlow, dear,' said her lover gravely. 'No doubt your father intended to feign death to escape Lestrange, but it would seem that he overdid it, and really died. I saw the manager of the Occidental Bank. He informed me that he had received a letter telling him that Beauchamp was dead.'

'How long ago was this?'

'A little over a week.'

'Who wrote the letter?'

'That he refused to tell me.'

'Had he seen this Mr Beauchamp, to whom the money was to be paid?'

'Never. Your father had informed him that he had left an income to Beauchamp, and that drafts for the money were to be sent to a certain place—where, I don't know. The manager sent a draft, but it was returned to him with a letter stating that the man was dead. For my own part, I believe that Mr Marlow was Beauchamp. His plan to hide himself from Lestrange has succeeded only too well.'

Mr Phelps now joined in.

'Then I understand, Alan, that you think Marlow is really dead?'

'I do. If he had only feigned death, then Beauchamp would be receiving his income. In my opinion, the two men are one and the same. I believe Lestrange's story so far.'

'Humph!' said the Rector, who was really of the same opinion. 'But let us leave this question for the moment and talk of the

118

other. You say that Lestrange arrived on the day and by the boat he asserted that he did?'

'I saw the passenger-list myself. If he had not been on board, his name would not have been there. Even he could not falsify a passenger-list.'

'Then our idea that Lestrange was the Quiet Gentleman is false?'

'It must be, sir. The man—Lestrange I mean—was not in England when the Quiet Gentleman lived in this village. I believe Brown had to do with the stealing of the body and the murder. But, then, Brown is not Lestrange. Who he is I don't know!'

'Alan!' cried Sophy—for if what Lestrange stated was true, this hypocrisy was detestable—'you are not straightforward with me!'

'Indeed I am,' he said, with a stare of astonishment. 'I have told you of my discoveries. Why should I deceive you?'

'Why, indeed!' said the girl bitterly. 'You know how much I love you, yet you keep me in the dark about matters which concern us both—matters which I, if anyone, have a right to know.'

He might have had some inkling of what she meant, for his face turned a dark red. Nevertheless, he held himself well in hand, and looked inquiringly at the Rector.

'What does she mean, sir?'

'I think you can guess,' said Phelps, more coldly than he had ever before spoken to Alan.

'No; upon my word, I—'

Sophy rose from her chair and closed his mouth with her hand.

'Don't! don't!' she cried despairingly.

'I can't bear it. Captain Lestrange—' She hesitated.

'Ah!' said Alan fiercely. 'I might have guessed he had been making mischief. Well, and what does he say?'

'That you stole my father's body, Alan!'

'I—I—stole the body?'

'Yes!' chimed in the Rector. 'And he further says that you took it to the hut on the heath, where Warrender's corpse was found.'

'Oh, indeed!' cried the young man derisively. 'And did I murder Warrender, too?'

'Alan! Alan! Oh, don't jest! If you love me, Alan, tell me the truth.'

'Sophy! What do you mean?' He pushed away his plate and rose. 'Do you believe this man's tale for one moment? Am I the man to violate a grave—to drag the remains of a man I respected and honoured to the light of day? You must be mad to think of such a thing! How dare he bring forward such a terrible—such a dastardly accusation? For what reason does he say that I did it?'

'Out of revenge, I expect,' said Phelps. 'He dislikes you, Alan. He says you took poor Marlow's body to dissect it.'

'And bases his lie upon some gossip of my having been a medical student, I suppose?' cried the young man, now thoroughly angry. 'I'll thrash the scoundrel within an inch of his life!'

'Oh, Alan, I am so glad—so thankful! I said so, didn't I, Mr Phelps? You didn't do it!'

'Do it—of course I didn't do it! Why should I? Phelps,'—Alan forgot his respect for the Rector in his rage—'do you believe this lying story?'

'Knowing you as I do, I don't believe it. But I must say that Lestrange—he is a very dangerous man—makes out a strong case against you.'

'Oh! Let me hear on what grounds.'

'Alan!' Sophy came forward and took him by the lapels of his coat, 'before we tell you anything, confess if you have kept anything from us.'

He looked at her in a puzzled manner. Then a light seemed to dawn upon him. He glanced at the Rector.

'Now I understand, Mr Phelps. Jarks has told you.'

'Told me what?' asked the Rector, with well-feigned ignorance.

'I see! I see!' Alan sat down again. 'It's all right, Sophy. I kept that from you only that you should not be worried. So Lestrange found out—from Jarks, I suppose—that I was at Heathton on the night of the funeral?'

'Yes, yes. Oh, Alan, is it true?'

'True—of course it is. Why should it not be true? Does the fact of my having been here corroborate this cock-and-bull story? You ought to know me better, Sophy, and you too, Phelps.'

'I couldn't believe it—I didn't,' cried the girl.

'Nor I. We both told him that he lied. But I must admit that things looked bad for you, as he put it. Why didn't you tell us you were at Heathton on that night? Why did you come? Was there any serious reason for such secrecy?'

'No reason whatsoever,' replied the young man frankly, 'save the trifling one that I did not want to bother Sophy with my suspicions. Yes, I came by the 8.30 train from Bournemouth, and I returned at half-past eleven. I had to go to another station to keep my secret, you know. Jarks saw me in the graveyard about ten, and as I wished to keep my visit quiet, for the reason I have told you, I gave him something to hold his tongue. It appears that he did not. I suppose Lestrange bribed him?'

'Well, no,' said the Rector, 'not exactly. Jarks, in his cups, told that scoundrel Gramp, and he told Lestrange.'

'Oh! So there are two of them in league to make trouble. A proper pair of scoundrels!'

'But,' said Sophy, more composedly, 'you have not told us why you came.'

'I came,' said her lover, determined now to make a clean breast of it, 'to look at the vault—to see that all was safe.'

The Rector uttered an exclamation of astonishment.

'Did you expect, then, that there would be some foul play?'

'Well, I hardly know, sir. It was this way: After Mr Marlow received that letter from the West Indies—which doubtless warned him that Lestrange was on his track—he was much worried. He would not tell me the reason, but kept speaking of some shock he had had which might cause his death. "And I don't know if the scoundrel will let my body rest in its grave," he said in a fit of passion. I asked to whom he alluded, but he would say no more. When he died so unexpectedly, his words came back to me. I wondered if he had enemies who might disturb his remains, and all that day after the funeral I felt so bothered about it that I could not rest without coming back to see if all was well.'

'And you found nothing wrong?'

'Nothing, sir. I was in the churchyard for about a quarter of an hour. I examined the door of the vault, and saw everything was right. As I came away I met Jarks; the rest you know.'

'You saw no signs of that tramp in the churchyard?'

'None! I expect he was sleeping when I was there. According to his story, it was after midnight when the vault was opened.'

'Alan,' said Sophy, much relieved, 'how is it they did not know at Heathton Station that you were here?'

'I did not go to Heathton Station. I stopped at Murbury, and walked from there across the heath. I went back the same way. I did so simply to keep the tongues of gossips quiet. I did not want you to be worried, Sophy; and after all,' he said, after a pause, 'beyond the chance words of your father I had no reason to think that anything was wrong. Ah! if I had only stayed in the churchyard all night, I should have prevented this trouble. The vault would never have been broken into, and poor Warrender would still be alive.'

The Rector nodded approval of this speech, and poured himself out a glass of wine, which, poor man, he sadly needed. Lestrange's accusation had been disproved; still, there remained the evidence of Cicero. Sophy put the question which was in the Rector's mind.

'Captain Lestrange brought Cicero here, Alan,' she said abruptly, 'and he—Cicero, I mean—declared that you were in the hut on the moor that night.'

'I was not!' cried young Thorold hotly. 'I was never near the hut. Why should I have been? Ask yourself, as I had to walk to and from Murbury, and spend a quarter of an hour in the churchyard, had I time to cross the moor all the distance to the hut?'

'Of course, you know I don't believe it. But Cicero—'

'Well, and how can he prove I was there?' he said impatiently.

'He found something there which belonged to you.'

'What?'

'A lancet.'

'A lancet! And why mine? Warrender was a doctor; he took away the body—why should the lancet not belong to him? If he had intended to dissect the body—which he might have, for all I know—he would want one.'

'No doubt,' Mr Phelps said drily. 'But this lancet had your initials on the ivory handle. It is your lancet, Alan, and it is now in Cicero's possession.'

'H'm! That's queer. Initials?—Yes, it might be mine. But how did it get there?'

'Did you ever lend a lancet to Dr Warrender?'

'No, not that I can remember.'

'Then there was the other man, his accomplice, Brown the—'

'Ha!' cried Alan, starting up and pacing the room. 'I see, I see!'

'See what?' cried Sophy eagerly.

'How the lancet came to be found in the hut. The Quiet Gentleman stole it.'

'Stole it?'

'Of course. Did he not steal the key of the vault from my desk? There was a case of lancets in the same drawer; he took one. Ha! this proves to me that Brown stole the body and murdered Warrender. A clever scoundrel! He stole my lancet to throw suspicion on me.' Alan clenched his hands and looked upward. 'In God's name, what does this roguery mean?'

It was indeed a perplexing case. They were all in the dark, and such gleams of light as came served only to confuse them the more. Lestrange could not be the Quiet Gentleman, for, as had been proved by Alan, he had landed in England only the week before. Brown was the *deus ex machina* who could put matters right, and Brown had vanished. He could reappear only at the risk of being charged with murder.

Why had the body been removed? If it were a case of black-mailing, the claim would have been made long since. The police were apparently as much at a loss as Alan himself. And Blair—

'Does Blair know of this accusation?' asked Mr Thorold suddenly.

'I am certain he does not,' answered the Rector emphatically. 'In the first place, it was only made today. Lestrange, I am sure, wants money, and would come to us before going to the police.'

'If he does not want money, Cicero does,' put in Sophy scornfully.

'In the second place,' resumed Mr Phelps, 'Blair is away.'

'Where has he gone?'

'I can't say, but he will be back in a fortnight.'

'Well,' said Alan moodily, 'I don't know if he will be much good when he does come. I shall see this firm of scoundrels at the Good Samaritan, and threaten them with the police, unless they tell all they know. Lestrange is as bad as Cicero, and I know *him* to be a scoundrel. What's that?'

This exclamation was drawn from him by the violent ringing of the door-bell. Before the sounds had ceased, Miss Vicky, red, hot and agitated, rushed in a most unladylike manner into the room.

'Oh, Sophy! Mr Phelps! Mr Alan! I really never! Joseph Brill—oh, that Joseph Brill! He's back again!'

CHAPTER XVII

JOE'S EVIDENCE

FOR a moment the three gazed in silence and amazement at the old maid. She stood before them, all tousled and red with haste, a figure of fun she would not have recognized for herself. Her buckram demeanour had for once given way to the real woman. Alan was the first to speak, and he jumped up from the table with a shout of joy. From an unexpected quarter, in the most unexpected manner, help had come, and at the moment when it was most needed.

'Joe Brill!' cried Mr Thorold. 'He is the very man I want. Where is he, Miss Vicky?'

'At the Moat House. I went to the kitchen for a moment; he was there—he had just come in. I thought he was a ghost,' declared the little lady solemnly; 'indeed I did until he convinced me that he was flesh and blood.'

'What explanation did he make?' asked Sophy anxiously.

'None—to me. He said he was ready to explain his absence to Mr Thorold.'

'Did he? Then he shall have the chance. Go back to the Moat House, Miss Parsh, and send on Joe to the Good Samaritan.'

'Why there of all places?' asked the Rector.

'Because I am going to see Lestrange, and force the truth out of him. There shall be an end to all this devilment. He accuses me, does he?' cried Thorold, with an ugly look. 'Let him have a care lest I accuse him, and prove my accusation, too, with the help of Joe Brill.'

'Joseph!' cried Miss Parsh, quite at sea. 'What can he do?'

'He can prove if Lestrange's story is true or false.'

'Story, Mr Alan! What story?'

'Never mind, Vicky,' put in Sophy, catching Miss Parsh's arm. She saw that Alan was growing impatient. 'Come back home, and we will send Joe on to the inn. Come, you look quite upset.'

'And I am upset,' wailed the poor woman. 'I ran all the way to tell you that Joseph had returned—like a thief in the night,' she added. 'Oh, dear me! and I'm so hot and untidy. I don't like these dreadful things!' Miss Vicky suddenly caught sight of herself in an adjacent mirror, and made a hasty attempt to arrange her disordered dress. 'Oh, what a spectacle for a genteel gentlewoman to present! A glass of wine, Mr Phelps, I beg of you.'

The Rector poured out the wine in silence, then turned to Alan.

'Shall I come with you?'

'No, sir. Joe and I are quite able to deal with this brace of blackguards.'

'Remember that Lestrange is a dangerous man, Alan.'

'So am I,' retorted the other grimly. 'If I happen to find a whip handy, I don't know what I might be tempted to do.'

'But if Joe declares that Lestrange is Sophy's father?'

'He is not my father!' cried Sophy. 'His story is a lie! I am the daughter of Richard Marlow.'

'Sophia! This man—your father!' wailed Miss Vicky. 'Oh dear, what is all this?'

'I'll tell you when we get home,' said the girl. 'Alan, I will send Joe to the inn at once.'

And she led the weeping Vicky from the room.

'Let me come, Alan. You will want a witness.'

'Joe will be witness enough,' said the young man decisively. 'No, sir; better let me see him alone; there may be rough work. Your cloth—'

'Deuce take my cloth!' cried the Rector. 'Bless me, may I be forgiven! My cloth might keep the peace.'

'I don't want the peace kept,' retorted Thorold. 'Unless that Creole Frenchman apologizes I'll thrash him!'

The Rector stared, and well he might. All the well-bred composure had gone from Alan's face and manner, the veneer of civilization was stripped off, and man, primeval man, showed naked and unashamed. He stared back at the clergyman, and for quite a minute the two looked at one another. Then the younger man turned and left the room, and Mr Phelps made no attempt to stay him. He knew that he might as well have tried to chain a whirlwind. He bowed to circumstances and sat down again to his wine.

'I hope to Heaven he'll keep himself in hand,' he muttered, without his usual self-apology for swearing. 'Lestrange is dangerous; but Alan, in his present mood, is more so. I should not care to be the man to meet him with that look on his face. Dear! dear!' The little man sighed. 'I wish all these mysteries were over and done with, and we could resume the quiet tenor of our way.'

Meantime, Alan was making for the inn. It was just on nine o'clock, and the night had turned out wet. As he had no overcoat, the rain was soaking him. But he did not care for that. His blood was on fire to meet this man and force the truth out of him. He was certain that Lestrange could explain much if he chose; and whether he chose or not, Alan intended that he should speak out. He was determined that an end should be put to these troubles.

The rain whipped his face and drenched him, but he walked on steadily. There was no gas in Heathton, which was so far uncivilized, and the roads were dark and miry. Not until he got into the principal street did he leave the mud and the darkness behind him. Then before him glimmered the feeble lantern over the door, with which Mrs Timber illuminated the entrance to her premises. Alan could hear the drowsy voices of the villagers sitting over their ale in the taproom—heard above the rest the pompous speech of Cicero, who was evidently playing his favourite part of Sir Oracle.

In the hall Mr Thorold was found by the landlady. The

woman pervaded the house like a fly, and was always to be discovered where she was least expected. She recognized Alan, curtsied and awaited instructions.

'Take me,' he said abruptly, 'to Captain Lestrange.'

'Lor', sir!' Mrs Timber, in her amazement, overstepped the bounds of class. 'You said he was no friend of yours, sir.'

'Nor is he. Come, show me his room. He is in, I suppose?'

'Catch him wetting himself!' she said, leading the way, with a sour smile. 'He's a furrin' Jack-o-dandy, that he is. Not but what he don't pay reg'lar. But I see the colour of his money afore my meat goes down his throat. This is the door, sir.'

'Very good. And, Mrs Timber, should Joe Brill come, show him in here.'

'Joe Brill!' yelped the landlady, throwing up her hands. 'You don't mean to say as he's back, Mr Alan? Well, I never did! And I thought he'd run away because of the murder.'

'You think too much, Mrs Timber. Some day you will get yourself into trouble. Now go, and don't forget my orders.'

Chilled by the severity of his tone, Mrs Timber crept away, somewhat ashamed. Alan knocked at the door, heard the thin voice of Lestrange call out '*Entrez*', and went in. The man was lying on the sofa, reading a French novel by the light of a petroleum lamp, and smoking a cigarette. When Alan appeared, he rose quickly into a sitting position, and stared at his visitor. Of all men, the last he had expected to see was the one he had so basely accused. The thought flashed into his mind that Thorold had come to have it out with him. But Lestrange, whatever his faults, was not wanting in a certain viperish courage. He rose to greet his enemy with a smile which cloaked many things.

'Good-evening, Mr Thorold,' he said, with a wary glance; 'to what am I indebted for this visit?'

'You shall know that before long,' replied Alan, closing the door. He was now considerably cooler, and had made up his mind that more was to be got out of this man by diplomacy than by blind rage. 'Have I your permission to sit down?' he asked, with studied politeness.

'Certainly, my dear sir. Will you smoke?'

'No, thank you.'

'Have some refreshment, then?'

'No, thank you.'

'Ah!' sneered Lestrange, throwing himself again on the couch, 'your visit is not so amiable as I fancied. You come as my enemy.'

'Considering your behaviour, it would be strange if I came as anything else.'

'My behaviour?'

'I refer to your interview with Mr Phelps and Miss Marlow.'

'Mademoiselle Lestrange, if you please.'

'Ah, that is for you to prove!'

'I shall prove it,' said the other, quite unmoved, 'in open court.'

'That will be a harder task than you imagine,' retorted Alan quickly. 'But I am not here to discuss Miss Marlow's parentage. My errand is to ask you why you have accused me of taking away the body of her father.'

'Richard Marlow was not her father,' replied the man with heat.

'So you say—we can pass that point, as I told you before. I speak of the charge you have thought fit to bring against me.'

'It is a true one. I am willing to take it into court.'

'You may be brought into court sooner than you expect,' remarked Alan drily; and from the sudden start the man gave he saw that the shot had gone home. 'On what grounds do you base this charge?'

'If Mr Phelps reported the interview correctly, you must know,' said he sullenly.

'To save time,' retorted Alan, 'I may as well admit that I do know. Jarks and Cicero speak the truth.'

Lestrange looked surprised.

'Then you admit your guilt?'

'No; that is quite another thing. I admit that I was in Heathton on that night when Jarks saw me. What I came for does not concern you, Captain Lestrange; but I can prove also that I was back in Bournemouth before twelve o'clock. You will observe that I can establish an alibi.'

'Upon my word, I really believed you guilty!' cried the Captain with sincerity.

'No doubt,' was the scornful reply. 'The wish is father to the thought. I will thank you not to accuse me falsely again.'

'You have to explain away the finding of the lancet.'

'That was stolen from my desk, with the key of the vault, by a man called Brown, whom I believe to have been guilty of a crime. You need not try to fasten the guilt upon me! I can defend myself—to use your favourite phrase—in open court, if necessary.'

'Your word is enough,' protested Lestrange. 'I was wrong to accuse you!'

'Very wrong. You did it out of spite—'

'No, no! I really believed—'

'What you wished yourself to believe,' interrupted Alan in his turn. 'It was my intention to have given you a thrashing, Captain Lestrange—'

'Sir!' the man started up white with rage.

'But I have changed my mind,' pursued Alan, without noticing the interruption. 'I now intend to take another course. If you do not at once leave Heathton, I shall bring a charge against you of defamation of character.'

'Oh!' Lestrange shrugged his shoulders. 'You are a true English shopkeeper. A man should protect himself by more honourable means.'

'I know very well what I am about, sir. I wish to bring you into contact with the law. For that reason—unless you go—I shall bring the action.'

'And what can the law do to me?' he asked defiantly. 'I have committed no wrong.'

'You intend to. Oh! I know that you are innocent of taking Marlow's body, and of murdering Warrender. But you are here to blackmail Miss Marlow on the threat of proclaiming her dead father a murderer.'

'I am here to claim my daughter!' shouted Lestrange fiercely. 'Sophia Marlow I know nothing of; but Marie Lestrange is the daughter of Achille Lestrange, and I'—the Captain struck his breast—'I am he!'

While he was still posing in a very effective attitude, the door opened, and Mrs Timber ushered in Joe Brill. Hardly had it closed, when Brill took a step forward, staring at Lestrange as though he had seen a vision. Lestrange turned white, this time not with rage but with fear. In the silence which ensued Alan looked from one to the other, wondering what revelation was about to be made. Joe was the first to speak.

'You swab!' cried Joe. 'D—d if it ain't Captain Jean!'

CHAPTER XVIII

A PORTION OF THE TRUTH

JOE was not in the least changed. Wherever he had been, in whatever nefarious transactions he had been engaged, he was still the mahogany-coloured, tough old sailor whom nothing could surprise or alarm. After having greeted Lestrange he hitched up his trousers in true nautical style and touched his forehead.

'You wished to see me, sir,' he said to Alan, and took a sidelong glance at the Captain. That polished scoundrel had, for once, lost his coolness, and, colourless with rage, was glaring at the seaman like a devil.

'Joe,' said the Squire, as soon as he could take in the situation, 'you are making a mistake.'

'Not me, sir! I knows a shark when I sees one.'

'But this is Captain Achille Lestrange.'

'Curse me if he is!' cried Joe vigorously. 'Achille weren't no Captain. This one's a Captain right enough, and a blazing fine lobster he is! Jean's his name, sir, but he ain't a Scotch girl, for all that. No, it's the French lingo for John.'

'I am Achille Lestrange,' persisted the Captain, very shrill and very short of breath. 'This man is a liar!'

'Say that again, and I'll knock the teeth down your throat!' growled Joe, like an angry mastiff. 'Achille be blowed! I know'd you twenty year ago in the islands, I did, and a bad lot you were then. Jean Lestrange—why, there never was a wuss lot! I never did think much of Achille, for all his money; but you—'

Joe spat to show his disgust.

'Then this man is not Sophy's father?' gasped Alan.

'Oh, he sez that, does he, the lubber? Missy's father! Why, he ain't fit to be her shoeblack!'

'Achille was the girl's father,' said Lestrange sullenly. He saw that it was useless to lie in face of Joe's positive knowledge. 'And if I'm not her father, I'm her uncle.'

'That's a d—d lie!' put in Joe. 'You weren't no more nor Achille's cousin. What you are to missy, I don't know. But she won't have nothing to do with you, you land-shark!'

'Joe, do you mean to say your late master is not Sophy's father?'

'I do, sir. It's got to come out somehow, if only to put a stop to that devil's pranks. She's the daughter of Achille Lestrange.'

'Who was murdered by Marlow!' finished the Captain savagely. 'Ah, my friends, I have still some cards left.'

'You'll have no teeth left!' growled Joe, making a step forward. 'You're a liar, Captain Jean—you always was! Mr Marlow—'

'Beauchamp,' corrected Lestrange, with a glance at Alan.

'Beauchamp it is,' continued Brill coolly. 'Oh, you needn't be afeared that I'm going to lie! But Mr Beauchamp never stabbed Munseer Achille, and you know it, you lubber! Let me get at him, Mr Thorold!'

'No, no, Joe!' Alan kept the irate seaman back. 'We'll deal with this gentleman in a better fashion. Sit down, Joe, while we talk it over.'

Joe nodded, and sat down on a chair, which he placed directly before the door.

With a glare that showed he noticed and resented this action, Lestrange resumed his seat. He was too clever a man not to recognize that Joe's cunning would dislocate his plans. But he was evidently determined to fight to the last. At present he held his tongue, for he wanted to hear what Joe would say. He preferred, for the moment, to remain strictly on the defensive.

It was with a thankful heart that Alan Thorold realized the value of Joe as an ally. At one time he had really believed that Lestrange was truly Sophy's father, and although she would never have admitted the relationship, still it was satisfactory to know that the man had no claim on her obedience. The knowledge of Lestrange's falsehood cleared the air somewhat. For one thing, it proved conclusively that the Captain had come to blackmail the girl. His claim to be her father was doubtless made in the hope that she would accompany him back to Jamaica, and would give him control of her money. Failing this—and Lestrange had long since realized that there was no doing anything with Sophy in a paternal way—there remained the chance that, to preserve Marlow's memory from stain, she might buy his silence.

Thus Lestrange argued, and Alan, with his eyes on the man's expressive face, guessed his thoughts and answered them.

'No, Lestrange,' he said, with decision, 'you won't get one penny.'

'We shall see about that,' was the rejoinder.

'Of course. We are going to see about it now. You will be brought to your bearings, sir. Joe, you say that this man is Jean Lestrange?'

'Yes, sir. But may I ask, Mr Thorold, how you know about the shark?'

'I have heard the story from his own lips, Joe. He claimed to be Achille Lestrange and Miss Sophy's father.'

'Did he, now, the swab! and you know, sir, how Mrs Lestrange ran away to Mr Beauchamp from the way her husband treated her?'

'I know—'

'Achille treated Zelia well,' interrupted the Captain; 'only too well.'

'That's another lie!' retorted Joe. 'He was fond-like of her the first year they were married, but it was you, Captain Jean, who made a mess of them. You made him jealous of Mr Beauchamp, and he treated her crool. No wonder she ran away, poor lass!'

'Did the way Achille treated Zelia give Beauchamp any right to murder him?'

'He didn't murder him. You know he didn't.'

'He did, I say. Achille was found stabbed to the heart on the veranda of Beauchamp's house. Zelia was dead, and your master took the child away to his yacht at Falmouth. You were on board.'

'Yes,' said Joe coolly, 'I wos; and it wos well for you, Captain Jean, that I wasn't near the house that same evening. I'd ha' wrung your neck, I would! Anyhow, master didn't kill Munseer Achille.'

'There was a warrant out for his arrest, however.'

'I know that, Captain Jean, and it was you who got it out. And I know as you came over here after master from seeing his picter in the papers. We both knowed you were coming, Captain Jean.'

Alan interposed:

'Was that the West Indian letter, Joe?'

'Yes, sir, it was. Master got a letter from a friend of his in Jamaica telling him this swab was after him to say as he'd murdered Munseer Achille, which,' added Joe, deliberately eyeing Lestrange, 'is a d—d lie!'

'Then who killed Achille?' sneered the Captain, quivering with rage.

'I dunno rightly,' replied Mr Brill stolidly. 'I wasn't in the house that night, or I'd ha' found out. But master ran away, because he knew you'd accuse him out of spite. But Mr Barkham, of Falmouth, believed master was innocent, and know'd where he was, and what was his new name. 'Twas he wrote the letter saying as Captain Jean was on his way to England to make trouble.'

'Barkham!' muttered Lestrange. 'Ah! he was always my enemy.'

'A shark like you, Captain Jean, ain't got no friends,' remarked Joe sententiously.

'Do you think that Barkham's letter caused Mr Marlow's death?' asked Alan.

'Do I think it, sir? Why, I knows it! After twenty years of hearing nothing, the shock, as you might say, killed my master.'

'Then he was guilty, and my accusation was a righteous one to make,' chimed in Lestrange. 'A clean conscience fears nothing.'

'Mr Beauchamp's conscience was a darned sight cleaner nor yourn, Captain Jean, but you had the whip-hand of him, as all those in Jamaica thought he'd murdered Munseer Achille, from them quarrelling about him coming after his wife. But master didn't do it—I swear he didn't! More like you did it yourself,' added Joe, with a look of contempt, 'though I dare say you ain't man enough to stick a knife into anyone.'

Alan thought for a few minutes, then turned to Lestrange.

'I think you must see that you have failed all round,' he said quietly. 'Your plot to pass as Miss Marlow's father is of no use now. The accusation against me is not worth considering, as I have shown. If necessary, I can defend myself. On the whole, Captain Lestrange, you had better go back to Jamaica.'

'Not without my price,' said the adventurer.

'Ah, blackmail! Well, I always thought that was at the bottom of it all. A man with clean hands and honourable intentions would not have joined hands with a confessed rogue like Cicero Gramp. But may I ask on what grounds you demand money?'

'I can prove that Beauchamp killed my cousin.'

'What good will that do? Beauchamp is dead, and beyond your malice.'

'Ay, that he is,' said Joe approvingly. 'He's gone where you won't get him. I reckon you'll go the other way when your time comes, you blasted swab!'

Lestrange, writhing under these insults, jumped up and poured out a volley of abuse, which the seaman bore quite unmoved.

'I'll not go without my money,' he raged, 'and a good sum, too, otherwise I shall see the girl—'

'If you annoy Miss Marlow again, I'll have you arrested,' said Alan sharply. 'We don't permit this sort of thing in England.'

'I shall put the story of Beauchamp's wickedness in all the papers.'

'As you please. It cannot harm the dead.'

'And will that girl stand by and see her father's memory disgraced?'

'You seem to forget,' said Thorold, with quiet irony, 'that he was not Miss Marlow's father. Well, there is no more to be said. If you make yourself a nuisance, the law shall deal with you.'

'And I'll deal with him myself,' said Joe. 'I'll make them eyes of yours blacker than they are by nature.'

'Leave him alone, Joe. He'll go now.'

'I won't go!' cried the man. 'I'll have my price.'

Alan shrugged his shoulders.

'I shall have to give you that thrashing, after all.'

'Let me do it, sir,' put in Mr Brill, who was simply spoiling for a row, and he stepped towards Lestrange.

The man's courage, genuine enough of its kind, suddenly gave way before the ferocity of the sailor. He sprang up, ran into an inner room and bolted the door.

Joe uttered the roar of a baffled tiger.

'Never mind, Joe; we're quit of him now. He will leave Heathton.'

'I'll wait for him at the station,' muttered Joe, following the young Squire out of doors. "T'ain't right that the swab should get off scot-free.'

Outside the rain had ceased. Alan looked at his watch, and finding that it was late, turned his face towards home. Suddenly he recollected that Joe had not explained his absence.

'Well, Joe, where have you been?' he asked sharply.

'After him.' Joe pointed his thumb over his shoulder. 'When master's body was carried away, I thought that shark might have done it. I know'd he was coming from Jamaica, so I went to Southampton to see when he arrived.'

'You did not see him?'

'No,' was the gloomy reply. 'But I seed the list of passengers in one of them boats, and his name wos on it. He couldn't have done it!'

'I found that out myself. No; Lestrange is innocent.'

'If I'd know'd he wos on his way here to make trouble with missy, I'd have waited,' said the sailor; 'but I thought if I dropped across him I'd keep him off.'

'He stole a march on you, Joe. And you have been at Southampton all this time?'

'I have, sir—there and in London. But it's all right now, Mr Alan. He won't worry Miss Sophy any more. But now you know, sir, why I gave a sov to that tramp. He talked about one as sent him, and I thought he wos talking of Captain Jean, so I hurried him away as soon as I could, lest Miss Sophy should hear.'

'I understand, Joe. But Cicero knew nothing at that time.'

'Ah!' Joe clenched his fist. 'He's another as needs a beating. Beg pardon, sir, but I suppose you ain't found out who killed the doctor?'

'No; I believe myself it was that man Brown, who was called the Quiet Gentleman. Do you know who he was, Joe?'

'No, sir, I do not,' replied Joe doggedly. 'Good-night, Mr Alan,' and he walked off in great haste.

The young Squire pursued his way to the Abbey Farm, and all the way wondered if Joe's sudden departure hinted at an unwillingness to talk of Brown.

'I'll ask him about the man tomorrow,' muttered Alan.

But on the morrow he had other matters to attend to. While he was at breakfast a card was brought to him and he jumped up with a joyful cry.

'Inspector Blair!' he said, throwing down the card. 'Show him up, Mrs Hester. Ah! I wonder what he has found out.'

CHAPTER XIX

A REAPPEARANCE

'I AM glad to see you, Blair. Sit down and have some breakfast.'

'Aha!' The inspector rubbed his hands as he looked at the well-spread table. 'I never say no to a good offer. Thank you, Mr Thorold, I will peck a bit.'

'You are looking well, Blair.'

'Never felt better in my life, Mr Thorold. I have good cause to look jolly.'

'Enjoyed your holiday, no doubt,' said Alan, as he assisted the officer liberally to ham and eggs. 'Where did you spend it?'

'In Brighton—pleasant place, Brighton.'

Blair looked so jocular, and chuckled in so pleasant a manner that the Squire guessed he had good news. However, he resolved to let Blair tell his story in his own way.

'What took you to Brighton of all places?' he asked tentatively.

'Well, you might guess. Joe Brill took me.'

'Joe Brill?'

The inspector nodded.

'I followed him there.'

'But I have seen Joe. He tells me he was at Southampton and in London.'

'No doubt—a clever fellow Joe. He knows how to hold his tongue. Well, Mr Thorold, I hope your troubles about this matter of the lost body will soon be at an end.'

'Blair!' Alan bent forward in a state of great excitement. 'You have found out something about it?'

'Yes, enough to gain me a thousand pounds.'

'Not enough to gain you two thousand pounds?'

139

'No.' Blair's face fell. 'But I intend to get that also. However, I have learned all about the theft of Mr Marlow's body—how it was removed, and why it was removed.'

'By Jove! How did you find out?'

'Through Joe Brill. Somehow I suspected Joe from the first. That sovereign he gave Cicero Gramp, you know—I always fancied there was something behind his anxiety to get that man away. So I had him watched, and applied for leave of absence. When he left Heathton I followed as a tourist,' chuckled Blair. 'Oh, I assure you, Mr Thorold, I make a very good tourist.'

'And he went to Brighton?'

'Yes, direct to Brighton. I went there and found out all about it.'

'You don't mean to say that he stole the body!'

'Ay, but I do and with the best intentions, too.'

'Was he the short man Cicero Gramp saw with Warrender?'

'He was the short man,' replied Blair, finishing his coffee.

'Then, why did he not tell me?' Alan burst out angrily. 'I saw him last night, yet he said nothing. He knew how anxious Miss Marlow is about the loss of her father's body.'

'Not her father,' corrected the inspector. 'Achille Lestrange was her father.'

'What!' Alan started from his seat. 'You know that?'

'I know all—the elopement in Jamaica; the kidnapping of Marie Lestrange, whom we know as Sophy Marlow; the coming of Jean Lestrange to blackmail the girl, and—and—all the rest of it. You see, Mr Thorold, I interviewed Joe Brill this morning, and he told me all about your conversation with that rascal. I am posted up to date, sir.'

'Joe Brill had no business to keep me in the dark,' said the Squire angrily. 'He should have relieved my mind and Miss Marlow's.

'Miss Lestrange,' hinted Blair.

'No, sir—Sophia Marlow she is, and Sophia Marlow she will remain until she changes her name for mine. Her father is dead, and Jean Lestrange has no claim on her. Sophia Marlow, Mr Inspector, if you please.'

'Well, well—as you please. We shan't quarrel about a name. Have you anything to smoke, Mr Thorold?'

Alan got him an excellent cigar, and returned to the point.

'Why did Joe keep me and Miss Marlow in the dark?' he asked.

'Acted under orders, Mr Thorold.'

'Whose orders?'

'Mr Marlow's, or rather, I should say Mr Beauchamp's.'

'Blair!'

Alan gasped out the name. His face was white and he was appalled at the news. For the moment he believed the inspector must have taken leave of his senses.

'Oh, I dare say your astonishment is natural,' said the inspector, lighting his cigar. 'I was astonished myself to find the dead man alive and kicking. Yet I should not have been, for I suspected the truth.'

Alan had not yet recovered from his amazement.

'You suspected that Mr Marlow was alive!' he said faintly. 'On what evidence?'

'On circumstantial evidence,' said Blair smartly. 'When I examined the coffin with Mr Phelps I noticed what he did not. At the sides small holes were bored in inconspicuous places, and the shell of the leaden case was pierced. Only one inference could be drawn from this—that the man had designedly been buried alive. The design must have been carried out by Warrender and the short man. I suspected Joe, from the fact of his having given that sovereign to Cicero, and I watched him. Presuming my belief to be correct, I made certain that sooner or later he would rejoin his master. As I say, he went to Brighton. I followed close on his heels to a boarding-house in Lansdowne Place. There I saw Mr Marlow.'

'Did he recognize you?'

'Of course. While he was living at Heathton I had seen Mr

Marlow several times on business. He made no attempt when I saw him at Brighton to disguise himself—not thinking, I suppose, that his clever scheme to frustrate Lestrange would come to light in this way.'

'But, Blair, you did not know about Lestrange then!'

'True enough; but I soon heard the whole story. Mr Marlow told it to me himself. As you may guess, he was in a great way about my having discovered him, and seeing no means of evading the truth, he told it. I insisted upon it, in fact; and now I know all.'

'And how did it come about?'

Blair held up his hand.

'No, Mr Thorold,' said he, 'I shall leave Mr Marlow—I think we had better continue to call him so—to tell his own history. He can do it better than I. Besides,' added the inspector, rising briskly, 'I have business to do.'

'What sort of business?'

'You can judge for yourself. I want you to come with me.'

'Where—what to do?'

'To see Mrs Warrender. You see, it was her husband who carried out this scheme of feigned death to deceive Lestrange. Marlow, accused of having murdered Achille in Jamaica, was afraid that this Captain Jean would have him arrested. Now, Warrender was in Beauchamp's house at Falmouth, Jamaica, when Mrs Lestrange died, and he knew all about it. It is my belief,' added the inspector slowly, 'that Beauchamp is innocent, as he asserts himself to be, and that Warrender knew as much.'

'But, my dear Blair,' protested Alan, 'in that case Warrender could have told Marlow the truth, and could have stopped Jean Lestrange from making mischief.'

'I dare say he could, but he did not. Warrender, my dear Mr Thorold, was a blackmailing scoundrel, who assumed the mask of friendship to bamboozle Marlow. I had considerable difficulty in impressing this view on Marlow, for, strange to say, he believed in the doctor. Joe did not, however, and Joe told me a few facts about Warrender's practice in Jamaica, which showed me that the doctor was not the disinterested person he pretended to be. No, I am sure Warrender knew Beauchamp to be innocent, and kept the fact quiet so as to retain a hold on the man, and get money out of him. Now, do you understand why I want to see his widow?'

'No,' replied Alan, not following the inspector's hypothesis, 'I do not. If Warrender kept the truth from Marlow, he would most certainly have kept it from his wife. The woman would have babbled, even against her own interests, as women always do. Mrs Warrender can tell you nothing—I feel sure of that.'

'You forget that the doctor may have left a confession of his knowledge.'

'Would he have done that?' said Alan doubtfully. 'It would have been a foolish thing.'

'And when do criminals do other than foolish things?' was Blair's response. 'The murderer usually returns to the scene of his crime—as often as not sets out its details in writing. It is impossible to account for the actions of human beings, Mr Thorold. It would not surprise me in the least to hear that Warrender had written out the whole story in a diary. If so, his wife must have found it amongst his papers, and she will be disposed to sell it—at a long price.'

'If she had found such a document, she would have shown it to me or to Sophy before now.'

'By no means. If she knew that Marlow were alive, then, of course, she would realize that the document was valuable. But she believes him to be dead.'

'Humph!' said Alan. 'You seem very certain that such a document exists.'

'Perhaps I am too sanguine,' admitted Blair; 'but Mr Marlow gave me a full account of what happened on the night Achille was murdered. Moreover, he swore that he was innocent, and I believe him. As to Warrender, he was a scoundrel, and I am sure that, like all scoundrels, he has left a record of his villainies in black and white. If this is so, I can prove Marlow's innocence, and he can defy Lestrange.'

By this time Alan and the inspector were walking along the road which led to Heathton. It was a bright, sunny morning, and Alan was in high spirits. How happy Blair's news would make Sophy!

'And Warrender, what about his death?' he asked. 'Does Marlow know who killed him?'

'Strange as it may seem, he does not, Mr Thorold. He is as ignorant as you or I. That death is a mystery still.'

'But if Warrender was killed on the heath—'

'I can't explain, Mr Thorold. Hear Marlow's story, and you will be as much in the dark as I am. But I suspect Lestrange.'

'So did I,' replied Alan, speaking in the past tense. 'But I learned for certain that Lestrange was not in England on the night of the murder.'

'I proved that, too,' said Blair thoughtfully; 'yet I can't help thinking there is some trickery. Lestrange is at the Good Samaritan?'

'Yes, dancing on Miss Marlow's doorstep in the hope of getting money.'

'Does he receive any letters?'

'I don't know. Why?'

'Merely an idea of mine. I'll tell you later on what I think.'

'You are keeping me very much in the dark, Blair,' said Alan, somewhat piqued.

'I don't care to show incomplete work,' replied the inspector bluntly. 'I believe I can unravel the whole of this mystery, but I don't want to show you the raw material. Let me work it out my own way, Mr Thorold, and judge me by the result.'

'As you please. So long as you do it, I don't care how you go about it.'

'I am working for two thousand pounds,' said Blair, 'and I don't intend to let anyone else have it. That blackguard tramp would like to be the man.'

Alan laughed.

'He has already made a clutch at it by accusing me of the theft of Mr Marlow's body.'

The inspector nodded and smiled grimly.

'The two are working in unison,' said he, rubbing his hands; 'but I'll catch them.'

'By the way,' said Thorold, 'is Mr Marlow coming back here?'

'To be caught by Lestrange? No, I think not. He is not such a fool. If you want to see him, you must go to Brighton.'

'I shall go tomorrow, Blair. I am most anxious to hear the story of that night.'

'A strange story—more like fiction than truth.'

'Truth is always stranger than fiction.'

Blair assented. They walked on through a steep lane, which led into the High Street of the village. As they breasted this, Mrs Marry, with a basket on her arm, met them. She was evidently excited.

'Well, Mrs Marry,' said Alan kindly, 'what is it?'

'The poor dear isn't dead, after all,' cried the panting woman. 'I declare, Mr Thorold, you could ha' knocked me down wi' a feather when I saw him.'

'Saw who?'

'Why, Mr Brown, sir—the Quiet Gentleman. He has come back!'

CHAPTER XX

THE AMAZEMENT OF ALAN THOROLD

MRS MARRY delivered her startling piece of news with an air of triumph. She did not guess for one moment how very important it was, or in what peril it placed the Quiet Gentleman.

'He came back last night,' she continued, 'and he told me with his fingers how he had been lying ill in London town. Poor dear! he took it into his head to go for a jaunt, he says, and went by the night train. He meant to have come back to me next morning, but a nasty influenza took him and kept him away. I'm that glad he's come back I can't tell!' cried Mrs Marry joyfully, 'for he do pay most reg'lar, and gives not a bit of trouble, innocent babe that he is!' and having imparted her news, she hurried on down the lane.

The two men stood looking at one another.

'Brown back again!' said Alan. 'Now we shall know the truth.'

'If he knows it,' said Blair drily—he was less excited than his companion—'but I doubt if we shall learn much from him, Mr Thorold. If he had anything to do with the murder, he would not have come back.'

'But he must have something to do with it, man! Have you forgotten that it was he who stole the key of the vault from my desk?'

'No,' said Blair pointedly, 'nor have I forgotten that he did not use the key. It was Joe Brill who opened the vault.'

'Indeed! And where did Joe get the key? Not from Mr Phelps, for he still has his key. Ha!' cried Alan suddenly, 'did Joe get it from Brown?'

'No, he did not. The key was not used at all. There was a third key in existence, of which neither you nor Mr Phelps were aware. Marlow had had it made to provide against the contingency which arose. He had always resolved to feign death, should Lestrange track him. So he kept the third key, and Joe used it on that night.'

'Well, even granting that such is the case, why should Brown have stolen my key? And how could he have known that it was in my desk?'

'I think we discussed that point before,' replied the inspector composedly, 'and that we came to the conclusion that Brown overheard your conversation with Mr Phelps on the day of the funeral. Where are you going?'

'To see Brown. I am determined to get the truth out of him.'

Blair looked at him.

'Well, Mr Thorold,' he said, 'I don't suppose it will do any harm for you to see the man. Meanwhile I will go on to Mrs Warrender's.'

'But you ought to come with me and arrest him.'

'I do not think I have sufficient evidence to procure a warrant, Mr Thorold. A charge of murder is serious, you see.'

'Pooh! pooh! I don't want him arrested for murder, but on the charge of breaking open my desk.'

'I could do that certainly. Well, you go and see him, Mr Thorold, while I interview Mrs Warrender. I'll call along at the cottage later. You needn't let Brown out of your sight until I come.'

'You'll arrest him?'

'If you wish it; I'll take the risk.'

'Very good, I'm off!' and with an abrupt nod Alan ran down the lane. Blair looked after him with a queer smile on his dry face. He had his own ideas regarding the termination of Alan's attempt to make Brown the mysterious speak out.

Mrs Warrender was at home when the inspector called. At first she felt she could not see him, for the idea of coming into contact with the police was abhorrent to her. She wondered if Blair could have discovered the relationship which existed between herself and Cicero, and it was her anxiety to ascertain this which made her grant the inspector an interview. If her brother were playing her false, the more she knew about his plans the better would she be able to frustrate them. Mrs Warrender was a capable woman, and had a genius for intrigue. She was quite decided that she could hold her own even against the trained intelligence of a police officer.

And so it came about that the gentleman in question was shown into the drawing-room, a meretricious, gaudy apartment, which betrayed in furniture and decoration the tawdry taste of the doctor's widow.

She came forward to receive him in an elaborate tea-gown of pink silk trimmed with lace, and, in spite of the early hour, she wore a quantity of jewels. Blair had an eye for beauty, and could not deny that this lady was a fine woman, though, perhaps, too much of the ponderous type. He wondered why she did not wear mourning. She could have cared but little for her husband, he thought, to appear in gay colours so soon after his untimely end. But, in truth, Mrs Warrender had never professed to be an affectionate wife. She had married for a home, and made no secret of it.

'Good-morning,' she said, with a sharp glance at Blair's impassive face. 'I understand that you belong to the police, and that you wish to see me—why, I cannot conceive.'

'If you will permit me to explain myself, I will soon give you my reasons,' said the inspector, in his best manner. 'May I sit down? Thank you. Now we can talk at our ease.'

'I suppose it is about the sad end of my poor husband,' she said, in tones of grief, which her gay attire somewhat belied. 'Have you found out the truth?'

'No; but I hope to do so—with your assistance.'

She looked up suddenly.

'If you think I killed the poor lamb, you are mistaken,' she said. 'I can account for all my actions on that night, policeman.'

This last was hurled at Blair with the object of keeping him well in mind of her condescension in receiving him.

'I never had the slightest suspicion of you,' he protested. 'My errand has to do with quite a different matter. And might I suggest,' he added, a trifle testily, 'that I am usually addressed as Inspector Blair?'

'Oh, of course, if you insist upon it!' she cried, with a shrug. 'Inspector Blair—will that do?'

'That will do very well, thank you.' He paused, and stared hard at the expensive tea-gown and the aggressive jewellery until the widow became restive. 'Are you rich?' he asked abruptly.

'What has that got to do with you?' cried Mrs Warrender furiously. 'Remember you are talking to a lady!'

'To a rich lady or to a poor one?'

'Upon my soul, this is too much! Mind your business, Inspector Blair!'

'This is my business,' he retorted, keeping himself well in hand. 'I merely asked you the question, because, if you are not rich, then I come to make you so.'

'What do you mean?'

'Answer my question first: Are you rich?' And he took another good look at the dress and the jewels.

'No,' she said sullenly, 'I am not. My husband left me fairly well off, but not with so much money as I expected.'

'Then you would not object to making some more?'

Her eyes lighted up with the fire of greed.

'I should! I should! I am dying to leave this dull village and take up a position in London; but I cannot do it without money.' She paused, then clapped her hands. 'I see,' she cried; 'Sophy Marlow is going to compensate me for the death of my husband. It would be easy enough with all the millions she has!'

'I am sure it would,' assented Blair coolly; 'but I don't mean to supply you with money for nothing.'

'You! What have you to do with the matter?'

'A good deal. Mr Thorold and Miss Marlow will rely on my advice.'

'Oh, Miss Marlow!' jeered Mrs Warrender, sitting up. 'That is her name, is it, Inspector Blair? Are you sure it isn't Marie Lestrange?'

He leaned forward and caught her wrist in a grip of steel.

'So you know the truth, then?' he said. 'Give me the confession.'

'What confession? What do you mean?' she cried, trying to release her hand.

'The confession left by your husband, in which he tells the story of Achille Lestrange's murder.'

'I—I—I don't know—'

'Yes, you do; yes, you do—no lies!' He shook her wrist. 'You know that Marlow never murdered Captain Lestrange.'

'Let go my wrist!' cried Mrs Warrender, and succeeded in wrenching herself free. 'What do you mean by behaving like this? I know nothing about the matter—there!'

Blair jumped up and made for the door.

'Very good. Then you lose the money I have got for you.'

'Come back! come back!' She followed him to the door and laid her hand on his shoulder. 'Don't be in a hurry. Is there—is there money in it?'

'If you have the confession, yes.'

'How much?'

'We will talk of that when I know the truth. Have you a confession?'

'Yes, I have.' She thought she might with safety admit as much. 'I found the whole story of Mr and Mrs Lestrange and Mr Beauchamp amongst my business papers—my husband's papers, I should say. It was signed and witnessed in New Orleans. It seems Warrender was dying there, and wanted to tell Mr Beauchamp—Marlow, I mean—the truth, so he had the confession drawn up by a lawyer. Afterwards, when he got well, he did not destroy it.'

'Beauchamp was innocent of the murder, then?'

'Yes. He knocked Achille Lestrange down, but he did not kill him.'

'Aha! I thought so!' chuckled Blair, rubbing his hands. 'Who did?'

Mrs Warrender drew back with a look of cunning on her face.

'That's tellings,' said she, relapsing into the speech of her people. 'I don't part with my secret unless I get my price.'

'Name your price.'

'Two thousand pounds.'

'What!' cried the inspector. 'Two thousand pounds for clearing the memory of a dead man! My dear lady, five hundred is nearer the mark.'

'Two thousand,' she repeated. 'If Sophy Marlow has the millions left by her supposed father, she can well afford that.'

'Humph! We'll see. I must speak to Mr Thorold first. You have the confession?'

'I have—safely put away. It was my intention to have seen Sophy Marlow about it, but I thought I'd wait.'

'To see what price you could get?' put in Blair.

'Quite so. I'm a woman of business. If I don't get my price, I burn that confession.'

'You dare not! I can have you arrested, remember.'

She snapped her fingers.

'Pooh!' she said. 'I don't care for your threats. This is my one chance of making money, and I'm going to take it. Two thousand pounds or nothing.'

'I'll think it over,' said Blair. 'I am to have the refusal of that confession, mind.'

'What! Do you want to make money too?'

'Certainly,' said Blair, with irony; 'I am a man of business.'

She laughed, and took leave of him in a very amiable frame of mind. When he had gone, she smirked in front of a mirror and took a long look at herself.

'Two thousand pounds,' she cried, 'and my own savings! I'm not so old, after all. I'll run away from Cicero and marry again. Ha ha! I've made a deal this time!' And she went in to luncheon with a most excellent appetite.

While this interview was taking place, Alan had been at Mrs Harry's cottage. Having received no orders to the contrary, she ushered him into the sitting-room. There sat the Quiet Gentleman in his grey suit. At sight of Alan he started violently.

'Good-day, Mr Brown,' said his visitor, looking closely at him. 'I have come to see you about that key you stole. You are dumb, I believe, but not deaf, so no doubt you follow my meaning.'

The Quiet Gentleman made a step forward, and, to the amazement of his visitor, he spoke.

'Alan,' he said—'Alan Thorold!'

The young man dropped into a chair, white and shaking. He knew that voice—he knew what was coming.

With a laugh the Quiet Gentleman pulled off his wig and beard.

'Don't you know me, Alan?' he asked.

'Richard Marlow!' gasped Alan.

'Herbert Beauchamp,' was the quiet reply.

CHAPTER XXI

THE STORY OF THE PAST

'COME, Alan,' said Beauchamp after a pause, 'you need not be tongue-tied with astonishment. I sent Blair on to tell you all that had happened, so you must have known that I was alive.'

'Yes, yes—but your disguise,' stammered the young man. 'I expected to see Brown. You are not Brown, never could have been; for when he was here, I have seen you and him at the same time.'

'That's all right, my boy. I was not Brown, as you say, and who Brown was I know no more than you do. But I am Brown now,' with emphasis, 'and Brown I shall remain until I can show myself with safety as Richard Marlow. Not that I intended to stick to that name. No; if Blair is right, and that scoundrel Warrender has left papers to prove my innocence, I shall take my own name. But this disguise! It is a plot between me and Blair. It was necessary that I should be on the spot, so we thought this was as good a mask as any. Oh, depend upon it, Alan, I am perfectly safe here from Jean Lestrange!'

As he spoke, Beauchamp was putting on his wig and beard. And when this was done to his satisfaction, he seated himself on a chair opposite to Alan, looking the very image of the Quiet Gentleman. Thorold did not wonder that Mrs Marry had been deceived—the completeness of the disguise would have deceived a cleverer woman.

'Still,' said he doubtfully, 'if the real Brown should reappear—'

'We will have him arrested for the murder of Warrender,' said Beauchamp quietly. 'Yes, I am convinced he is guilty, else why did he steal the key of the vault? Blair told me about that.

He must surely be some tool of Jean Lestrange's. No, not the man himself—I am aware of that. Blair saw the passenger-list.'

'Are you certain that the Quiet Gentleman killed Warrender?'

'No, because I did not see the blow struck. I was insensible at the time—but it is a long story, and to make things perfectly clear, I must begin at the beginning. One moment, Alan.' Beauchamp crossed to the door and turned the key. 'I don't want Mrs Marry to come in.'

'She will hear your voice, and believing you to be dumb—'

'I'll speak low. Come nearer to this chair. First tell me how Sophy is.'

'Very well, but much cast down. She thinks you are dead, and that your body has been stolen. Oh, Beauchamp!' cried Alan passionately, 'why did you not trust Sophy and me? You would have spared us both many an unhappy hour.'

'I wish now that I had told you, but I acted for the best. I had little time for thought. I expected daily that Lestrange would appear. If I had only considered the matter rather more—but there, it's done and we must make the best of it. Sophy's tears will be turned to smiles shortly—if, indeed, she still loves me, knowing that I am not her father,' and the old man sighed.

'You need have no fear on that score,' said Alan, with a faint smile. He was getting over the first shock of surprise. 'Sophy would have nothing to do with Jean Lestrange, although she half believed his story. She always insists that you are her true father. She will welcome you back with the greatest joy.'

'She must welcome me secretly.'

'Secretly—why? Should your innocence be established, you would surely reappear as Richard Marlow?'

'What! And have the whole story in the papers? No, Alan, I shall spend the rest of my life under my true name of Beauchamp, and live on the two thousand a year I left myself in my will. You and Sophy can marry and take the rest of the money. I shall travel, and take Joe with me.'

'Well, perhaps it is the best thing to do,' said Thorold. 'But tell me, how was it that the manager of the Occidental Bank reported you dead?'

'Joe wrote to him by my order to say so. When Joe came to me at Brighton and told me how the death of Warrender had complicated matters, I was afraid lest I should be traced, and perhaps accused of a second murder. So I thought it best to put it about that I was dead, and end all pursuit.'

'If you had only trusted me, sir, all this trouble would have been avoided. I merited your confidence, I think.'

'I know—I know. Indeed, on that day when I spoke to you of the probability that my body would not be allowed to rest in its grave, I had half a mind to tell you. But somehow the moment passed. Even then I had designed my plot of feigning death. It was the only way I saw of escaping Lestrange.'

'Tell me the story from the beginning,' said Alan. 'I know only scraps.'

'The beginning was in Jamaica, Alan,' said Beauchamp sadly. 'All this trouble arose out of the love I had for Sophy's mother. Poor Zelia! If only she had married me, I would have made her a good husband. As it was, she chose Achille Lestrange, a roué and a gambler, a spendthrift and a scoundrel. I could never tell Sophy what a bad man her father was. He treated poor Zelia abominably.'

'But was that altogether his fault, Beauchamp? Joe hinted that Jean Lestrange caused much of the trouble.'

'So he did, the scoundrel! Jean was, if anything, worse than his cousin, though there was not much to choose between them. But Jean was madly in love with Zelia—worshiped her with all the fierce passion of a Creole. When he lost her he vowed he would be revenged—he sowed dissension between them on my account.'

'He hinted that you were in love with her, I suppose?'

'Yes, and he was right!' cried Beauchamp with emphasis. 'I was in love with Zelia, and pitied her from the bottom of my heart. Well, a year after Sophy was born things came to a crisis.

I was at Kingston, and my yacht in the harbour there. I saw a good deal of Zelia, and one night she came on board with her child, and asked me to take her away. Lestrange had struck her, the beast! and she had refused to live with him any longer. At first I hesitated, but she was in such a state of agony that I consented to take her away from her wretched life. I had to go first to Falmouth to fetch some things which I did not wish to leave—I had sold my plantation some time before, having made up my mind to leave Jamaica. So we sailed, reached Falmouth in safety, and I went to my estate, leaving Joe Brill on board.'

'Ah! that was why Joe could not say who killed Achille?'

'Precisely. Joe knew little of the events of that night; but he believed in me, and stood by me like the noble, faithful fellow he is. But to continue: Zelia arrived at my house only to die; worry and melancholy had brought her to a low state of health, and she caught a fever. On the very night Jean and her husband came in pursuit she died. I had made all arrangements to sail; I had sold my estate, and had sent the proceeds to England. It had been my intention to have married Zelia when Achille had divorced her, to adopt little Marie, and to start life afresh in a new land. Her death put an end to these plans.'

'But the murder, Beauchamp?'

'I am coming to that. Warrender was attending Zelia when she died, and he was in the house when Achille and Jean arrived. I was quite determined he should not get the child; for Zelia had left some money, and I knew well that Achille would soon squander it. Well, Lestrange demanded his wife. I told him she was dead; he declined to believe me, and we quarrelled. I am naturally of a fiery temper,' continued Beauchamp with some agitation, 'and I knocked him down on the veranda. The blow stunned him, and he lay there like a dog.'

'Was Jean present?'

'Yes. He saw me knock Achille down; then he went away to see the body of Zelia. I had to look for the child, intending to take her to my yacht until such time as I could obtain the guardianship. When I came out again I found Warrender kneeling down beside the body of Achille. He was dead!'

'Not from the effects of your blow?' cried Alan incredulously.

'No. He had been stabbed to the heart while senseless.'

'By whom—Warrender?'

'I don't know. Warrender always swore that his hands were clean of blood, and certainly he had no reason to murder Achille. I suspected Jean, but Warrender told me that Jean had been in Zelia's room praying beside the body. He advised me to fly.'

'Yes, yes; but who killed Achille?'

'Well, I supposed it must have been a negro whom Achille had brought with him—a Zambo, called Scipio, who was devoted to his mistress and who hated his master. On hearing that Zelia was dead—knowing, as he did, that her husband's brutality had probably had a good deal to do with it—he might have stabbed Achille as he lay senseless on the veranda. At any rate, Warrender said that he found him dead when he came out. To this day I don't know who killed him. It must have been either Warrender, Scipio, or Jean. I am inclined to suspect Scipio. However, at the time there was nothing for it but flight if I wanted to escape an accusation of murder. You see how strong the evidence was against me, Alan? I had taken away Achille's wife and child; he had come in pursuit; I had quarrelled with him and knocked him down; he had been found dead. Therefore I fled with the child. Can you blame me?'

'No,' said Alan decisively. 'Under the circumstances, I don't see what else you could do. So you escaped?'

'I did. I went on board my yacht and told Joe all. Of course, he believed in my innocence, and strongly advised me to leave at once. We sailed down the coast of South America, round the Horn, and home to England. I called myself Richard Marlow, and I sold the yacht under another name at a French seaport. I had plenty of money, and there was no one who suspected my past.'

'I suppose the news of the murder had not reached England?'

'No. I believe there was a casual reference in one of the papers, but that was all. The yacht was supposed to have foundered. I felt secure from pursuit, and determined to start a new life. I gave out that Marie was my daughter, and I called her Sophy. Then I placed her in the convent at Hampstead, with a sum of money for her education, and besides that, I secured a certain sum on her for life in case of my death. When this was settled I went to Africa. There Fortune, tired of persecuting me, gave me smiles instead of frowns. I made a fortune in the gold-mines, and became celebrated as Richard Marlow the millionaire. The rest of my story you know.'

'Up to a point,' said Alan significantly. 'I know how you bought this place and settled here with Sophy. But the letter from Barkham—'

'Ah! Joe told you about that, did he?' said Beauchamp composedly. 'Yes, the letter was from an old friend of mine called Barkham. He told me that Jean Lestrange had recognized my portrait in an illustrated paper, and that he intended to come to England to hunt me down. The letter was sent to the office of the paper, and by them forwarded here. You may guess my feelings. I thought myself lost. I showed the letter to Warrender, and he suggested that I should feign death. I jumped at the idea, made a will, allowing myself an income under my true name of Herbert Beauchamp, got another key of the vault fashioned from the one which afterwards was taken to Phelps, and took Joe into my confidence. Then Warrender drugged me.'

'What did he give you?' asked Alan. 'You looked really dead.'

'I can't tell you the name of the drug. He said it was some vegetable preparation used by the negroes. Then I died—apparently—and I was buried. They had bored holes in the coffin, and that night, when you were all absent, Joe and Warrender took me out of the vault and carried me to the hut on the heath, where Warrender revived me. It was while he was doing this that he heard a noise, and ran out. He never came back, and when I was myself again we went out to find his body. He was quite dead, stabbed to the heart, and lying some distance from the hut. Who killed him I do not know.'

'But how did his body get into the vault?'

'Joe did it. After he had got me away, he dragged the body into the hut, and next night came back and took it to the vault. He put it into the coffin, never dreaming that anyone would look for it there. Nor would they, and all would have been well had it not been for that man Cicero Gramp. He saw too much, and—'

He was interrupted by a sharp knock at the door.

CHAPTER XXII

THE BEGINNING OF THE END

ALAN started to his feet at that imperative summons. Had Beauchamp been overheard by Mrs Marry? Had his disguise been penetrated? Had she brought someone to witness the discovery? These thoughts rushed through his mind with lightning speed, and for the moment he lost his presence of mind. Not so the man who was truly in danger. Adopting the peculiar shuffle of the Quiet Gentleman, he crossed the room and opened the door. As the key turned in the lock Alan fully expected to see Lestrange, menacing and sinister, on the threshold. But the newcomer proved to be Blair.

'How are you getting on, Mr Thorold?' he said, stepping through the door, which Beauchamp locked behind him. 'You know now who the Quiet Gentleman is. Don't look so scared, sir.'

'Can't help it,' muttered the young man.

'This business has been rather too much for me. I thought when you knocked, that Lestrange had run his prey to earth.'

'He won't get much out of his prey if he does,' said Blair, with a nod to Beauchamp. 'I have seen Mrs Warrender.'

The old man turned as white as the beard he wore.

'And—and—what does she say?' he stammered.

'Say!' Blair seated himself and chuckled. 'She says two thousand pounds will pay her for that confession.'

'Then it does exist! Warrender knew the truth!'

'Of course. Didn't I tell you the man was a blackmailing scoundrel? Faith! and his wife is not much better. Two thousand pounds for a bit of paper!'

'And for my freedom!' said Beauchamp excitedly. 'Oh to think of being free from the horror which has hung over me all these years! And Warrender knew the truth! What a scoundrel! He always swore that he knew nothing, and I paid him money to hold his tongue about my supposed guilt. Ungrateful wretch! He and his wife arrived in England almost penniless. I met him in London, and, as he knew my story, I brought him down here. I helped him in every way. How was it he left a confession behind him?'

'It is an old confession,' replied Blair. 'It seems that Warrender fell ill of fever in New Orleans. His conscience smote him for his villainy, and he made a full confession, signed it, and had it witnessed. When he recovered he did not destroy it, but kept it safely with the rest of his papers. There Mrs Warrender found it, and she is now prepared to sell it for two thousand pounds. A nice sum, upon my word!' grumbled Blair.

'She shall have it,' said Beauchamp eagerly. 'I would pay five thousand for that confession—I would indeed!'

'I dare say. But Mrs Warrender will give it to you for the lesser sum, sir.'

'Does she know that I am here? Did you tell her?'

'Not such a fool, Mr Beauchamp. She'd have asked five thousand if she had known that. The woman has the black-mailing instinct.'

'Like her brother,' put in Alan. Then, observing the looks of surprise directed at him by the other two, he added: 'Didn't you know? Cicero Gramp is Mrs Warrender's brother. I found that out in London.'

'A nice pair of jail-birds!' cried Blair. 'I'd best get that confession at once, or she'll be giving it to Cicero, and they'll demand more money. Mr Beauchamp, can you give me a cheque?'

'No,' he said, shaking his head. 'You forget, Blair, I am dead and buried, and, what's more, I do not intend ever to come to life again as Marlow. But Mr Thorold, as Sophy's trustee, can give you the money.'

'If Blair will come to the Abbey Farm, I will do so,' said Alan, rising. 'I agree that the sooner the confession is obtained the better, or Cicero may give trouble. By the way, who was it killed Achille, Blair? Was it the doctor himself?'

'No, no!' cried Beauchamp. 'It was Scipio, the negro.'

'I can't tell you that;' and the inspector shook his head. 'Mrs Warrender declares that you are innocent, Mr Beauchamp; but she declines to give any further information until she has received her pound of flesh.'

'She shall have it this very day,' said Alan, putting on his cap. 'Come, Blair. Mr Beauchamp, will you remain here?'

'Yes. I am safer as the Quiet Gentleman than as anything else.'

'You don't want me to bring Sophy here?'

'Not until we get that confession, Alan. Sophy might make a scene when she met me. Mrs Marry would learn the truth, and the news would spread. If Lestrange knew, all would be lost. Get the confession, Alan.'

'Yes, I think that is the best plan. Good-day, Mr Brown,' said the inspector, speaking for the benefit of Mrs Marry, and with Alan he left the house.

Alone again, Beauchamp fell on his knees and thanked God that his innocence was about to be vindicated. For years he had lived in dread of discovery; now he was about to be relieved of the nightmare.

Talking as they went of the strange and unexpected turn the case, as Blair called it, had taken, the two men walked through Heathton and out on to the country road. On turning down a quiet lane which led to the Abbey Farm, they saw a ponderous man behaving in a most extraordinary manner. He danced in the white dust, he shook his fist at the sky, and he spun round like a distracted elephant. Blair's keen eye recognized him at once.

'Very pretty, Mr Cicero Gramp,' he observed drily. 'Are you in training for a ballet-dancer?'

The man stopped short, and turned a disturbed face on them.

'I'll be even with him!' he gasped, wiping his streaming forehead. 'Oh, the wretch! oh, the Judas! Gentlemen, proceed, and leave an unhappy man to fight down a whirl of conflicting emotions. *E pluribus unum!*' quoted Cicero, in a pathetic voice; 'that is me—Ai! Ai! I utter the wail of Orestes.'

'And, like Orestes, you seem to be mad,' observed Alan, as the fat man returned to his dancing.

'And no wonder, Mr Thorold. I have lost thousands. Lestrange—'

Cicero could say no more. He was choked with emotion, and gave vent to his feelings by shaking his fist at the sky.

'Ah,' said Blair, who had been taking in the situation, 'Lestrange! You have found a cleverer villain than yourself.'

'He has gone away!' roared Cicero, with the voice of an angry bull. 'Yes, you may look. He went this morning, bag and baggage. I don't know where he is, save that he roams the wilderness of London. And my money—he paid his bill to mine hostess of the hostel with my money!'

'The deuce he did!' said Alan. 'And how did you come to lend him money?'

'I do not mind explaining,' said Mr Gramp, with a defiant glance at the gentleman who represented the police. 'I went into partnership with Lestrange. He had no money; I lent him a goodly part of your fifty pounds, Mr Thorold, on an undertaking that I should get half of what he received from Miss Marlow.'

'A very creditable bargain,' remarked Alan grimly; 'but you invested your cash in a bad cause, Mr Gramp. I saw Lestrange last night, and assured him that he would not get one penny of the blackmail he proposed to extort. I dare say, after my visit, he found the game was up, and thought it advisable to clear out. I should recommend you to do the same.'

'So should I,' put in Blair significantly, 'or I'll have you arrested as a vagabond without proper means of support.'

'I am a professor of eloquence and elocution!' cried Cicero, his fat cheeks turning pale at this stern hint. 'You dare not arrest me; and you, Mr Thorold, will be sorry if you do not employ me.'

'Employ you? In which way?'

'To hunt Lestrange down.'

Alan shrugged his shoulders.

'I do not wish to see the man again.'

'But I know something about him. Promise to pay me some money, and I'll show you a letter written to Captain Lestrange, which came to the inn after he left. I took it and opened it to find out his plans.'

'Well, you are a scoundrel!' said Alan, looking Mr Gramp's portly figure up and down. 'By opening another person's letter you have placed yourself within reach of the law.'

'I don't care!' cried Cicero recklessly. 'I am desperate. Will you pay me for a sight of that letter?'

'Yes,' said the inspector before Alan could reply, 'if it is worth paying for. On the other hand, you could be arrested for opening it. Come, the letter!'

Cicero produced the document in question, and kept firm hold of it while he made his bargain.

'How much, Mr Thorold?'

'If it proves to be of use,' replied the young Squire leisurely, 'I'll pay you well. Leave the amount to me.'

The tramp still hesitated, but Inspector Blair, becoming impatient, snatched it out of his hand and proceeded to read it aloud. It was a short note to the effect that if the writer did not receive a certain sum of money 'at once' (underlined), he would come down to Heathton and 'tell all' (also underlined) to Miss Marlow. These few lines were signed, 'O. Barkham.'

'Barkham!' exclaimed Alan. 'That must be the man who warned Beauchamp that Lestrange was coming. I wonder what he knows.'

'Humph!' grunted Blair, putting the letter into his pocket, 'very likely he will be able to tell us sufficient to enable us to dispense with Mrs Warrender's confession. I am not particularly anxious to pay her two thousand pounds for nothing.'

'Two thousand pounds!' wailed Cicero, with his eyes staring out of his head. 'Oh, Clara Maria! Has she got that out of you? My own sister—my very own!' wept the old scamp, 'and she won't go shares! Yet I offered to work with her!' he finished.

'I don't think you'll get a sixpence out of her,' said Alan; 'a desire to grab money evidently runs in your family. However, if this letter turns out to be of any assistance in clearing up these mysteries, I'll see what I can do.'

Mr Gramp, seeing no other alternative, accepted this offer. 'When am I to get it?' he asked sulkily.

'When I choose,' Alan replied tartly. 'Go back to the Good Samaritan, and don't let me catch you annoying your sister, or I'll make it hot for you!' and he moved away, followed by Blair.

Cicero shook his fist at them, and spent the rest of the day making futile guesses as to how much they would give him.

'What's to do now, Blair?' asked Thorold abruptly.

'I shall pay Mrs Warrender and get the confession. You can take it to Mr Beauchamp and set his mind at rest.'

'And you—what will you do?'

'Catch the 6.30 train to London. I shall go straight to the address given in this letter'—Blair tapped his breast-pocket—'and see Barkham, and,' he added, 'I shall see Lestrange.'

'Will he be with Barkham?'

'I think so. He—Lestrange, I mean—went away before he got this letter. It is likely enough that he has gone to London to see his accomplice.'

'If Barkham were an accomplice, he would not have written, warning Beauchamp of Lestrange's departure from Jamaica.'

'It is on that point I wish to be clear,' retorted Blair. 'It seems to me that Barkham is running with the hare and hunting with the hounds.'

'Well, I hope you'll find out sufficient to solve the mystery,' said Alan, bringing the conversation to a close; 'but I confess I am doubtful.'

The cheque duly written and safely deposited in the inspector's pocket, the two men set out on their visit to Mrs Warrender, who was graciously pleased to accept the money, in exchange for which she handed over the confession. Alan and Blair read it on the spot, and were greatly astonished at the contents. Then the inspector hurried away to catch the London train, and Alan set out for Mrs Marry's cottage, taking with him the precious document. Mrs Warrender—fearful lest the cheque should be stopped—left for London by a later train. She had decided that she would cash it herself the moment the bank opened the following morning. Her business capacities were indeed undeniable.

Alan returned home, tired out with the day's work, and was glad enough to sit down to the excellent meal provided by Mrs Hester. But his troubles and excitements were not yet over. Hardly had he finished his dinner when a note from Sophy was brought in.

'Come at once,' she wrote; 'Lestrange is here.'

CHAPTER XXIII

ONE PART OF THE TRUTH

AFTER his interview with Alan, Captain Lestrange had come to the conclusion that it would be the best and wisest course to retreat before the enemy. Alan knew much, Brill knew more, and the two together might prove too much for him. Moreover, since his design of passing as Sophy's father had been rendered useless, it was not necessary that he should remain in Heathton. Therefore, he paid his account at the inn with money borrowed from Cicero, and departed in hot haste before that gentleman was afoot. It was not until he got to the Junction that he began to wonder if he was acting judiciously. It struck him that he should have made at least one attempt to get money out of Sophy.

For some time he pondered over this question, and finally decided to leave his baggage in the Junction cloak-room and steal back to Heathton under cover of darkness. True, his accomplice Barkham was waiting for him in London, but he would not get much of a welcome from that gentleman unless he brought money with him. Moreover, after Joe's intimation that it was Barkham who had warned Beauchamp of the plot to hunt him down, Lestrange had had no confidence in him. But that Barkham knew enough to be very dangerous, he would have left him out of his calculations altogether. He decided at last that he must get money out of Sophy, bribe Barkham to return to Jamaica, and then deal alone and unaided with the lucrative business of extracting further blackmail. Having made up his mind to this course of action, he loitered about at the Junction until he could with safety return to Heathton.

It was during this time that he had a surprise. While lurking in the waiting-room, he saw Blair arrive by a local train and catch the London express. What could he be doing? Was he hunting him down? The very idea terrified him, and he began to congratulate himself on having remained at the Junction. Had he known that Blair was now on his way to see Barkham, he would have had still greater cause for alarm. Matters were indeed coming to a crisis, but Lestrange did not guess that the crisis was so near at hand.

When he had seen the lights of the London express disappear, he took his seat in a local train, which was timed to leave shortly after eight o'clock. On arriving at Heathton, he left the station hurriedly, and stole through deserted by-ways to the Moat House. Here he asked for Miss Marlow, and sent in his card, on which he had scribbled, 'News of your father'. The lie, which was not all a lie, gained him the interview he sought; but before seeing him, Sophy sent off the note to Alan. Then she induced Miss Vicky to retire, and received her visitor alone in the drawing-room.

The Captain entered the room with a somewhat cringing air. His nerve was gone, and with it a goodly portion of his courage. Miss Marlow, on the contrary, was quite mistress of herself and of the situation. She had heard from Joe Brill, amongst other things, that this man was not her father, and she now felt no fear of him. He was anxious and ill at ease, like a culprit before a judge.

'Good evening, Captain Lestrange,' said Sophy, sitting very erect in her chair. 'You wish to see me, I believe. Why have you come?'

'To make reparation, Miss Marlow.'

'Oh,' she said ironically, 'then I am not your daughter?'

'I expect you have heard as much from Joe Brill,' replied Lestrange, looking at her gloomily. 'No, you are not my daughter, but you are my cousin, Marie Lestrange, although you choose to keep your name of Sophia Marlow.'

'I keep the name of the man who has been a father to me.'

'In that case, you should call yourself Beauchamp,' he retorted. 'May I sit down? Thank you. Well, I suppose you are wondering why I have come to see you?'

She glanced at the card.

'To give me news of my father, I presume,' she said. 'Do you mean my real father?'

'No, I mean the false one. Your real father died long ago. He was murdered by Beauchamp.'

'He was not!' cried Sophy vehemently, and started from her seat. 'I have heard the story from Joe, and I know now why you came here. But nothing will induce me to believe that he killed my father. My mother fled to him from the cruelty of her husband, and you were at the bottom of all the trouble.'

'Yes,' he cried fiercely, 'I was! I loved your mother dearly. She gave me up for Achille, and I swore I would be revenged. I sowed dissension between them. It was through me that Zelia fled with Beauchamp. Do you think I am sorry for what happened? I am not. I hated Achille; but he is dead. I hate Beauchamp, for your mother loved him—'

'And he also is dead,' interrupted Sophy; 'you cannot harm him.'

'Are you so sure he is dead?' sneered Lestrange.

'I saw his dead body!' cried the girl, with emotion.

'You saw him in a state of insensibility, brought about by Warrender's devilish drugs!' said the Captain sharply. 'I don't believe Beauchamp is dead. If he had been, why should his body have been carried off?'

'You declared that Mr Thorold did that, and—'

'I do not say so now. Thorold had nothing to do with it; but I am quite sure that Warrender had. In order to escape me, Beauchamp allowed himself to be drugged by Warrender, and that was why Warrender assisted at the removal of the supposed dead body. I feel certain that Beauchamp is alive.'

'Alive! Oh! I hope so, I hope so! My dear father!' cried Sophy.

'Only prove that he is alive, Captain Lestrange, and I will forgive you all!'

'You forget that I am his enemy,' was the fierce reply. 'Were I able to prove that he is alive, I should at once have him arrested for the murder of your father—my cousin.'

'It is not true! it is not true!'

'It is, and you know it. Beauchamp must have had some very good and strong reason for allowing himself to be buried alive so as to escape me. But for your sake and for my own I will leave Beauchamp, should he be indeed alive, to the punishment of his conscience.'

'What do you mean?'

'I mean that I want money. You are rich, and you can pay me. Give me a thousand pounds, and I will go away and never trouble you again.'

'I refuse!' She walked up and down the room in a state of great agitation. 'If you were certain that Mr Beauchamp was alive—if you were certain he had committed that crime, you would not let him escape so easily.'

'I would! I would! I am tired of the whole business.'

'No, no,' insisted the girl; 'I don't believe you. If I gave you money, I should only be supplying you with the means to cause further trouble. If my dear father—for I shall still call him so—is alive, I will leave the matter in his hands.'

'And hang him.'

'And save him,' retorted the girl firmly. 'You can go, Captain Lestrange. I shall not give you one penny!'

Lestrange made a bound and caught her wrist.

'Take care!' he cried, shaking with rage; 'I am desperate—I will stick at nothing. If you do not give the money I want, I shall go to the police!'

'Go! go! I defy you!'

'Little devil!' muttered Lestrange, and he gave her arm a sharp twist.

She screamed for help, and as though in answer to her

summons, Alan appeared at the door. With an exclamation of rage he sprang forward, seized Lestrange, and flung him on the floor.

'You hound!' he cried, panting. 'You dog!'

'Alan! Alan! Thank Heaven you are here! Let me sit down, Alan; I—I feel faint.'

While Alan was assisting the girl to a chair, Lestrange rose slowly from the ground. The sudden and opportune arrival of the young Squire disconcerted him greatly, and he began to think it was time to retire. If Sophy refused him money when alone, she would most certainly not yield to his demand now that her lover was beside her. So with deadly hatred in his heart, he stole towards the door, which was still open. On the threshold he recoiled with a shrill cry of fear. Before him stood Herbert Beauchamp, alias Richard Marlow.

'You—you here, after all?'

Beauchamp, shutting and locking the door after him, strode into the room.

'Yes, I live to punish you, Jean Lestrange. Hold him, Alan, while I speak to Sophy.'

The girl, with a pale face and staring eyes, was looking at the man who had come back from the grave. He approached and took her hands.

'My poor child!' he said in caressing tones, 'do not look so alarmed! I am flesh and blood.'

'You are alive, father?' gasped Sophy, amazed and somewhat terrified.

'Yes.' He kissed her. 'I feigned death to escape from this man. Come, Sophy, have you no welcome for me? It is true that I am not your father; but—after all—'

'You are as dear to me as ever!' she cried, putting her arms round his neck. 'You are my true father—my real father! I shall never think of you as anything else. Oh, thank God—thank God!' And she wept and kissed him by turns.

'Amen!' said Beauchamp in a solemn tone. 'But we have

much to do before things are put straight. There is the cause of all my trouble, and I must deal with him.' He rose and crossed to where Lestrange, white and shaking, was in the grip of Thorold. 'What have you to say for yourself, Lestrange?'

The man made a violent effort to recover his self-control, and partially succeeded.

'I have to say to you what I shall shortly say to the world: You are a murderer!'

'That is a lie!'

'It is no lie. You murdered that girl's father!'

'That is a lie!' repeated Beauchamp sternly. 'Do you think I am a Judas, to kiss that innocent girl if I knew myself to be her father's murderer? I knocked your cousin Achille senseless, and well he deserved it; but it was not I who stabbed him to the heart. It was you, Jean Lestrange!'

'I—I—' gasped the wretch, his lips white, his limbs shaking under him. 'You dare—to—to—accuse—me—of—'

'I do not accuse you,' said Beauchamp solemnly. 'Out of the mouth of the dead you are condemned. Here is the confession of Warrender, and in it he tells the truth. You are the murderer of Achille!'

Sophy uttered a cry of horror, and throwing herself back on the couch, hid her face from the guilty wretch. He strove to speak, but no words came, and he continued to look silently on the ground. But for the support of Thorold he would have fallen.

'Warrender,' continued Mr Beauchamp, 'himself almost as great a villain as you, knew the truth these twenty years. But he kept silence in order to terrorize me, to extort money from me. It was he who proposed that I should escape you by feigning death, knowing, as he did, that I was innocent. Well, he has been punished!'

'I did not kill him, at all events!' cried Lestrange savagely.

'I know you did not; you were not in England at the time. But you killed Achille. Yes, you left the room where Zelia lay dead, you found Achille senseless on the veranda, and you stabbed him to the heart. Warrender saw you commit the crime. It is all set out here, and signed by Warrender, in the presence of two witnesses. Can you deny it?'

Lestrange moistened his dry lips, looked at Sophy, at Beauchamp, then suddenly shook off Alan's hold.

'No, I don't deny it,' he said in a loud, harsh voice. 'You have been one too many for me. I am so poor as to be almost starving, so I don't care what becomes of me. Hang me if you like. I hate you, Beauchamp—I have always hated you, the more so when I found how much Zelia cared for you. And I loved her, though that was not the reason I killed her husband; for she was dead then, and could never be mine. But I killed him so that blame might rest on you. And I wanted the custody of the child, because I should have been able to handle the money. I found Achille senseless where you had knocked him down. I did not intend to do it; but I had a knife—and the devil put it into my head to stab him. Then you fled, and the murder was laid at your door.'

'And had you not done me harm enough, wretched man, without hunting me down?' said Beauchamp sternly.

'I wanted money,' he cried recklessly. 'I saw your portrait in the paper, and I arranged with Barkham, who was as hard-up as I, that we should come to England and get some of your money. He played the traitor, and wrote you that letter—why, I don't know, as he stood to make as much as I did. But for that letter I should have found you alive, and I should have forced you to pay me. As it turned out, you escaped me.'

'And will you escape me, do you think?' asked Beauchamp with emphasis.

'I don't know—I don't care. Call in the police and have me arrested if you like. I have played a bold game, and lost—do your worst!'

He folded his arms, and stared defiantly at the man whose life he had ruined.

Beauchamp looked irresolutely at him, then he turned to Sophy, who, pale and quiet, was clinging to her lover's arm.

'The daughter of the man whose life you took shall be your judge,' said the millionaire. 'Sophy, is he to go free, or shall the law take its course?'

'Let him go—let him go,' murmured the girl. 'His death shall not be upon my soul. Let him go and repent.'

'I agree with Sophy,' said Alan Thorold. 'Let him go.'

'And repent,' finished Mr Beauchamp. 'Go, Jean Lestrange, and seek from an offended God the mercy you denied to me.'

Lestrange pulled himself together, and put on his hat with a would-be jaunty air. He tried to speak, but the words would not come, and he slunk out of the room like a beaten hound.

And that was the last they ever saw of Jean Lestrange.

CHAPTER XXIV

THE OTHER PART OF THE TRUTH

SHORTLY afterwards Mr Beauchamp returned to his lodgings as the Quiet Gentleman. Having been informed by Alan, on his way to the Moat House, that Lestrange was there with Sophy, he had taken off his false wig and beard to confound him; but now, in spite of the girl's protestations, he put them on again.

'No, child, no,' he said; 'I am as dead as Richard Marlow, and I shall not come to life again. What purpose would it serve? It would only cause a scandal, and the papers would be full of the story. I have no wish to be a nine days' wonder.'

'But, father, what will you do? Where will you live?'

'Oh,' said he, with a smile, 'I dare say you will carry out the terms of the will and let me have that two thousand a year. I shall take my departure from Mrs Marry's as the Quiet Gentleman, and appear in London as Herbert Beauchamp. You can join me there, and we can go on our travels.'

'But what about me?' cried poor Sophy, who had found her adopted father only to lose him again.

'You shall marry Alan.'

'But I want you to be at the wedding, father.'

'I shall be at the wedding, child, and I shall give you away.'

Alan looked at him in surprise.

'Then you will be recognized, and the whole story will come out.'

'So it would if you were married here,' answered Beauchamp composedly. 'But the wedding must take place in London. Can't you see, Alan, that Sophy must be married to you under her true name—Marie Lestrange?'

'Oh, must I?' cried the girl in dismay.

'I think so; otherwise I doubt if the marriage would hold good.'

'You are right,' said Alan, after a pause. 'We must do as you say. But I am sorry. I wanted to be married here, and I wanted Phelps to marry us.'

'There is no reason against that. Bring him to London and tell him the whole story.'

'But I will never be called Marie!'

'No, no; you will always be Sophy to us,' said her lover, kissing her. 'And we will go abroad with Mr Beauchamp for our honeymoon.'

'With my father!' cried Sophy, embracing the old man; 'my dear and only father!'

He sighed as he kissed her good-bye. He was devoted to his adopted daughter, and felt deeply parting with her even to so good a fellow as Alan Thorold. But he comforted himself with the thought that they could be much together abroad. And so, taking this cheerful view of the situation which had been created by the villainy of Lestrange, the ex-millionaire, as he may now be called, withdrew to his lodgings. It was there that Alan took leave of him, promising to call the next morning. A thankful heart was Herbert Beauchamp's that night. The sorrow of his life was over, the dark clouds had lifted, and now, under his own name, and with a good income, he could spend the rest of his days in peace. Lestrange had slunk back into the night whence he had emerged, leaving one part of the mystery cleared up by his confession. It still remained to discover who had been the murderer of the unlucky Warrender. And that came to light the very next day.

Alan did not wait until Beauchamp had departed for London to acquaint his revered tutor with all that had taken place. On the afternoon of the next day he proceeded to the Rectory, and told the whole story to the amazed and delighted Phelps. Nothing would serve but that he must go at once to Mrs Marry's and see with his own eyes the man who had been buried alive.

But Alan restrained the Rector's impetuosity by pointing out that Mrs Marry supposed Brown, the Quiet Gentleman, to be dumb. If by any chance she should hear him speak all secrecy would be at an end.

'Ay, ay,' assented Mr Phelps, 'true enough, Alan, true enough. Mrs Marry is a terrible gossip, and we must keep the matter quiet. I don't want my churchyard to be made the subject of another scandal. But I must see Marlow—I mean Beauchamp. God bless me! I shall never get his name right—may I be forgiven for swearing! Bring him here, Alan—bring him at once. I must see my old friend after all he has suffered.'

This Alan agreed to do, and an hour later appeared with Beauchamp and Sophy. Phelps received his old friend as one returned from the dead, and insisted upon having several points cleared up which he felt to be obscure.

'How about getting away, Marlow?' he asked. 'You had no clothes. How did you manage?'

'But I had clothes,' replied Beauchamp. 'We prepared all our plans very carefully. Joe took a suit of clothes to the hut, and brought money with him. Then I walked to the nearest town and caught the train for London. There, at a quiet hotel, a box in the name of Beauchamp was waiting for me. I slept there, and went on to Brighton, and took rooms in Lansdowne Place. I was comfortable, you may be sure. Joe came down to see me, and told me all the trouble which had ensued upon the death of Warrender.'

'Ah!' said Alan reflectively; 'we don't know who murdered him, and we never shall know. It could not have been Lestrange, and if it were the Quiet Gentleman, he has escaped us.'

'I wonder who that Quiet Gentleman was,' said Sophy.

'We all wonder that, my dear,' put in the Rector; 'but I fear we shall never know.'

'Well, what does it matter?' said Beauchamp, with more asperity than he usually showed. 'Whoever murdered Warrender gave him no more than he deserved. The man was a blackmailer, although the money he got out of me was obtained under the guise of friendship. He could have saved me years of agony had he only spoken the truth—ay, and honesty would have paid him better than dishonesty.'

'No doubt. But the man is dead; let us not speak evil of the dead,' said Phelps. 'But there is one question I wish to ask you, Marlow—Beauchamp, I mean. How was it that the page-boy swore Joe Brill was never out of the room on that night?'

'Joe drugged the lad's supper-ale, and slipped out when he was fast asleep. He did the same the next night when he had to take Warrender's body to the vault. That was my idea, for I was terrified lest I should be traced by the murder, and I wanted to get rid of the evidence of the crime. That tramp, confound him! spoilt it all.'

They were interrupted by the entrance of a servant, with the card of Inspector Blair. He was admitted at once, leaving a companion whom he had brought with him in the hall.

'You must excuse my intrusion, sir,' he said, addressing Mr Phelps; 'but I have already been to the Moat House and to the Abbey Farm in search of Mr Thorold.'

'Here I am,' said Alan. 'What is the matter, Blair? You have some news?'

'I have, sir. I have been to London, and I have brought back with me a gentleman whom Mr Beauchamp may know;' and he summoned the gentleman in the hall.

'Barkham!' exclaimed Mr Beauchamp; 'you here!'

Mr Barkham was a dapper dark man, not unlike Lestrange, with an expression which a schoolboy would have called 'sneaky'. He did not recognize Mr Beauchamp until that gentleman stripped off beard and wig. Then he hastened to acknowledge him.

'Mr Beauchamp,' he said, in a servile voice, 'I hope, as I warned you of Lestrange's plot, you will hold me blameless.'

'Why? What have you been doing?'

'I will tell you,' interposed Blair. 'This gentleman, as you see, bears a slight resemblance to Captain Jean Lestrange. He and the Captain were hard up in Jamaica, and seeing your portrait, Mr Beauchamp, in the papers, they thought they might have a chance of extorting money from you. In case Lestrange got into trouble here, he wished to have an alibi, so he left for England under another name, and Mr Barkham here came to Southampton in the *Negress* as Captain Lestrange.'

'Yes, yes,' said Barkham nervously; 'but I warned Mr Beauchamp that Lestrange was coming.'

'Quite so; but you did not tell him that Lestrange was masquerading as a dumb man in Heathton.'

'What!' cried Alan and Sophy in one breath. 'Was Lestrange the Quiet Gentleman?'

'Yes,' replied Blair, with triumph. 'He confessed as much to Barkham here. That was why he wore the grey wig and beard and assumed dumbness—oh, a most effective disguise; quite a different person he made of himself! He came down to keep a watch on you, Mr Beauchamp, in order to plunder you when he thought fit. Your unexpected death took him by surprise and upset his plans. Then Barkham, as Jean Lestrange, arrived at Southampton, and our Quiet Gentleman disappeared from his rooms here, to reappear from London in his own proper person, as Captain Jean Lestrange. No wonder that, with so carefully-prepared an alibi, we did not guess it was he who had been masquerading here.'

'Ha!' exclaimed Alan, 'and he stole the key of the vault?'

'Mr Barkham can explain that, and other things,' said Blair significantly.

'Wait!' cried Sophy, rising excitedly, 'I know—I know! It was Lestrange who murdered Dr Warrender!'

'Yes,' admitted Barkham, 'he did.'

There was a deep silence, which was broken at length by Beauchamp.

'The scoundrel!' he said hoarsely, 'and I let him escape!'

'What!' cried Blair, jumping up. 'You let him escape, Mr

Beauchamp—and when you knew that he killed Achille Lestrange?'

'It was my wish,' struck in Sophy; 'I thought he might repent.'

'Such scoundrels never repent, Miss Marlow,' said Blair; 'he has committed two murders, he may commit two more. But I'll hunt him down. He can't have gone far yet.'

'No, I don't suppose he has,' said Alan. 'He was here last night. By the way, how did he kill Dr Warrender, and why?'

'Barkham!'

The little man obeyed the voice of the inspector, and meekly repeated his story.

'Lestrange,' he said, 'did not believe that Mr Beauchamp was dead. He heard Mr Thorold say something to the Rector about the key of the vault—'

'God bless me!' cried Phelps, 'so you did, Alan.'

'Yes,' said the little man, nodding, 'then he stole the key. He sent for the doctor to ask him about the burial. The doctor came, but Lestrange was out.'

'Did Warrender recognize him?' asked Beauchamp abruptly.

'No, sir, he did not—at least, not then. Well, Lestrange waited and waited to enter the vault. When he went at last he found Warrender and another man taking the body out. He followed them to the hut on the heath; he tried to look in, and he made a slight noise. Warrender came out, and in the moonlight he recognized Lestrange, who turned to run away, but the doctor caught him and they struggled. Then Lestrange, knowing that he would be arrested for the murder of Achille in Jamaica, stabbed the doctor to the heart. Terrified at what he had done, he lost his head, and hurried up to me in London. At first he refused to tell me anything, but I made him drink,' said Barkham, with a leer, 'and so I got the whole truth out of him.'

'You scoundrel!' cried Thorold.

'Call me what you like,' was the sullen rejoinder. 'I wanted to get money out of Beauchamp myself, and wrote to warn him that I might have a claim on his gratitude. I was afraid to come here. I sent a letter to Lestrange asking him for money, and it got into this policeman's hands. He traced me, and brought me down here. That is all I know; but as Mr Beauchamp is alive, I ought to have something. After all, it was I who warned him.'

'You shall have fifty pounds,' said Beauchamp sternly. 'But you must leave England.'

'I don't know that I will let him,' said Blair. 'He should have communicated with the police.'

'I'll turn Queen's evidence if you like,' said Barkham. 'I don't care if I am arrested or not. I have had nothing but this fifty pounds—and you call that gratitude, Mr Beauchamp!'

'Let him go, Blair, if you can consistently with your duty,' said Beauchamp.

'I'll see,' was the reply. 'Hullo! what's that! Gramp, what do you mean by rushing into the room?'

It was indeed Cicero who stood, hot and puffing, at the door. He took no notice of Blair, but addressed himself to Alan.

'Mr Thorold,' he said, 'I have information if you will pay me well.'

'You shall be paid if what you have to say is worth it.'

'Then I must tell you that Lestrange was the Quiet Gentleman. You see this lancet? He stole it out of your desk, and gave it to me to say that I found it in the hut. This proves that he was the Quiet Gentleman, and I believe he murdered Dr Warrender.'

'You do, you scoundrel!' cried Mr Beauchamp. 'But you are too late—we know all!'

'Too late!' cried Gramp. 'Good heavens! to think of my getting nothing, and Clara Maria two thousand pounds!'

*

Little remains to be told. Lestrange was traced to Southampton, but there the trail was lost, much to the disappointment of Inspector Blair, who, although he duly received the two thousand pounds, never ceased to regret the man's escape. Alan paid him the reward gladly, for without him the mystery would never have been solved, and Mr Beauchamp's innocence would never have been established.

Sophy and Alan were married in the presence of the ex-millionaire and of Miss Vicky. After the ceremony, the former left England with Joe. He bought a small yacht, in which he and his faithful servant sail the waters of the Mediterranean. No one has ever guessed the truth.

Mrs Marry continues to lament the loss of the Quiet Gentleman, but she has always believed him to have been one and the same person. That Mr Beauchamp was the second representative of the part, she never dreamed. Mr Marlow is dead to the Heathton villagers, and to this day they talk of the mystery which surrounded the disappearance of his corpse—indeed, the vault has the reputation of being haunted.

Barkham left England with his fifty pounds, and Mrs Warrender returned to America with her two thousand and her many jewels. There she married a Canadian doctor, and vanished altogether. Cicero received a small sum, and now spends his time frantically hunting for Clara Maria, in the hope of extorting a share of her money; but Clara Maria is a clever woman, and he is not likely to come across her.

Sophy and Alan are supremely happy in their life at the Abbey Farm. They make frequent trips to the Continent, where they meet Mr Beauchamp.

Miss Vicky, too, is happy. She has Sophy's son and heir to care for, and what more can she want?

'The heir to millions,' says the old lady, 'and what a mystery there was about it all! To this day, I don't understand everything.'

'Few people do,' is Alan's reply. 'The millionaire's mystery will always remain a mystery in Heathton.'

THE END

THE GREENSTONE GOD
AND THE STOCKBROKER

As a rule, the average detective gets twice the credit he deserves. I am not talking of the novelist's miracle-monger, but of the flesh and blood reality who is liable to err, and who frequently proves such liability. You can take it as certain that a detective who sets down a clean run and no hitch as entirely due to his astucity, is young in years, and still younger in experience. Older men, who have been bamboozled a hundred times by the craft of criminality, recognize the influence of Chance to make or mar. There you have it! Nine times out of ten, Chance does more in clinching a case than all the dexterity and mother-wit of the man in charge. The exception must be engineered by an infallible apostle. Such a one is unknown to me—out of print.

This opinion, based rather on collective experience than on any one episode, can be substantiated by several incontrovertible facts. In this instance, one will suffice. Therefore, I take the Brixton case to illustrate Chance as a factor in human affairs. Had it not been for that Maori fetish—but such rather ends than begins the story. Therefore it were wise to dismiss it for the moment. Yet that piece of greenstone hanged—a person mentioned hereafter.

When Mr and Mrs Paul Vincent set up housekeeping at Ulster Lodge they were regarded as decided acquisitions to Brixton society. She, pretty and musical; he, smart in looks, moderately well off, and an excellent tennis-player. Their progenitors, his father and her mother (both since deceased), had lived a life of undoubted middle-class respectability. The halo thereof still environed their children, who were, in consequence of such inherited grace and their own individualisms, much sought after by genteel Brixtonians. Moreover, this popular couple were devoted to each other, and even after three years of marriage they posed still as lovers. This was as it should be, and by admiring friends and relations the Vincents were regarded as paragons of matrimonial perfection. Vincent was a stockbroker; therefore he passed most of his time in the City.

Judge, then, of the commotion, when pretty Mrs Vincent was discovered in the study, stabbed to the heart. So aimless a crime were scarce imaginable. She had many friends, no known enemies, yet she came to this tragic end. Closer examination revealed that the escritoire had been broken into, and Mr Vincent declared himself the poorer by two hundred pounds. Primarily, therefore, robbery was the sole object, but, by reason of Mrs Vincent's interference, the thief had been converted into a murderer.

So excellently had the assassin chosen his time, that such choice argued a close acquaintance with the domestic economy of Ulster Lodge. The husband was detained in town till midnight; the servants (cook and housemaid), on leave to attend wedding festivities, were absent till eleven o'clock. Mrs Vincent, therefore, was absolutely alone in the house for six hours, during which period the crime had been committed. The servants discovered the body of their unfortunate mistress and raised the alarm at once. Later on Vincent arrived to find his wife dead, his house in possession of the police, and the two servants in hysterics. For that night nothing could be done, but at dawn a move was made towards elucidating the mystery. At this point I come into the story.

Instructed at nine o'clock to take charge of the case, by ten I was on the spot noting details and collecting evidence. Beyond removal of the body nothing had been disturbed, and the study was in precisely the same condition as when the crime was discovered. I examined carefully the apartment, and afterwards interrogated the cook, the housemaid, and, lastly, the master of the house. The result gave me slight hope of securing the assassin.

The room (a fair-sized one, looking out on to a lawn between house and road) was furnished in cheap bachelor fashion; an old-fashioned desk placed at right angles to the window, a round table reaching nigh the sill, two armchairs, three of the ordinary cane-seated kind, and on the mantelpiece an arrangement of pipes, pistols, boxing-gloves, and foils. One of these latter was missing.

A single glimpse showed how terrible a struggle had taken place before the murderer had overpowered his victim. The tablecloth lay disorderly on the floor, two of the lighter chairs were overturned, and the desk, with several drawers open, was hacked about considerably. No key was in the door-lock which faced the escritoire, and the window-snick was fastened securely.

Further search resulted in the following discoveries:

1. A hatchet used for chopping wood (found near the desk).
2. A foil with the button broken off (lying under the table).
3. A greenstone idol (edged under the fender).

The cook (defiantly courageous by reason of brandy) declared that she had left the house at four o'clock on the previous day and had returned close on eleven. The back door (to her surprise) was open. With the housemaid she went to inform her mistress of this fact, and found the body lying midway between door and fireplace. At once she called in the police. Her master and mistress were a most attached couple, and (so far as she knew) they had no enemies.

Similar evidence was obtained from the housemaid with the additional information that the hatchet belonged to the wood-shed. The other rooms were undisturbed.

Poor young Vincent was so broken down by the tragedy that he could hardly answer my questions with calmness. Sympathizing with his natural grief, I interrogated him as delicately as was possible, and I am bound to admit that he replied with remarkable promptitude and clearness.

'What do you know of this unhappy affair?' I asked when we were alone in the drawing-room. He refused to stay in the study, as was surely natural under the circumstances.

'Absolutely nothing,' he replied. 'I went to the City yesterday at ten in the morning, and, as I had business to do, I wired my wife I would not return till midnight. She was full of health and spirits when I last saw her, but now—' Incapable of further speech he made a gesture of despair. Then, after a pause, he added, 'Have you any theory on the subject?'

'Judging from the wrecked condition of the desk I should say robbery—'

'Robbery?' he interrupted, changing colour. 'Yes, that was the motive. I had two hundred pounds locked up in the desk.'

'In gold or notes?'

'The latter. Four fifties. Bank of England.'

'You are sure they are missing?'

'Yes. The drawer in which they were placed is smashed to pieces.'

'Did anyone know you had placed two hundred pounds therein?'

'No! Save my wife, and yet—ah!' he said, breaking off abruptly, 'that is impossible.'

'What is impossible?'

'I will tell you when I hear your theory.'

'You got that notion out of novels of the shilling sort,' I answered drily. 'Every detective doesn't theorize on the instant. I haven't any particular theory that I know of. Whosoever committed this crime must have known your wife was alone in the house and that there was two hundred pounds locked up in that desk. Did you mention these two facts to anyone?'

Vincent pulled his moustache in some embarrassment. I guessed by the action that he had been indiscreet.

'I don't wish to get an innocent person into trouble,' he said at length, 'but I did mention it—to a man called Roy.'

'For what reason?'

'It is a bit of a story. I lost two hundred to a friend at cards and drew four fifties to pay him. He went out of town, so I locked up the money in my desk for safety. Last night Roy came to me at the club, much agitated, and asked me to loan him a hundred. Said it meant ruin else. I offered him a cheque, but he wanted cash. I then told him I had left two hundred at home, so at the moment could not lay my hand on it. He asked if he could not go to Brixton for it, but I said the house was empty, and—'

'But it wasn't empty,' I interrupted.

'I believed it would be! I knew the servants were going to that wedding, and I thought my wife, instead of spending a lonely evening, would call on some friend.'

'Well, and after you told Roy that the house was empty?'

'He went away, looking awfully cut up, and swore he must have the money at any price. But it is quite impossible he could have anything to do with this.'

'I don't know. You told him where the money was and that the house was unprotected, as you thought. What was more probable than that he should have come down with the intention of stealing the money? If so, what follows? Entering by the back door, he takes the hatchet from the wood-shed to open the desk. Your wife, hearing a noise, discovers him in the study. In a state of frenzy, he snatches a foil from the mantelpiece and kills her, then decamps with the money. There is your theory, and a mighty bad one—for Roy.'

'You don't intend to arrest him?' asked Vincent quickly.

'Not on insufficient evidence! If he committed the crime and stole the money it is certain that, sooner or later, he will change the notes. Now, if I had the numbers—'

'Here are the numbers,' said Vincent, producing his pocket-book. 'I always take the numbers of such large notes. But surely,' he added as I copied them down—'surely you don't think Roy guilty?'

'I don't know. I should like to know his movements on that night.'

'I cannot tell you. He saw me at the Chestnut Club about seven o'clock and left immediately afterwards. I kept my business appointment, went to Alhambra, and then returned home.'

'Give me Roy's address and describe his personal appearance.'

'He is a medical student, and lodges at Gower Street. Tall, fair-haired—a good-looking young fellow.'

'And his dress last night?'

'He wore evening dress concealed by a fawn-coloured overcoat.'

I duly noted these particulars, and I was about to take my leave, when I recollected the greenstone idol. It was so strange an object to find in prosaic Brixton that I could not help thinking it must have come there by accident.

'By the way, Mr Vincent,' said I, producing the monstrosity, 'is this greenstone god your property?'

'I never saw it before,' replied he, taking it in his hand. 'Is it—ah!' he added, dropping the idol, 'there is blood on it!'

''Tis the blood of your wife, sir! If it does not belong to you, it does to the murderer. From the position in which this was found I fancy it slipped out of his breast-pocket as he stood over his victim. As you see, it is stained with blood. He must have lost his presence of mind, else he would not have left behind so damning a piece of evidence. This idol, sir, will hang the assassin of Mrs Vincent!'

'I hope so, but unless you are sure of Roy, do not mar his life by accusing him of this crime.'

'I certainly should not arrest him without sufficient proof,' I answered promptly, and so took my departure.

Vincent showed up very well in this preliminary conversation. Much as he desired to punish the criminal, yet he was unwilling to subject Roy to possibly unfounded suspicions. Had I not forced the club episode out of him I doubt whether he would have told it. As it was, the information gave me the necessary clue. Roy alone knew that the notes were in the escritoire, and imagined (owing to the mistake of Vincent) that the house was empty. Determined to have the money at any price (his own words), he intended but robbery, till the unexpected appearance of Mrs Vincent merged the lesser in the greater crime.

My first step was to advise the Bank that four fifty-pound notes, numbered so and so, were stolen, and that the thief or his deputy would probably change them within a reasonable period. I did not say a word about the crime, and kept all special details out of the newspapers; for as the murderer would probably read up the reports so as to shape his course by the action of the police, I judged it wiser that he should know as little as possible. Those minute press notices do more harm than good. They gratify the morbid appetite of the public, and put the criminal on his guard. Thereby the police work in the dark, but he—thanks to the posting up of special reporters—knows the doings of the law, and baffles it accordingly.

The greenstone idol worried me considerably. I wanted to know how it had got into the study of Ulster Lodge. When I knew that, I could nail my man. But there was considerable difficulty to overcome before such knowledge was available. Now a curiosity of this kind is not a common object in this country. A man who owns one must have come from New Zealand or have obtained it from a New Zealand friend. He could not have picked it up in London. If he did, he would not carry it constantly about with him. It was therefore my idea that the murderer had received the idol from a friend on the day of the crime. That friend, to possess such an idol, must have been in communication with New Zealand. The chain of thought is somewhat complicated, but it began with curiosity about the idol, and ended in my looking up the list of steamers going to the Antipodes. Then I carried out a little design which need not be mentioned at this moment. In due time it will fit in with the hanging of Mrs Vincent's assassin. Meanwhile, I followed up the clue of the banknotes, and left the greenstone idol to evolve its own destiny. Thus I had two strings to my bow.

The crime was committed on the twentieth of June, and on the twenty-third two fifty-pound notes, with numbers corresponding to those stolen, were paid into the Bank of England. I was astonished at the little care exercised by the criminal in concealing his crime, but still more so when I learned that the money had been banked by a very respectable solicitor. Furnished with the address, I called on this gentleman. Mr Maudsley received me politely, and he had no hesitation in telling me how the notes had come into his possession. I did not state my primary reason for the inquiry.

'I hope there is no trouble about these notes,' said he when I explained my errand. 'I have had sufficient already.'

'Indeed, Mr Maudsley, and in what way?'

For answer he touched the bell, and when it was answered, 'Ask Mr Ford to step this way,' he said. Then turning to me, 'I must reveal what I had hoped to keep secret, but I trust the revelation will remain with yourself.'

'That is as I may decide after hearing it. I am a detective, Mr Maudsley, and you may be sure, I do not make these inquiries out of idle curiosity.'

Before he could reply, a slender, weak-looking young man, nervously excited, entered the room. This was Mr Ford, and he looked from me to Maudsley with some apprehension.

'This gentleman,' said his employer, not unkindly, 'comes from Scotland Yard about the money you paid me two days ago.'

'It is all right, I hope?' stammered Ford, turning red and pale and red again.

'Where did you get the money?' I asked, parrying this question.

'From my sister.'

I started when I heard this answer, and with good reason. My inquiries about Roy had revealed that he was in love with a hospital nurse whose name was Clara Ford. Without doubt she had obtained the notes from Roy after he had stolen them from Ulster Lodge. But why the necessity of the robbery?

'Why did you get a hundred pounds from your sister?' I asked Ford.

He did not answer, but looked appealingly at Maudsley. That gentleman interposed.

'We must make a clean breast of it, Ford,' he said with a sigh. 'If you have committed a second crime to conceal the first, I cannot help you. This time matters are not at my discretion.'

'I have committed no crime,' said Ford desperately, turning to me. 'Sir, I may as well admit that I embezzled one hundred pounds from Mr Maudsley to pay a gambling debt. He kindly and most generously consented to overlook the delinquency if I replaced the money. Not having it myself I asked my sister. She, a poor hospital nurse, had not the amount. Yet, as non-payment meant ruin to me, she asked a Mr Julian Roy to help her. He at once agreed to do so, and gave her two fifty-pound notes. She handed them to me, and I gave them to Mr Maudsley who paid them into the bank.'

This, then, was the reason of Roy's remark. He did not refer to his own ruin, but to that of Ford. To save this unhappy man, and for love of the sister, he had committed the crime. I did not need to see Clara Ford, but at once made up my mind to arrest Roy. The case was perfectly clear, and I was fully justified in taking this course. Meanwhile I made Maudsley and his clerk promise silence, as I did not wish Roy to be put on his guard by Miss Ford, through her brother.

'Gentlemen,' I said, after a few moments' pause, 'I cannot at present explain my reasons for asking these questions, as it would take too long and I have no time to lose. Keep silent about this interview till tomorrow, and by that time you shall know all.'

'Has Ford got into fresh trouble?' asked Maudsley anxiously.

'No, but someone else has.'

'My sister,' began Ford faintly, when I interrupted him at once.

'Your sister is all right, Mr Ford. Pray trust in my discretion. No harm shall come to her or to you, if I can help it — but, above all, be silent.'

This they readily promised, and I returned to Scotland Yard, quite satisfied that Roy would get no warning. The evidence was so clear that I could not doubt the guilt of Roy. Else how had he come in possession of the notes? Already there was sufficient proof to hang him, yet I hoped to clinch the certainty by proving his ownership of the greenstone idol. It did not belong to Vincent, or to his dead wife, yet someone must have brought it into the study. Why not Roy, who, to all appearances, had committed the crime, the more so as the image was splashed with the victim's blood? There was no difficulty in obtaining a warrant, and with this I went off to Gower Street.

Roy loudly protested his innocence. He denied all knowledge of the crime and of the idol. I expected the denial, but I was astonished at the defence he put forth. It was very ingenious, but so manifestly absurd that it did not shake my belief in his guilt. I let him talk himself out—which perhaps was wrong—but he would not be silent, and then I took him off in a cab.

'I swear I did not commit the crime,' he said passionately. 'No one was more astonished than I at the news of Mrs Vincent's death.'

'Yet you were at Ulster Lodge on the night in question?'

'I admit it,' he replied frankly. 'Were I guilty I would not do so. But I was there at the request of Vincent.'

'I must remind you that all you say now will be used in evidence against you.'

'I don't care! I must defend myself. I asked Vincent for a hundred pounds, and—'

'Of course you did, to give to Miss Ford.'

'How do you know that?' he asked sharply.

'From her brother, through Maudsley. He paid the notes

supplied by you into the bank. If you wanted to conceal your crime you should not have been so reckless.'

'I have committed no crime,' retorted Roy fiercely. 'I obtained the money from Vincent, at the request of Miss Ford, to save her brother from being convicted for embezzlement.'

'Vincent denies that he gave you the money!'

'Then he lies. I asked him at the Chestnut Club for one hundred pounds. He had not that much on him, but said that two hundred were in his desk at home. As it was imperative that I should have the money on the night, I asked him to let me go down for it.'

'And he refused!'

'He did not. He consented, and gave me a note to Mrs Vincent, instructing her to hand me over a hundred pounds. I went to Brixton, got the money in two fifties, and gave them to Miss Ford. When I left Ulster Lodge, between eight and nine, Mrs Vincent was in perfect health, and quite happy.'

'An ingenious defence,' said I doubtfully, 'but Vincent absolutely denies that he gave you the money.'

Roy stared hard at me to see if I were joking. Evidently the attitude of Vincent puzzled him greatly.

'That is ridiculous,' said he quietly. 'He wrote a note to his wife instructing her to hand me the money.'

'Where is that note?'

'I gave it to Mrs Vincent.'

'It cannot be found,' I answered. 'If such a note were in her possession it would now be in mine.'

'Don't you believe me?'

'How can I against the evidence of those notes and the denial of Vincent?'

'But he surely does not deny that he gave me the money?'

'He does.'

'He must be mad,' said Roy in dismay. 'One of my best friends, and to tell so great a falsehood. Why, if—'

'You had better be silent,' I said, weary of this foolish talk.

'If what you say is true, Vincent will exonerate you from complicity in the crime. If things occurred as you say, there is no sense in his denial.'

This latter remark was made to stop the torrent of his speech. It was not my business to listen to incriminating declarations, or to ingenious defences. All that sort of thing is for judge and jury; therefore I ended the conversation as above, and marched off my prisoner. Whether the birds of the air carry news I do not know, but they must have been busy on this occasion, for next morning every newspaper in London was congratulating me on my clever capture of the supposed murderer. Some detectives would have been gratified by this public laudation—I was not. Roy's passionate protestations of innocence made me feel uneasy, and I doubted whether, after all, I had the right man under lock and key. Yet the evidence was strong against him. He admitted having been with Mrs Vincent on the fatal night; he admitted possession of two fifty-pound notes. His only defence was the letter of the stockbroker, and this was missing—if, indeed, it had ever been written.

*

Vincent was terribly upset by the arrest of Roy. He liked the young man and he had believed in his innocence so far as was possible. But in the face of such strong evidence, he was forced to believe him guilty. Yet he blamed himself severely that he had not lent the money and so averted the catastrophe.

'I had no idea that the matter was of such moment,' he said to me, 'else I would have gone down to Brixton myself and have given him the money. Then his frenzy would have spared my wife and himself a death on the scaffold.'

'What do you think of his defence?'

'It is wholly untrue. I did not write a note, nor did I tell him to go to Brixton. Why should I, when I fully believed no one was in the house?'

'It was a pity you did not go home, Mr Vincent, instead of to the Alhambra.'

'It was a mistake,' he assented, 'but I had no idea Roy would attempt the robbery. Besides, I was under engagement to go to the theatre with my friend Dr Monson.'

'Do you think that idol belongs to Roy?'

'I can't say. I never saw it in his possession. Why?'

'Because I firmly believe that if Roy had not the idol in his pocket on that fatal night he is innocent. Oh, you look astonished, but the man who murdered your wife owns that idol.'

The morning after this conversation a lady called at Scotland Yard and asked to see me concerning the Brixton case. Fortunately, I was then in the neighbourhood, and, guessing who she was, I afforded her the interview she sought. When all left the room she raised her veil, and I saw before me a noble-looking woman, somewhat resembling Mr Maudsley's clerk. Yet, by some contradiction of nature, her face was the more virile of the two.

'You are Miss Ford,' I said, guessing her identity.

'I am Clara Ford,' she answered quietly. 'I have come to see you about Mr Roy.'

'I am afraid nothing can be done to save him.'

'Something must be done,' she said passionately. 'We are engaged to be married, and all a woman can do to save her lover I will do. Do you believe him to be guilty?'

'In the face of such evidence, Miss Ford—'

'I don't care what evidence is against him,' she retorted. 'He is as innocent of the crime as I am. Do you think that a man fresh from the committal of a crime would place the money won by that crime in the hands of the woman he professes to love? I tell you he is innocent.'

'Mr Vincent doesn't think so.'

'Mr Vincent!' said Miss Ford, with scornful emphasis. 'Oh, yes! I quite believe *he* would think Julian guilty.'

'Surely not if it were possible to think otherwise! He is, or rather was, a staunch friend to Mr Roy.'

'So staunch that he tried to break off the match between us. Listen to me, sir. I have told no one before, but I tell you now. Mr Vincent is a villain. He pretended to be the friend of Julian, and yet he dared to make proposals to me—dishonourable proposals, for which I could have struck him. He, a married man, a pretended friend, wished me to leave Julian and fly with him.'

'Surely you are mistaken, Miss Ford. Mr Vincent was most devoted to his wife.'

'He did not care at all for his wife,' she replied steadily. 'He was in love with me. To save Julian annoyance I did not tell him the insults offered to me by Mr Vincent. Now that Julian is in trouble by an unfortunate mistake Mr Vincent is delighted.'

'It is impossible. I assure you Vincent is very sorry to—'

'You do not believe me,' she said, interrupting. 'Very well, I shall give you proof of the truth. Come to my brother's rooms in Bloomsbury. I shall send for Mr Vincent, and if you are concealed you shall hear from his own lips how glad he is that my lover and his wife are removed from the path of his dishonourable passion.'

'I will come, Miss Ford, but I think you are mistaken in Vincent.'

'You shall see,' she replied coldly. Then, with a sudden change of tone, 'Is there no way of saving Julian? I am sure that he is innocent. Appearances are against him, but it was not he who committed the crime. Is there no way?'

Moved by her earnest appeal, I produced the greenstone idol, and told her all I had done in connection with it. She listened eagerly, and readily grasped at the hope thus held out to her of saving Roy. When in possession of all the facts she considered in silence for some two minutes. At the end of that time she drew down her veil and prepared to take her departure.

'Come to my brother's rooms in Alfred Place, near Tottenham Court Road,' said she, holding out her hand. 'I promise you that there you shall see Mr Vincent in his true character. Good-bye till Monday at three o'clock.'

From the colour in her face and the bright light in her eye, I guessed that she had some scheme in her head for the saving of Roy. I think myself clever, but after that interview at Alfred Place I declare I am but a fool compared to this woman. She put two and two together, ferreted out unguessed-of evidence, and finally produced the most wonderful result. When she left me at this moment the greenstone idol was in her pocket. With that she hoped to prove the innocence of her lover and the guilt of another person. It was the cleverest thing I ever saw in my life.

The inquest on the body of Mrs Vincent resulted in a verdict of wilful murder against some person or persons unknown. Then she was buried, and all London waited for the trial of Roy. He was brought up, charged with the crime, reserved his defence, and in due course he was committed for trial. Meantime I called on Miss Ford at the appointed time, and found her alone.

'Mr Vincent will be here shortly,' she said calmly. 'I see Julian is committed for trial.'

'And he has reserved his defence.'

'I shall defend him' said she with a strange look in her face. 'I am not afraid for him now. He saved my unhappy brother. I shall save him.'

'Have you discovered anything?'

'I have discovered a good deal. Hush! That is Mr Vincent,' she added, as a cab drew up to the door. 'Hide yourself behind this curtain and do not appear until I give you the signal.'

Wondering what she was about to do, I concealed myself as directed. The next moment Vincent was in the room, and then ensued one of the strangest of scenes. She received him coldly, and motioned him to a seat. Vincent was nervous, but she might have been of stone, so little emotion did she display.

'I have sent for you, Mr Vincent,' she said, 'to ask for your help in releasing Julian.'

'How can I help you?' he answered in amazement—'willingly would I do so, but it is out of my power.'

'I don't think it is!'

'I assure you, Clara,' he began eagerly, when she cut him short.

'Yes, call me Clara! Say that you love me! Lie, like all men, and yet refuse to do what I wish.'

'I am not going to help Julian to marry you,' declared he sullenly. 'You know that I love you—I love you dearly, I wish to marry you—'

'Is not that declaration rather soon after the death of your wife?'

'My wife is gone, poor soul. Let her rest.'

'Yet you loved her?'

'I never loved her,' he said, rising to his feet. 'I love you! From the first moment I saw you I loved you. My wife is dead! Julian Roy is in prison on a charge of murdering her. With these obstacles removed there is no reason why we should not marry.'

'If I marry you,' she said slowly, 'will you help Julian to refute this charge?'

'I cannot! The evidence is too strong against him!'

'You know that he is innocent, Mr Vincent.'

'I do not! I believe that he murdered my wife.'

'You believe that he murdered your wife,' she reiterated, coming a step nearer and holding out the greenstone idol—'do you believe that he dropped this in the study when his hand struck the fatal blow?'

'I don't know!' he said, coolly glancing at the idol. 'I never saw it before.'

'Think again, Mr Vincent—think again. Who was it that went to the Alhambra at eight o'clock with Dr Monson and met there the captain of a New Zealand steamer with whom he was acquainted?'

'It was I,' said Vincent defiantly, 'and what of that?'

'This!' she said in a loud voice. 'This captain gave you the greenstone idol at the Alhambra, and you placed it in your breast-pocket. Shortly afterwards you followed to Brixton the man whose death you had plotted. You repaired to your house, killed your unhappy wife who received you in all innocence, took the balance of the money, hacked the desk, and then dropped by accident this idol which convicts you of the crime.'

During this speech she advanced step by step towards the wretched man, who, pale and anguished, retreated before her fury. He came right to my hiding-place, and almost fell into my arms. I had heard enough to convince me of his guilt, and the next moment I was struggling with him.

'It is a lie! a lie!' he said hoarsely, trying to escape.

'It is true!' said I, pinning him down. 'From my soul I believe you to be guilty.'

During the fight his pocket-book fell on the floor and the papers therein were scattered. Miss Ford picked up one spotted with blood.

'The proof!' she said, holding it before us. 'The proof that Julian spoke the truth. There is the letter written by you which authorized your unhappy wife to give him one hundred pounds.'

Vincent saw that all was against him and gave in without further struggles, like the craven he was.

'Fate is too strong for me,' he said, when I snapped the handcuffs on his wrists. 'I admit the crime. It was for love of you that I did it. I hated my wife who was a drag on me, and I hated Roy who loved you. In one sweep I thought to rid myself of both. His application for that money put the chance into my hand. I went to Brixton, I found that my wife had given the money as directed, and then I killed her with the foil snatched from the wall. I smashed the desk and overturned the chair, to favour the idea of the robbery, and then I left the house. Driving to a higher station than Brixton, I caught a train and was speedily back at the Alhambra. Monson never suspected my absence, thinking I was in a different corner of the house.

I had thus an alibi ready. Had it not been for that letter, which I was fool enough to keep, and that infernal idol that dropped out of my pocket, I should have hanged Roy and married you. As it turns out, the idol has betrayed me. And now, sir,' he added, turning to me, 'you had better take me to gaol.'

I did so there and then. After the legal formalities were gone through, Julian Roy was released and ultimately married Miss Ford. Vincent was hanged, as well deserved to be, for so cowardly a crime. My reward was the greenstone god, which I keep as a memento of a very curious case. Some weeks later Miss Ford told me the way in which she had laid the trap.

'When you revealed your suspicions about the idol,' she said, 'I was convinced that Vincent had something to do with the crime. You mentioned Dr Monson as having been with him at the Alhambra. He is one of the doctors at the hospital in which I am employed. I asked him about the idol and showed it to him. He remembered it being given to Vincent by the captain of the *Kaitangata*. The curious look of the thing had impressed itself on his memory. On hearing this I went to the docks and I saw the captain. He recognized the idol and remembered giving it to Vincent. From what you told me I guessed the way in which the plot had been carried out, so I spoke to Vincent as you heard. Most of it was guesswork, and only when I saw that letter was I absolutely sure of his guilt. It was due to the greenstone god.'

So I think, but to Chance also. But for the accident of the idol dropping out of Vincent's pocket, Roy would have been hanged for a crime of which he was innocent. Therefore do I say that in nine cases out of ten Chance does more to clinch a case than all the dexterity of the man in charge.

THE END

THE RAINBOW CAMELLIA

COUNTRY solicitors have fewer opportunities than their urban brethren of handling exceptional cases. The friction of metropolitan life develops numerous strange episodes, which are of rarer occurrence in provincial centres. Human nature is no doubt the same in country as in town; but the lack of a concentrated population, by demanding less ingenuity on the part of the criminal, reduces the level of crime. Moreover bucolic wits are not so keen as those sharpened by the necessities of London life. Agrarian wrong-doers are usually commonplace rogues, who sin in a crude fashion unworthy of notice. Crime, which in the capital is a fine art, is in the country commonly the result of a childish outburst of temper. These remarks apply peculiarly to the inhabitants of inland market towns, and to the rural population of their intervening pasture-lands.

Yet at times a case not easily to be paralleled, even in the metropolis, comes under the notice of a country solicitor. Such a one is that of the Rainbow Camellia, which is, to my mind, unique in the annals of crime. It was simply a case of theft, but sufficiently noticeable for the skilful way in which it was planned and executed. My first intimation of the affair came from my wife, who one morning entered the breakfast-room with a face expressive of consternation.

'Fred,' said she, in an awestruck tone, 'do you remember Eliza Drupp the housemaid who left six months ago?'

'Was that the red-haired minx who smashed our best dinner-service, and who carried a bottle of diamond cement in her pocket to mend breakages?'

'Yes, she has been arrested.'

'I'm not surprised. Whose dinner-service is it this time?'

'Don't jest, Fred. I am very sorry for the poor girl, though

201

she has been stealing. Cook told me all about it. She is so excited.'

'Who is excited, cook or Eliza?'

'Cook, of course.'

'Then the dinner won't be fit to eat. I wish cook would gossip less, and attend more to her stewing and frying. Give me my breakfast, Nell; I must be off early this morning. Well,' I added, as my wife poured out the coffee, 'and what has Eliza Drupp been stealing?'

'The rainbow camellia.'

'What, the whole plant?'

'No, only a bud. She went into the Gardens yesterday and picked it.'

'Audacious creature, she'll get six months for that. Old Bendel is on the Bench, and as he is a prominent member of the Horticultural Society, Eliza need expect no mercy.'

'I don't know what possessed her to do such a thing,' said Nell reflectively; 'and the worst of it is, that George Beanfield gave information about the theft.'

'Who is George Beanfield, and why shouldn't he give information?'

'Because he kept company with her. It is a piece of spite on his part to punish Eliza for taking up with the greengrocer.'

'I congratulate you on your knowledge of kitchen gossip, Nell. But you have not answered my question. Who is George Beanfield?'

'A gardener in the service of the Horticultural Society. I suppose he will be the principal witness against poor Eliza. How can a man be so mean!'

'A man scorned is as dangerous as a woman scorned my dear. Eliza should not have 'walked out' with the greengrocer. By the way, was George the man who used to hide in the coal-cellar?'

'No, that was a soldier.'

'Oh, then he was the Gargantua who devoured all the cold meat.'

'Don't talk nonsense, Fred. Go to your office, and if you hear anything of the case, tell me when you come home. I am so sorry for poor Eliza.'

This was very charitable on the part of Nell. So far as I could remember Eliza Drupp had been a sore trial, and I had frequently heard my wife express a hope that the Drupp sins would come home to the Drupp sinner. Now that they had come in the most satisfactory manner, she regretted the accomplishment of her wishes, and pitied the recreant Eliza. I did not. It was impossible to pity a girl who had cost me over twenty pounds in breakages.

When I reached my office, I received a message from Eliza, requesting me to step round to her cell and discuss the matter. As fish did not come to my net in sufficient quantities to make me despise even such small fry as Eliza, I accepted the invitation, and speedily found myself in the presence of my former housemaid. She was to be brought before Bendel that very morning, so there was no time to be lost in learning what defence she proposed to make.

To judge of the heinousness of Eliza's offence, it is necessary to state that the Horticultural Society of Foxton is the sole owner of the famous rainbow camellia. That unique plant had been brought from China many years ago by a vagrant Foxtonian, and it was the only one in existence on this side of the world. The Foxton Society prided itself on the possession of this rarity, the more so as such possession excited the envy of all rival societies. Of these many had attempted to beg, borrow, buy or steal slips of the plant in order to raise rainbow camellias on their own account; but hitherto not one had secured even a single bud. It was reserved for Eliza to commit that crime.

The blossom was streaked with the seven colours of the rainbow—hence its name—and as a further priceless qualification it emitted a distinct odour. Now as, with this exception, a scented camellia is absolutely unknown, it was only natural that the Foxton horticulturists should set a high value on their ownership. I thought myself that their enthusiasm was exaggerated, as the prosperity of Foxton did not entirely depend on the possession of that striped and scented flower; but then I am not a flower-fancier, and I cannot appreciate the passions of horticulturists. Those of Foxton were quite offensive in their pride. If Eliza Drupp had stolen the Crown Jewels the theft would have been a mere venial transgression: but that she should cull a single bud of the rainbow camellia placed her beyond the pale of ordinary sinners.

Eliza was tearful but voluble. She had been born within sound of Bow Bells, and talked with a strong cockney accent, which became more marked with increasing agitation. How this child of the London pavement had drifted to Foxton I do not know, but she had served as housemaid in various houses for the last four years, and was accustomed when out of a situation, which happened frequently on account of her destructive propensities, to visit her parents at Hackney. Her town graces and brazen good looks—our cook said they were brazen—attracted many admiring swains. The vengeful George was one of these, but Eliza had jilted him in favour of the more opulent greengrocer. Nemesis in the person of the deserted gardener was now punishing her for such perfidy.

''Ow 'e's treated me shaimful,' said the tearful Eliza; 'jest 'cause I wouldn't taike 'im 'e shows me up loike this.'

'If you play with fire, Eliza, you burn your fingers as a natural consequence. But this is not the point. Have you any defence to this charge?'

'I should soigh so, sir. 'Tain't trew es I stole thet measly kemmelliar. Whoy, it was my own.'

'Come now, that's nonsense. The Foxton rainbow camellia is the only one of its kind in England.'

''Tain't the only one in the world anyhow, sir,' retorted Eliza, with some heat. 'I hev a rinebow kemmelliar et 'Ackney. If you don't b'li've me jest send up to my father an' see.'

'Do you mean to say that you possess a plant of the same species?' I asked, rather astonished at this information.

"Course I do, sir. My brother 'e's a steward 'e is; 'e goes to Chiner on the Three Star Loine, sir. 'E browght it to me fower years ago from furren parts 'e did.'

'And the flower you wore was off your own bush?'

'Yuss. I kim 'ere yesterdaiy from 'Ackney, an' I browght it with me jest to see if moine was loike this 'un 'ere.'

'Did you wear it when you entered the Gardens?'

'No, sir, I 'ed it in a paiper beg, an' when I was in the green'ouse I takes it hout. When I sawr it wure the saime, I pins it in moy dress. Then that bloomin' gonoph collared me. D'ye see, sir?'

'I see, but how is it that a blossom is missing from the tree?'

'I don'no, sir. 'Tworn't me as took it, sir. You jist telergrarf to moy father at 'Ackney an' arsk 'im to bring down moy kemmelliar, sir.'

'Yes, I'll do that, but as he cannot be down in time for the case today, I'll ask for a remand, so that I may ascertain the truth of your story.'

'Thenk 'ee, sir. Em I to staiy 'ere, sir?'

'I hope not, I will be security for your bail myself.'

'Thet is 'ensome on yer, sir. An' if yer sees thet there George Beanfield, sir, jist tell 'im as 'ow I'll scretch 'is eyes out of 'is 'ed.'

There was no necessity for me to deliver this agreeable message. She did so herself when brought before the magistrate. Beanfield seemed to appreciate the situation, and to congratulate himself that Eliza was restrained from violence by two stout policemen. As long as possible he remained modestly in the background, and it was with manifest reluctance that he came forward when called upon to enter the witness-box. The lady in the dock glared at him with a mixture of scorn and rage, and again proclaimed her determination to 'scretch 'is eyes out'. When ordered to be silent she relapsed into tears and said she was being 'put upon'. I had heard her make this remark before when gently corrected for breaking three plates in succession.

The court was filled with infuriated members of the Horticultural Society, who wished Eliza to be forthwith hanged and quartered. It was commonly reported that my client had not only picked the flower but had also stolen a slip of the plant, which she designed to sell to a rival society. Believing that Eliza thus intended to rob Foxton of the glory of solely possessing the rainbow camellia, the horticulturists thought no punishment too severe for so abandoned a creature. I applied for a remand, which old Bendel (who was a rabid member of the society) was disposed to refuse. I pointed out that, in the interests of justice, the prisoner should be granted sufficient time to communicate with her friends, and prove herself innocent of the charge. Bendel did not believe she had a defence, and said as much, but after considerable argument I managed to obtain an adjournment for three days. In the matter of bail I was unsuccessful, as the magistrate declined to allow Eliza to be at large until the matter had been legally threshed out. He was supported in this decision by his angered confreres, who had already judged and condemned the delinquent housemaid. The ultimate outcome of my application was the removal of Eliza to her former captivity.

When instructing the parental Drupp by letter as to the misfortune which had befallen his daughter, I suggested that, to clear her character, he should forthwith bring with him to Foxton the Hackney camellia. As to the existence of this plant I had my doubts, expecting that Eliza had mistaken the variegated scentless camellia for the unique plant of Foxton. But the bush brought by Drupp proved to be of the same genus. It was streaked with seven colours, it was scented, and, as a proof that Eliza was innocent, it still bore the stem whence the bud, alleged to have been stolen from the Foxton greenhouse, had been reft. Her story thus proved to be true, but I thought it strange that, at such a juncture, a blossom should also be missing from our local plant. The coincidence was peculiar, the inference doubtful.

'Moy daughter growed this 'ere,' explained Drupp, who was quite as cockney in speech as Eliza; 'et was browght from Chiner by moy son Sam, es is a steward on the *Mendeloy*. Ses Lizer t' me t'other doy, "Oi'll jest tike a flower t' Foxton an' see if thet kemmelliar es th' saime es moine." Which she did, an' now thi've put 'er in quod. Oi 'opes, sir, es 'ow thi'll let 'er orf.'

With so clear a defence I thought it extremely probable that they would let her off; but as old Bendel was on the Bench I knew the fight would be a tough one. Had Eliza worn the bud when she entered the Gardens, her innocence would have been proved beyond all doubt. Still as the matter stood I had every hope of clearing her character.

When Eliza was again placed in the dock the court was even more crowded than on the former occasion. A rumour had originated—I know not how—that a plant similar to that owned by the society would be put in evidence by the defence. As in duty bound no horticulturist believed this fable. As well say there were two Queens of England, as two rainbow camellias. The Foxton plant was displayed in all its glory, and, lost in admiration, the onlookers exclaimed that there was none like unto it. This biblical exclamation is suitable to the scene, for the plant might have been the golden image of Nebuchadnezzar, so abjectly did its worshippers grovel before it. The mere sight of the missing bud roused them to wrathful denunciations against its ravisher.

When brought before the magistrate, Eliza wept loudly; but on the appearance of George in the witness-box, she recovered her spirits, and called him names. Then she again relapsed into tears, and sniffed provokingly during the subsequent proceedings.

Beanfield deposed that Eliza was not wearing the flower when she entered the Gardens, but he admitted that she had carried a paper bag, which he feebly conjectured to contain biscuits. He had exchanged no words with her, as they were not on friendly terms, but he declared that she had made a face at him, and had derisively put out her tongue. When he saw her again, the bud—produced in court—was fastened in the bosom of her dress. He at once inspected the rainbow camellia, and found a blossom missing, upon which evidence he had given Eliza in charge for theft.

Another gardener proved that no buds were wanting when he saw the plant half an hour before Eliza's visit. He was followed by the President of the Horticultural Society, who stated that outside China, to which the species was indigenous, there was no rainbow camellia in existence. The bud produced in court could only have been taken from the Foxton green-house. His assertion of the uniqueness of the plant was received with great applause by his fellow-horticulturists.

Their jaws dropped when old Drupp brought forward Eliza's specimen. At first they insisted that the petals were painted, but when by direction of old Bendel the plant was handed round, and handled, and smelt, and thoroughly examined, they were reluctantly compelled to admit that it was a genuine rainbow camellia. The admission almost drew tears from their eyes, and they mourned Ichabod! Ichabod! The two plants placed on either side of the magistrate appeared to closely resemble one another, save that Eliza's was the smaller of the two. I forgot to mention that the Hackney plant had eight buds while the Foxton plant showed twelve. As a blossom had been plucked from each, these were respectively reduced to seven and eleven.

Drupp's evidence in conjunction with the production of the plant turned the scale in favour of Eliza. It was all plain sailing when he opened his mouth. The plant belonged to his daughter; it had been brought from China by her brother the steward; under her care it had grown and flowered; and she had plucked a bud to compare with the blooms of the Foxton bush. No link was wanting in the chain of evidence to prove the innocence of the prisoner, and Bendel was reluctantly compelled to discharge her without a stain on her character. I say reluctantly, because he could not forgive Eliza for owning a duplicate of the Foxton fetish, and, taking every possible advantage, he delivered a smart lecture to its iniquitous possessor. There was no applause when Eliza left the dock.

Restored to freedom, she sought George Beanfield; but he, mindful of her threat, had departed long since. He left the town, he even left the country, for a letter addressed from the Continent was received by the president of the society, which cleared up the mystery of the missing Foxton bud. George stated that in attending to the plant he had accidentally knocked off a blossom and, fearful of a reprimand, had burnt it in the greenhouse fire. The appearance of Eliza with a similar bud to that destroyed had afforded him an opportunity of hiding his delinquency, by making her the scapegoat. He did not offer any opinion as to how he thought Eliza had become possessed of the blossom when the one missing from the bush had been destroyed by himself.

Thus was the innocence of Eliza proved beyond all doubt, and, angered by the unjust aspersions cast on her, she proceeded forthwith to turn the tables on her accusers. The morning following her acquittal, she appeared in my office with a wrathful countenance.

'Now, sir,' said she viciously, 'I'm agowin' to hev a action agin thim Gardins fur lockin' me up.'

But the action never came off. The society, knowing it had no defence, owned that it was in the wrong, and offered to compromise. Moreover they feared lest Eliza should sell her plant to a rival society, and thus rob Foxton of the glory of solely possessing the rainbow camellia. After some correspondence, they agreed to settle the action for five hundred pounds, provided Eliza gave them her plant. This she did, and having received her damages, and paid my fees, she disappeared from Foxton.

A month afterwards my wife again brought up the subject of Eliza Drupp. As usual, the cook was her informant.

'Fred,' said she; 'Eliza Drupp?'

'Well, what has she been doing now? Stolen another camellia?'

'No. She has married George Beanfield.'

'The fellow who gave evidence against her? Impossible.'

'It is true. Cook has this morning received a piece of the wedding cake.'

'Well, all I can say is that Eliza is of a most forgiving disposition.'

'I have no patience with her,' replied my wife. 'But I think she is ashamed to return to Foxton. She and George have gone to South America.'

'A very sensible step to take,' said I, weary of the subject. 'They can set up on the proceeds of the trial At all events we have heard the last of Eliza Drupp.'

The remark was premature, for in less than twelve months I was again discussing Eliza, and learning the reason of her eccentric behaviour.

It was on board the *Mandalay* that I heard the truth concerning the matrimonial alliance of our former housemaid. I was ordered to take a sea voyage for the benefit of my health, and as Nell refused to come on the plea of being a bad sailor, I was obliged to make the journey alone. One place was much the same as another to me, provided the instructions of my physician were carried out; so, taking the first chance that presented itself, I embarked for China on a Three Star Liner. The ship was comfortable, the passengers sociable, and the table excellent, so the voyage promised to be very pleasant. As a description thereof is not pertinent to the story, I proceed at once to the episode which brought up again the name of Eliza Drupp.

Among the stewards figured a red-haired creature, freckled and stumpy. He was neither my table nor berth attendant, yet he never failed, when by accident I caught his eye, to salute me with a knowing grin. This mark of recognition led me to examine him closely, in the expectation of finding a former client or servant. I could not recall his features, yet they seemed to be familiar to me. We were in the Bay of Biscay when I spoke to him. The ship was rolling heavily, and on my way to lie down in my cabin, I met with my red-polled friend. He smiled as usual, whereupon I asked him if he knew me.

'No, sir,' said he with a grin, 'but 'Lizer knows y', sir.'

''Lizer?'

'M' sister, sir, 'Lizer Drupp es was.'

'Ah, that accounts for the familiar look of your face. You are her brother Sam.'

'Yessir. Shell I 'elp y' long t' y' bunk, sir?'

'If you please.'

By this unexpected meeting the circumstances of the case recurred to my mind, and I was pleased to meet with Sam. It was he who had brought the camellia to Eliza, and I wished to learn where he procured it, and also why his sister had married her enemy. Sam was not unlike my former client, but, owing to his vocation, he had a less pronounced cockney accent. At times, however, the Londoner peeped out.

'How is Eliza?' I asked, when safely bestowed in my bunk. 'And where is Eliza?'

'In Paraguay with 'er 'usband, sir. They're es 'eppy es th' doy es long.'

'That is rather curious, Drupp, considering her husband was a witness in that case of—'

Sam interrupted me at this moment by laughing violently. I checked his untoward mirth with a frown, whereupon he wiped his eyes and apologized.

''Scuse me, sir, but I ken't 'elp laufin' when I thenk of thet 'ere caise. Y' got 'Lizer foive 'un'red, y' did, sir. She an' George 'ave bowght a ranch in Paraguay an' are gitting on fine. Don Jorge 'e is now, sir, an' 'Lizer's quite t' laidy.'

'Her bad luck was the cause of her good luck,' said I epigrammatically; 'it was a fortunate thing for Eliza that you brought her that rainbow camellia from China.'

Sam grinned, and again apologized.

'Bless y', sir, I didn't bring no camelliar fro' Chiner, sir.'

'Then how did Eliza become possessed of the second plant?'

'George, sir; 'e got er a slip off t' Foxton plant.'

'George!' repeated I in amazement; 'but he gave evidence against her. If he got her the slip he must have known that—'

''Course 'e did, sir. It was all ploy-actin'. 'Lizer wrote 'ome an' told all about it.'

'Then you can tell me all about it, Drupp. As I conducted the case I should like to hear the sequel. It may explain why Eliza married Beanfield.'

'Thet it do, sir,' said Sam, grinning. 'It were this waiy, sir. 'Lizer 'ad no money, an' George 'adn't enough to marry on. Th'y wanted to git spliced, an' so 'it on a plan to git money. 'Lizer she was readin' about a cove es got a thousan' poun's fur bein' put in quod when 'e was innercent, so she ses t' George, "Cawn't we try the saime gaime on an' git enough t' marry on?" An' George, sir, 'ad an idear—'e's a long-'eaded chap, sir—fur bein' a gardiner to t' Foxton Society 'e knew whot a lot th'y thought of thet blessed camelliar. So 'e steals a slip an' tells 'Lizer to mek it grow, an' to tell father es I browght it fro' Chiner. She arsked me t' soy so, an' not knowin' 'er gaime I sid so. But I never knowed anythin' about it, sir. Then 'Lizer meks it grow es George ses, tho' 'twas a long toime growin'. When t' flowers come, she taiks one t' Foxton an' walks into th' green'ouse an'—'

'I see, it was all arranged between them so as to sue the society and get damages?'

'Yessir. George nipped off a bud an' burnt it, 'e did. Then 'Lizer, wearin' 'er own, comes out an' 'e puts 'er in quod.'

'And between the two of them they clear £500?'

'Yessir, an' then 'e marries 'er. D'y' see, sir?'

'I see, Drupp, and I must say they are a nice pair.'

'Thet th'y are, sir. I'd 'a spilt their gaime 'ad I know'd it.'

After delivering this opinion Drupp departed and I was left to ruminate over his story. I quite believed that he was ignorant of the plot, but I was satisfied that had he known he would only have held his tongue if well paid. It was useless to give the benefit of the doubt to one who was of the same stock as Eliza. That artful girl knew her family too well to entrust them with her secret, and, less legal expenses, she and her fellow-conspirator got the whole of the damages to themselves. Much as I condemned their rascality, I could not but admire the cleverness with which they had planned and carried out their scheme. They had deceived Drupp, they had deceived the society, they had deceived me. Their comedy was extremely well acted, and ended quite to their satisfaction. Therefore I say that country wits are at times equal to those of townbred folks, for though the idea was Eliza's, the conception and execution of the scheme emanated from the bucolic brain of George.

I told the whole story to my wife when I returned home, and she was very severe on her former housemaid. Naturally enough she could not keep it to herself, and in a short time the history of the deception soon became town talk. At first the members of the Horticultural Society were angered at being so treated, but as the delinquents were in South America, it was wisely concluded to let the matter drop. They possessed both rainbow camellias, and, warned by the trickery of George and Eliza, watched the plants with renewed vigilance. I do not think that anyone else will have the chance of stealing a slip of the Foxton fetish, but should a third rainbow camellia make its appearance in the market, old Bendel is quite resolved not to be hoodwinked a second time. He often regrets that he did not give Eliza six months, but is too late now, as the conspirators are farming in Paraguay. They ought to rear a rainbow camellia, if only to remind them of their iniquity.

THE END

THE DETECTIVE STORY CLUB

"The Man with the Gun."

THE SELECTION COMMITTEE HAS PLEASURE IN RECOMMENDING THE FOLLOWING NOVELS OF OUTSTANDING MERIT

The Terror   EDGAR WALLACE

There are many imitators—but only one EDGAR WALLACE. *The Terror* is a most sensational thriller, and has had a great success both as a play and as a film.

The Leavenworth Case   ANNA K. GREEN

What did MR. BALDWIN say in 1928 ? He said : " *The Leavenworth Case* is one of the best detective stories ever written."

The Crime Club
By an Ex-Supt. of the C.I.D., SCOTLAND YARD

Here is the real straight thing from G.H.Q. A detective thriller that is different, by FRANK FRÖEST, the Scotland Yard man, assisted by GEORGE DILNOT, author of the *Famous Trials* Series.

Called Back   HUGH CONWAY

A clever and exciting thriller which has become world-famous.

The Perfect Crime   ISRAEL ZANGWILL

This very ingenious detective novel, by the distinguished novelist and play-wright, is the subject of one of the most successful films of the year.

The Blackmailers   EMILE GABORIAU

All detective writers worship at the shrine of Gaboriau—master of the French crime story. *The Blackmailers* is one of his best, replete with thrills and brilliantly told.

LOOK FOR THE MAN WITH THE GUN